THE BOYZIE TRILOGY

John Broome

All characters and most of the places in this novel are entirely
fictitious.
No reference to anyone alive or dead is intended.

Trafford
PUBLISHING

Order this book online at www.trafford.com/07-2765
or email orders@trafford.com

Most Trafford titles are also available at major online book retailers.

Edited by: Jill Todd

Note for Librarians: A cataloguing record for this book is available from Library
and Archives Canada at www.collectionscanada.ca/amicus/index-e.html

Printed in Victoria, BC, Canada.

ISBN: 978-1-4251-6088-3

*We at Trafford believe that it is the responsibility of us all, as both individuals
and corporations, to make choices that are environmentally and socially sound.
You, in turn, are supporting this responsible conduct each time you purchase a
Trafford book, or make use of our publishing services. To find out how you are
helping, please visit www.trafford.com/responsiblepublishing.html*

*Our mission is to efficiently provide the world's finest, most comprehensive
book publishing service, enabling every author to experience success.
To find out how to publish your book, your way, and have it available
worldwide, visit us online at www.trafford.com/10510*

www.trafford.com

North America & international
toll-free: 1 888 232 4444 (USA & Canada)
phone: 250 383 6864 ♦ fax: 250 383 6804
email: info@trafford.com

The United Kingdom & Europe
phone: +44 (0)1865 722 113 ♦ local rate: 0845 230 9601
facsimile: +44 (0)1865 722 868 ♦ email: info.uk@trafford.com

10 9 8 7 6 5 4 3 2

To Mum and Dad, with love and thanks.

ABOUT THE AUTHOR

John Broome was born in New Silksworth, Sunderland, County Durham in June 1947.

He has been blind since birth, and was educated in a number of "special" schools in various parts of the country.

At the age of 16 years, he went to an Assessment Centre in Reigate, Surrey, where he met his future wife, Kathleen. The couple have been married for 37 years and live amicably and comfortably in the East Midlands.

John Broome moved from the South-East to Derbyshire in August of 1969, and he and Kathleen were married in June 1970.

John works for a Charitable Association, and has been attempting to write a novel for over 30 years. But two and a half years ago, after a long illness and several major operations, he decided to endeavour to make his dream a reality. Now, he is about to see the culmination of his dream as his first novel is published.

John Broome has just turned 60 years old, and has also recently undergone training with his fifth guide dog. He loves life and lives it to the full, despite his visual impairment.

Book One

Portrait of my Love

Introduction

I T WAS 8 p.m. on the evening of Thursday, 28th December, 1989. I was leaning my elbows on the counter in the crowded public bar of the Gunners in Allerton. Young Ru Henry behind the bar, with whom I always enjoyed a laugh, a joke and a good chat whenever I was in the Gunners those days, had just served me with my third pint of ice-cold cider. I was swilling it down to calm my nervous excitement. In a short while I would be embarking upon an 80-hour music marathon from midnight that night until 8 a.m. on Monday, the first day of 1990, the start of a new decade.

Soon Simon (my driver) would arrive to take me down to the Laughing Cow for Playback, 'The last supper', we had been joking about that, and then we would drive to the studios of Sunny Gold Radio, 'the new and exciting sound all year round', and I would commence my broadcast.

The event would culminate at 8 a.m. on Monday, 1st January, 1990, with a big party in the reception room at the studios with all the station staff, directors etc., present! There would be drinks, plenty of food, decorations, balloons, a huge tree and a very special cake for 1990, and I had even heard the rumour that there might be fireworks outside, as long as there were none inside, my worst fear! Before all that would be my 80-hour music marathon, for which I had been preparing for ages.

I felt a sense of tremendous excitement welling up inside me, but that was tinged with concern and a feeling of nervous tension. Would everything go according to plan? Would it all be okay? Oh, please, please make it be all right! No major hitches, no dramas, oh, please, no dramas.

The door of the pub swung open again and Simon, my driver and a good friend too, stomped in. He shouldered his way forward until he stood beside me where I was leaning my elbows on the counter, and he leaned against my right shoulder. Simon Wallis was in his late twenties. Tall, lean and athletic, he was one of five brothers who ran a minicab business in the town, the big rivals of Phoenix Cars. Simon and I had become friends over the past couple of years, and he drove me around a good deal those days.

"Ready to go then, Boyzie?" he asked.

I finished my pint, placed my tankard on the counter and called out cheerio to Dennis Parkin, the landlord of the Gunners, and his family. They all wished me a Happy New Year and Ru Henry shook my hand across the counter and wished me good luck for the duration of my 80-hour music marathon upon which I was about to embark. I was then following Simon Wallis out of the pub, with my right hand resting on his left shoulder. Outside, the cold night air hit me, and it was very welcome after the smoky atmosphere of the pub.

"Ooh, that's better!" I said as we stood side by side for a few moments in the car park before walking quickly towards his yellow minicab.

We climbed in and he started the engine.

"The Laughing Cow then, Boyzie?" he asked.

"Yes please, Simon!" I replied.

We drove slowly and carefully out of the congested car park at the Gunners, and turned right to drive into town. Now we had approximately a 20-minute drive before we reached the Laughing Cow, a popular cafe/milk bar situated in the town centre. A chance for me to relax! A chance for me to think, and my mind went roving back over the years! Back to the late seventies! Back to a time when my life seemed far less complicated than the present turmoil in which I found myself!

Sitting beside Simon Wallis, as we drove towards the town centre and the Laughing Cow, I relaxed completely and allowed my mind to wander where it would.

Playback

Chapter 1

Wednesday, 3rd May, 1978.

AFTER THE ambulance had taken her to hospital on that Wednesday morning, I got ready and went to work. I had put my smoking jacket on over my pyjamas to see her off. She had wanted me to go with her in the conveyance, but I had firmly resisted. Instead, I had telephoned her brother, Mick. His wife, Trudy, would go down to the County Hospital and would be there to see her admitted, to establish which ward she went onto and to ensure that she was comfortable. I knew Dr Janet Perry would also visit her on the ward, and I would go in after work that night to take her anything she needed. We had already packed a few essentials into two large carrier bags, which accompanied her in the ambulance that morning!

She cried and clung to me, but eventually she allowed me to kiss and hug her tightly to me, and then, after more tears, she walked to the waiting vehicle on the arm of Andy Lee, the tall, well-built, good-humoured young medic. She allowed Andy and Barry, the two medics, to escort her into the vehicle and settle her comfortably into the seat. She waved and called out 'goodbye' to me as she was driven away to the County Hospital.

I went back into the house in a daze! I was very tired. I sat down in the chair after she had gone, with a large mug of hot chocolate and two thick toasted doorsteps with plenty of butter and smeared with strawberry jam. I had slightly burned the toast at the edges, but it didn't matter. I had been up with her since before 2 a.m. and had not had much sleep, but those days, when Susan was so very ill, that was par for the course. I should have been used to it by then. I ate my breakfast and drank a second mug of hot chocolate then I went upstairs and made the bed, tidied around, washed my hands and face, cleaned my teeth, ran a comb through my hair and finished preparing for work. I would be able to catch the 7.50 a.m. bus from the end of the close if I was quick!

At 7.45 a.m. I threw my bag over my shoulder, the bag she had bought me for Christmas, took my white cane, unfolded it and set off for work, ensuring that the house was securely locked behind me. I was in a hurry. I did not want to be late for work that morning. Why the white cane? Oh yes, I forgot to tell you that I have been registered blind since birth!

I ran for the bus. As I did so, Terry Whaley, my milkman, called out to me.

"Aw saw the ambulance, Boyzie, how's your wife?"

"Very poorly," I replied.

I could not stop, or I would miss my bus.

"Well, if there's owt you need, you know who to ask for, eh?" Terry shouted.

I was touched. Terry always impressed as a tough little guy. He was only about five feet six inches tall, but he had the reputation of being a hard man and a fighter. I felt I had to stop for a few seconds and respond.

"Thanks, Terry!" I called back and then, as I moved off again towards the end of the close, Dean Sadler, the 14-year-old son of my next-door-but-one neighbours, rode up on his bike.

"Hi, Boyzie!" said the friendly youngster. "Aw saw the ambulance, aw'll tell Mam an' Dad, an' aw'm sure they'll be rahnd to see yo', Boyzie."

I could feel tears welling up in my eyes.

"Ta, Deano," I said, and ran to catch my bus.

If I had not caught that one, I would have been later into work and even though I had good cause to be, I did not want to make Susan's admission to hospital an excuse for lateness at the office. The bus had stopped for me and I scrambled aboard, folding my white cane and thanking the driver. A hand landed on my right shoulder.

"On'y jus' med it in time!" said Steve Lambert.

He was in his twenties, another near neighbour of mine in the close.

"Yes, a bit of a rush this morning" I said, as we sat down side by side at the back of the vehicle.

"I saw the ambulance at your house," said Steve. "Sharon and I hope you know where to come if there's owt you need."

I wanted to cry, but I bit my lip. The neighbours in Rutland Close were so friendly, so caring! Just like the network that built up around us when we lived on The Circle, in the midst of the vast Mount Carmel Estate. We had lived at number 23 for just under two years, and everyone had made us feel most welcome! Ours had been the second house from the end on the left-hand side of the close. It was a three-bedroomed, semi-detached council property and was very well appointed and comfortable.

With the help of the neighbours and friends, we tore the guts out of it prior to moving in. Well, we had to, it was such a God Almighty mess, but thanks to a lot of good mates and a great deal of goodwill, we eventually had a home to be proud of, and the rent was not too expensive either. I had a good steady income!

My only sorrow was my lovely wife's failing health. Susan had been poorly for some years, but since the previous Christmas, her health had really deteriorated. In March of that year, she was admitted to ward 20 of the County Hospital for almost three weeks. I visited on the first evening she was there and was seen by Dr Mervyn Fraser. He told me in a very direct, matter-of-fact way, but kindly nonetheless, that my darling Susan had cancer. He explained that it was inoperable, that it would eventually spread to her brain and that her life expectancy could not be very long. He said he had sat beside her bed and held her hand while he imparted the same information to her.

He was a bloke about my own age, and I had a lot of time and respect for Doe Merv, as we both christened him. He was blunt and straightforward without any prevarication, but that was good. At least we knew where we stood, and as I travelled into work on that bright, but cool, May morning in 1978, I was pretty sure that Sue's time was very near and that in all probability she would not be coming home again! Sue and me, Dr Merv and probably Dr Janet Perry, our own GP, were the only ones who knew that, at that time anyway.

§≈≈§

Sue and I had first met in January of 1965. I had been a new student at a college for blind and partially sighted adolescents near Fordingbridge in Shropshire. Susan, who was approximately 14 months older than me, was a trainee-nurse at the Coptall Hospital for Sick Children in Fordingbridge. She and a small group of her student colleagues had come over one Saturday afternoon. That was the very first Saturday following my arrival at Queen Mary College! I was standing on my own for a short while and she approached me.

"Hello!" she said brightly.

"Hello, yourself!" I responded.

She came and stood beside me.

"What's your name?" she asked.

Her voice was friendly and I noted a sense of humour about that young woman.

"I'm Ian, Ian Richard Dickson, known to all my nearest and dearest as Boyzie," I

told her.

"Hi, Boyzie!" she responded. "I'm holding out my hand," she added.

As she spoke, she stepped right in front of me. I held out my own right hand and we shyly shook hands, then both started to giggle. A good start, anyway!

"And you?" I asked her, "Who are you?"

"I'm Susan," she told me, "Susan Smith."

༺══༻

The bus was pulling up outside the bank on Chequers Road, and I alighted at the stop to wait for the bus into Allerton. Steve Lambert got off at the same stop and waited with me. The 8.35 a.m. bus to Allerton was crowded. Steve and I found seats together and the vehicle lurched on its way towards Gunners Lane and the enormous Hyland Road Industrial Estate at Allerton.

Allerton was a very poor area of the large North Midlands town in which I lived. I worked at the Family Support Centre on Bread Street, which was the tenth turning on the right off Gunners Lane. The vast Hyland Road Industrial Estate was situated on the right-hand side at the top of Hyland Road. After stopping there to let most people get off, the bus continued on its way, around an island then turned left. That was my stop. I got off on Hyland Road, outside James Blume's Bakery. I then walked along and crossed two roads on the left-hand side, before arriving at the crossing on Gunners Lane. That was almost directly outside the newly built Gunners Lane Sixth Form College for boys and young men, part of the Gunners Lane Boys' School.

Until recently, that establishment of education had been a grammar school, but although it had remained 'single sex', almost five years previously it had amalgamated with two other boys' schools in the area. The school was now under new headship, took boys from the ages of 11 years up to 16 years and they then either left or moved on to the newly built and equally vast Sixth Form College. There, the average length of course for a young man was up to three years. There were some 2,200 boys in the main school, and well over 2,500 at the Sixth Form College. None of the students in either establishment was a boarder, but they had come from all over the county and from other parts of the North and East Midlands to the new Sixth Form College. The billeting officers there helped some of the young gentlemen to find lodgings with families in the area.

The two massive council estates in the area were the Mount Carmel Estate and the Morleston Estate. There was also the Heath Road Estate, which was not far from Gunners Lane, travelling towards the centre of the rather rundown area of Allerton. The Heath Road Estate was smaller than the other two. It was Morleston School and Heath Road School that merged with Gunners Lane Grammar School to form the then vast establishment. The new headmaster of the establishment, including the Sixth Form College, was Mr Timothy Waterhouse. He was only 32 years of age! He was someone I had come to know very well through working at the Bread Street Family Support Centre.

The crowded bus lurched on its way. We had been joined at the back of the vehicle by two more blokes who were regular travellers with us of a morning—Chris Lambert, brother of Steve, and Roy Pearson. Steve, Chris and Roy all worked on the Hyland Road Industrial Estate. They alighted from the bus at the stop before mine. The four of us sat and chatted amiably together until they reached their stop. After they had alighted, saying they would probably see me later on that night, I moved down towards the doorway of the vehicle, so I could exit more quickly at my stop. I had a few words with the driver, Colin Fleck, a bloke in his mid-forties, and someone I knew well. That was the joy of living in that town; people were really very friendly.

"A nice bright mornin' eh, Boyzie?" said Colin Fleck as we pulled up at my stop outside James Blume's Bakery.

"Yeh!" I rejoined as I dismounted.

There was a queue of people waiting to board the vehicle. I waved a hand to Colin and walked on towards my destination.

I was still thinking about Susan. We had seen plenty of one another after that first Saturday. The following day, Sunday, which was cold, but fine, we had walked together in the woods nearby the establishment in which I was currently dwelling; the Queen Mary College at Fordingbridge. That was right in the heart of beautiful Shropshire countryside and, had it not been so far from my home and family in Thamesford, Essex, and in South-East London, I would have greatly relished the time spent there.

As it was, I grew to love it more because of Susan, but at the time we met again, on that first long Sunday afternoon after a huge dinner, I was feeling pretty homesick. Susan seemed to notice how I was feeling. She told me she was homesick too! She told me she came from a large North Midlands town called Gaynsford. I had never heard of it! I told her I came from Thamesford, where my parents and brother lived, but that originally we were an East End family. My mother's people were true East Enders. Unfortunately, I never knew either of my grandfathers, and my dad's mother died in the mid-fifties, in the village of Blackhorton in County Durham, where I was born in June of 1947.

My grandma on my mother's side kept a lodging house after the family had grown up and left home. She had had four daughters and one son, making five offspring in all, of whom my mum, Mary Frances, was the eldest. At one time Granny Annie had had as many as eight male lodgers, and she had cooked, cleaned, washed, ironed etc., for them all, and she had loved it, every last minute! Despite that, she had always had time for her own family. My Granny Annie had died in 1968, and I greatly missed her. My only joy was that she had been able to be present at my wedding in 1966.

Susan and I had become engaged in the December of 1965, to the great joy of my family and the considerable concern of the older members of hers. However, after I went to live up in Gaynsford in the March of 1966, just a few weeks before our marriage, things improved vastly between myself and her parents, who took me to their hearts.

On that wonderful day in August 1966 when we got married, the sun shone and more than 90 people sat down to a sumptuous repast in the Georgian Suite at the Co-op. We had met with the manager of the Co-op, Mr Reedy, and he had been most accommodating, so had the Reverend John Lammie, who married us.

He was a man in his mid-thirties, and we had both taken to him immediately. Susan's mother and father were not regular church-goers, but nevertheless, the Reverend Lammie had been kindness itself and because he had a delicious sense of the ridiculous, he had immediately endeared himself to both of us.

More than 40 of my friends, neighbours and members of my family travelled up from the south and from other places to be with me on my wedding day. In the evening, loads more people came to join us and the band we had booked and paid for, since Susan's parents had only wanted a small affair for their daughter and we had wanted something spectacular, played for an extra half hour because we asked them to do so. Ernie Wilde and his 'Wildcats' were truly wonderful and could play anything from waltzes, quicksteps, foxtrots etc., to the latest pop tunes. Their singer, who was Ernie's wife, Frances, was absolutely brilliant. She danced with me before the evening was over. A wonderful, happy occasion!

The only people who didn't really enjoy it were Susan's grand-parents, Alice and Joe Cunliffe. They were the parents of Lizzie, Susan's mother, and Annie, her elder sister. Lizzie and Annie both enjoyed themselves hugely, and both were a little tiddly at the end of the evening! Both had deigned to dance with me before the night was over.

No one was very concerned about Alice and Joe sitting in the corner scowling at everyone who was enjoying the occasion. That was fairly typical of the couple, who were both dead within four years of our marriage anyway.

Granny Annie, my own grandmother on my mother's side, had a whale of a time. She danced and 'carried on' with most of the blokes her age, including Susan's dad, Frank. Everyone praised the reception, which had been a sit-down meal for 90 people and then, later on, we had a massive buffet for at least 200 people at night. That had all been undertaken by the women who lived on and around The Circle, where Sue and I were to live now that we were newlyweds.

We had acquired a three-bedroomed council house at 48 The Circle, Mount Carmel. The neighbours had been fantastic. The blokes in the neighbourhood had completely rewired, redecorated and carpeted the house all through, according to our wishes. They had fitted our cooker, plumbed in the washer etc., etc., all to the highest standard. My father and brother, Eric, had inspected everything and were highly delighted with all that had been achieved by our soon-to-be neighbours.

Lizzie and Frank Smith, Sue's parents, plus her Aunt Annie, and Trudy and Mick, her brother and sister-in-law, had been over and helped us to hang curtains, put up pictures, place ornaments etc., and Frank had put up a couple of wall cabinets in the kitchen and bathroom, but the vast majority of the work in the house had been undertaken by the men and women who were soon to be our new neighbours. The women, apart from undertaking the catering at our reception, had cleaned the house all through once all the rewiring, plastering, painting, papering etc., had been done, and, in truth, they had made a wonderful job of it. We were absolutely delighted. Susan had done plenty as well, but she had been glad of the help, as she was working as a nurse right up until the time we married. So already, a network of people was beginning to form around us.

§✿✿§

It was approximately 8.50 a.m. when I alighted from the bus outside James Blume's. The smell of hot bread was very tempting. I loved the bread from that bakery. I usually treated us to a couple of loaves a week, and made up my mind that the following morning I would buy two more large white and a small brown, but not then, no, not then!

I unfurled my long white cane and set off at a brisk pace towards the crossing at Gunners Lane and Hyland Road. That would take me onto Gunners Lane and thus, onto Bread Street and my office at the Family Support Centre. I did not have to be there until 9.15 a.m. My hours of work were 9.15 a.m. to 12.15 p.m. then an hour for lunch. I then worked from 1.15 p.m. until 5.45 p.m. I caught the bus to town at around 6.10 p.m., and that night I would probably eat my dinner at the Laughing Cow before going on to the hospital to see my darling Susan.

On a Friday we finished at 5.15 p.m. Thus, we worked a 37-hour week, at least we admin staff did, unless there was an emergency and we had to work overtime on an evening, and that was not unusual either. I hoped it would not occur that night, as I wanted to spend as much time as possible with my lovely one. I knew I could take time off to be with her, but that would be abusing my situation, and since my boss, Pat Lenham, and her second in command, Chris Braun, were both very good to me, I did not want to do that, but I did want to be away on time that night.

I walked on, lengthening my stride. I had thought seriously about having a guide dog once upon a time, but had decided I would not do so—at least not for the present—as I already had two dogs at home. Badger, almost 12 years old, came to us from the Royal Society for the Prevention of Cruelty to Animals. He was nine weeks old when he came to live with us, soon after our marriage in August 1966. Meggie, also a mongrel, was only 18 months old. She had been spayed, and was rather plump, but nevertheless, she was full of life and was a superb watchdog, as indeed Badger was. Now he was becoming rather slow and had the beginnings of arthritis. Still, he got around pretty well, and coped with Meggie with great patience and a deal of diplomacy. She always knew when he had had enough, but ultimately, she was the 'boss dog'. They got along fine together, and when I was not at home, Badger and Meggie were looked after by the three Williams brothers, who were the sons of my next door neighbours in the close.

୧᠁୨

Parkside, the area of Gaynsford in which Sue and I had lived for almost two years then, was a very pleasant quiet spot. Most of the people who lived around about there were young families, and many were buying their houses under the new Labour Government's policy.   .

I was thinking seriously about buying 23 Rutland Close, but as yet, I had done nothing about it because my main concern then was for my wife's health. Certainly, if anything happened to her, it would be too large for me on my own and I didn't know if I would want to stay there once she had left me for good. I could feel tears beginning to sting my eyes, so I turned my thoughts from that possibility and continued to walk briskly towards the pedestrian crossing at the junction of Hyland Road and Gunners Lane.

The morning had turned dull and cool. It corresponded well with my mood.

Chapter 2

SUSAN AND I had settled well into life at 48 The Circle. After our wedding on 27th August, we spent our honeymoon down in Seaport, West Sussex. My Auntie Nelly, Mum's youngest sister, and her husband, my Uncle Alf, had a boarding house down there. They usually kept at least one family room available for any of us who might want to go down for a few days. They were delighted when we expressed a wish to go there for our fortnight's honeymoon. In the event, we did not stay for the whole fortnight, but travelled down on the Sunday by coach, and then returned to Gaynsford on the Wednesday week.

The sun shone almost all the time. My Auntie Nelly and Uncle Alf, who had several young children, and the boarding house to run, had not been able to get up to Gaynsford for our wedding, so we had another small party down in Seaport on our arrival. We were made most welcome and had a fabulous time, although we almost ran out of money during the first part of our stay. Mum, Dad, Yvonne, Eric, plus other members of the family came down to see us on the Sunday, and we all had a lovely day together and, at the end of that fantastic day, Dad gave me another £30, so we were okay for money for the rest of our holiday in Seaport.

On arriving back in Gaynsford, we had the remainder of the week to do with as we pleased. We had dinner and tea with Susan's parents on the Saturday, and tea with Trudy, Mick and their son, David, on the Sunday. On the Monday, 12th September, we both recommenced at work—Sue at the Cottage Unit of the Princess Alice Hospital for Children and me at Brady Engineering, on the Hyland Road Industrial Estate, where I worked on the switchboard and on reception. I worked at Brady's until Christmas of 1975 then in January of 1976, I commenced my employment with the borough council, working in the Family Support Centre at Bread Street, off Gunners Lane.

ईৰৼৡ

I was now standing at the junction of the two main roads, beside the pedestrian crossing. What a lot of people seemed to be around me; boys and young men from the school and the sixth form college. They did not start their day until 9.15 a.m., but I thought most of them ought to have been in school or college by then. What a lot of them there were, just milling about in such vast numbers around the junction, the crossing and me. They were pushing, jostling, laughing and chattering all around me. I had never seen so many of them altogether before.

I stood patiently waiting to cross, but the noise all around me was so great that I could not hear when the bleeping sound was being emitted, which would tell me it was safe to cross over. So I just stood waiting, waiting until the noise died down, but instead, it seemed to be increasing, and so did the numbers of boys and young men crowding around me on the crossing. So many! So very, very many, all pushing, jostling, laughing, chattering among themselves, struggling and striving to get near me, or so it seemed to me, anyway, it was very frightening. I felt totally overwhelmed by the vastness of their numbers. Suddenly someone grabbed my white stick out of my hand and started playing around, wafting it about, handing it from one young man to another and generally behaving in a very immature manner. I tried to say, 'Please give me back my white cane!', but nobody would have heard me even if I had been able to speak and I could not, because the muscles in my throat seemed tense and the words would not come.

I was becoming very frightened. There were so many boys and young men packed altogether on the pavement, and I seemed to be right on the edge. Suddenly I felt hands pushing me and the next thing I remember, I was sprawling in the middle of that very busy road.

As I fell to my knees, there was a great deal of whooping and roaring from behind me, then the screech of brakes as a lorry pulled up just before I went right under its wheels. A nightmare! I lay where I was in the road. The lorry driver had alighted and was standing over me. He lifted me to my feet and was about to start shouting when two women came out into the road with the pieces of my broken white stick in their hands, and showed them to him.

"He was pushed out into the road, we saw it, we saw it happen, didn't we, Ma?" said the younger of the two women excitedly.

She was helping me back onto the pavement with her arm around my shoulders. I was shaking. The pavement was now completely clear of boys and young men. They must have all run off into their various venues after seeing me go sprawling in the middle of the busy road. The cowards, and what a way to behave!

The lorry driver and the older woman were earnestly engaged in conversation. A young police constable had arrived at the scene on foot and he was engaged in talking to the woman and the trucker whom, now that he believed I was going to be all right, seemed anxious to be on his way. Eventually, the young PC let him go, and he and the older woman joined us on the pavement.

I was still shaking and apparently I looked very pale. The younger woman still had an arm around my shoulders. She was still very excited, but had been talking quietly to me, trying to calm me down.

"We saw it, we saw what happened, didn't we, Ma?" she said again, excited, like a child.

"Wisht, wisht, Alice May!" said the older woman, who now stood on my left-hand side. "Now then, ma dear, how are you? I saw everything that happened, an' I've bin tellin' this young mon here all aboot it!"

She had a strong Scottish accent. She now introduced herself and her daughter.

"Aw'm Councillor Marjorie McNault and this is ma daughter,

Alice May."

Alice leaned forwards and kissed me on my right cheek. The young police

constable seemed a little unsure of how to proceed.

"Aw think aw'll go an' have a word with the headteacher at the school," Councillor McNault said.

"Okay, if you do that, then we'll tek' him ower to wor house an' get him a wee dram or summat."

"Ooh ay!" said Alice May, whom I judged to be about 40 years old.

She was about five feet three inches tall, and she still had a comforting arm around me.

"Aw'll cum to your house an' see you there in a little while, ma'am!" said the young police constable.

Councillor McNault, her daughter and I started to walk towards their house, which was on Hay Street, the eighth street on the right off Gunners Lane and two streets down from Bread Street. They lived at number 26, and I was taken into the lounge and made very comfortable. Alice May took my coat and I removed my shoes. Now the shock was coming out and I was very shaky and very tearful.

Marjorie McNault, a woman in her early sixties, very Scottish and extremely warm and caring, brought me a large mug of hot sweet coffee with 'summat in it' as she put it.

"Now wisht, laddie!" she said comfortingly. "Ye've had an awful shock, you ken!"

I sat and drank the beverage she offered me and was very glad of it and the other comforts around me. Councillor McNault sat quietly beside me and held my right hand, and Alice May, whom I now judged to be slightly retarded, although not badly so, went into the kitchen and brought me some fruit loaf. She set it down on a plate on the table beside my mug. I drank and ate with relish. The shock was beginning to subside now, I still felt a bit shaky, however.

"Now then, son, how do you feel?" asked Marjorie McNault.

"Better thanks," I replied, adding, "it was very kind of you to bring me back here and all."

"Aw wisht! It wor the least we cud dee for ye, ma laddie," said Councillor Marjorie McNault. "Will ye hae another drink now?"

I thanked her and said I would. Alice May went off into the kitchen to get it for me. She seemed very eager and anxious to please, like a friendly dog. I smiled to myself.

The doorbell rang. PC Joe Capper and Mr Timothy Waterhouse, principal of the Gunners Lane Academy and Sixth Form College now walked together into the large living room of number 26 Hay Street. After we had all sat down and Alice May had brought more coffee for everyone, plus shortbread and fruit loaf, we began to discuss my situation and what had occurred.

"What happened exactly, Sir? Can you tell me please?" asked the young police constable.

I told him what I remembered. Alice May and her mother interjected and told him what they knew. Alice May had to be calmed down by her mother, and was eventually dispatched to the kitchen to make more coffee.

"Aw'm sorry aboot her," apologised the good councillor, "she gets a wee bit excitable, you ken."

We all nodded understandingly. Tim Waterhouse was most apologetic and said that he would certainly investigate what had transpired, and he was most concerned about me and my situation.

I was crying again, and Marjorie McNault had an arm around me trying to console me. I told them that that morning my wife, Susan, had been rushed into the County Hospital, and that I knew she did not have long to live. Everyone was most sympathetic. The young PC wanted to take me to the hospital there and then, and both Mr Waterhouse and Councillor McNault thought I ought to go, but I told them I was on my way to work and that I should have been there ages ago.

Marjorie dispatched her daughter to make a phone call telling the Family Support Centre at Bread Street that I would be there as soon as possible, and said that she could tell them I had had an accident, but not to elaborate.

"She's gud on the phone, you ken," said Marjorie with some degree of pride.

I gave a statement to the police constable, who duly departed. With him went Tim Waterhouse, vowing he would resolve the situation that very morning. Marjorie McNault then walked with me to the Family Support Centre and left me at the end of the driveway. I shook her hand warmly and thanked her once again for all she had done to help me that morning.

"Och! It's nae a problem, ma lad. Cud aw hev left ye in the road like that? Nae, aw cudnae hev done that. Now then, ye look after yoursel', eh?"

I thanked her profusely and told her I would endeavour to do so.

"An' mek sure as how ye get another white stick tonight," she called as she set off back towards Hay Street.

"Oh yes, I had better do that."

Chapter 3

I WALKED INTO the reception area at the Family Support Centre and on into my office where the switchboard was located, along with my typewriter, the photostat machine etc., etc. As I walked into my office, there was a chorus of:

"Oh, Boyzie, you're all right then?"

There was a reception committee to greet me that morning. They were all there; Sandra Couchman, Mandy Moss, Jacky Paternoster, Chris Braun, and even my boss, Pat Lenham, the 'big chief' over all the admin staff, was there. They were all very concerned about me, even Chris Braun, who was the second in command among the admin staff. He was called the office manager.

I walked to my desk and removed my coat. I hung it on the hook near the door and then turned to face my audience. I explained about Susan. Pat immediately called me into her office, which was situated in a corridor a little way from our typing pool, the switchboard and Chris's office, which was a small room off the main reception area.

I sat with Pat for about 20 minutes. I had known her for some time. She had married a guy who had been my boss when I worked at Brady Engineering. Dave Lenham and I had become good mates, and he and Pat had visited Sue and me at home on several occasions, but that did not impinge on our working relationship. Pat was very easy-going, a good boss for whom to work. She had three children, Sarah, Mark and Usa, and she still managed to hold down a very demanding job. I had enormous respect for her.

"Now, don't forget, if there is anything we can do, you only have to let me know, or else talk to Chris, and we'll do all we can. It must be a terrible time for you!" she said as I stood up to leave.

"Yes," I said, holding my head down.

She came to me and stood beside me.

"You know you have lots of friends here, Boyzie, don't keep your feelings bottled up inside. We're all here to help you, you know that don't you, Boyzie?" she said.

"Thanks, Pat," I said, and squeezed her hand in a friendly way.

She drew me to her and gave me a peck on the right cheek.

"Off you go now, love, and don't forget what I've said, eh?"

I left the office of my boss and returned to take up my duties as receptionist/switchboard operative at the Family Support Centre in Bread Street, Gaynsford.

Chapter 4

I HAD MY lunch at the Gunners. It was a smashing pub that stood on the right at the very top of Gunners Lane. I often went in there for lunch. It was pleasant, comfortable and friendly, with a good atmosphere. Dennis Parkin, the 20-stone landlord was in his early forties, and he and his wife, Joan, with the help of three of their four children, ran the establishment very efficiently and well. It was a popular meeting place for lunch. They did a fantastic menu, and the ale was good too! Their pies and ploughman's lunches were out of this world, and very large indeed. You wondered how they got all that food onto one big platter, but somehow they did.

I walked into the lounge bar. George and Mary Parkin were both behind the bar. Both greeted me warmly. George served me with a pint and I ordered a ploughman's pie with French fries and all the salad. George said he would bring it to me as soon as it was ready. I thanked him.

Rob McCallasky, a young man about my height, well made, tough, with a strong Gaynsford accent, came and stood beside me.

"Shall we find a table an' sit dahn, mate?" he asked.

"Hi Rob!" I said, and took his elbow so he could lead me to the table.

He carried my foaming pint of bitter shandy for me and we sat down together. Rob showed me, by taking my right hand, whereabouts my drink was located on the table and he then asked me if I wanted a smoke. I declined. I did smoke sometimes, but I did not wish to do so, anticipating eats. He sat back, lit himself a cigarette and we both took long pulls at our drinks. Rob McCallasky worked in one of the smaller factories on the Hyland Road Industrial Estate. He had become a mate of mine since we met one day the previous winter.

We sat long into the afternoon on that occasion, talking about motorbikes, sport, all kinds of music, British comedy, soccer, girls, cars, where to get a good haircut and all kinds of other trivialities, nothing serious whatsoever. We had eaten, and enjoyed several convivial hours together, drinking one another's health. Rob had then driven me home on the back of his 1,000cc motorcycle. It had been a wonderful, relaxing winter's afternoon, on a day when I had half a day's holiday, which I was endeavouring to use up before the end of the leave year.

Our holidays were usually 25 days, plus days off for bank holidays. Those began in the April of each year and ran out in the March of the following year, and if one did not use up all one's allotted time, it was taken away. At one time you could carry it over, but not any more, unless you had a really good reason for so doing.

Rob and I sat and chatted. He was a single bloke, and the eldest of a family of ten. His dad was deceased, but his mum and several of his brothers and sisters lived in a house on the Morleston Estate in the Allerton area. Rob, however, lived alone in those days. He had his own flat and seemed to enjoy life to the full, as far as one could tell. He was a great bloke, and very easy to get on with. We clicked almost as soon as we met.   We both enjoyed a sumptuous repast, although I had not really wished for a great deal to eat, but the meals at the Gunners were almost always massive, and George had really pushed the boat out for me that afternoon. He came and served us and then Celia, his younger sister, brought us more drinks.

Later, Rob walked back to the corner of Bread Street with me and I shook his hand warmly as he left me to return to the factory. I had told Rob about what had happened to me that morning. He was angry, I could tell.

"Yo' be careful nah!" he said to me as he left.

I could hear him muttering as he walked quickly away towards his place of work on the Hyland Road Industrial Estate, and I returned to work on reception and the switchboard at the Family Support Unit. We were very busy for the remainder of the day.

Chapter 5

CHRIS BRAUN came into my small office where my desk and the switchboard were located, just off the main reception area where the typists sat. It had a window where people stood to wait for admission to the unit, and there was a button on the counter that they pushed. That caused a light to flash and a bell to ring, so that, if I was engaged on the switchboard, one of the typists or Chris, if he was in the vicinity, could answer the call from the person needing entry to our very busy Family Support Unit.

Chris Braun was 31 years old. The eldest of six brothers, he lived with his five younger brothers, his parents, plus 11 cats and seven dogs, in a two-bedroomed council house on Flint Street. The six young men, all aged between 17 and 31 years, shared one very large bedroom, but there was no privacy and the situation must have been very traumatic for all the family. That probably explained why Mr Christopher Braun was not the most friendly and well-mannered individual in God's world, but he had got a heart and, when he chose, could be very pleasant, even conspiratorial on occasions, especially with me.

That afternoon he walked into my little office, flung his five foot ten inch body onto one of the two sofas that stood side by side along the right-hand wall, and stretched out his long legs. He wanted to talk, and the switchboard was very busy, so it was going to be difficult.

"Tea?" he asked.

"Aw please!" I said.

I had not had a drink since lunchtime, and I was parched. Chris asked Tina Jobling, the office junior, if she would make us two large mugs of tea, then he flung himself down onto the couch again.

The switchboard was not lit up or buzzing at that time, so I could give him my attention, since the girls were looking after reception at that moment. Chris sat for a while then cleared his throat; he was not the most chatty bloke who ever inhabited God's earth! Sometimes, as I said, he would open up to me, but very rarely. We were certainly not 'best buddies', and he had a reputation among the staff there at the Family Support Unit for being somewhat morose. However, I knew he wanted to say something to me and because he had closed the door on entry, I guessed it must be fairly private, so I waited. He cleared his throat again and lit a cigarette. He sat back on the couch and stretched his long legs out before him. He had removed his shoes, and sat in his stockinged feet.

"Pat says you can go early tonight if you want, Boyzie," he said at last.

"Thanks," I said, "but I've made my plans for tonight."

Chris took a pull on his cigarette then spoke again.

"Well, any time you need to go early while Sue is so ill, you know all you have to do is ask."

I thanked him once again. He still showed no signs of moving.

"What you doin' Saturday?" he asked me. "Me an' all my brothers an' loads o' ahr mates are goin' dahn to Wembley on one o' the many coaches. I 'ope the Tahn lads win, eh?"

I had temporarily forgotten. On Saturday, Gaynsford United were in the FA League Challenge Cup Final at Wembley. A great occasion indeed for the people of the large, industrial North Midlands town!

"Aw," I said, "I suppose I'll be at the hospital with Sue." I thought for a moment, then added, "If not, I'll be over my brother-in-law's.

He and his lad, Dave, my nephew by marriage, they'll be watching it, no danger."

We chatted for a few moments more before he put on his shoes and stood up to leave. Before doing so, he came and stood beside me. He placed a hand on my right shoulder and stood for a moment.

"Don't forget nah," he said, in a voice that was full of bonhomie, "don't forget what I said, any time you need to go early, jus' let me or one o' the girls know. That'll be okay. All right, Boyzie?"

"Yes, and thanks again, Chris," I said.

He turned and left my office. The switchboard was buzzing. I bent to my task.

Chapter 6

SISTER WENDY Smith from ward 20 at the County Hospital telephoned me at work that afternoon at around five o'clock. She said she had just come on duty. Susan was comfortable, but that was all she was able to tell me, except that when I went in that evening, she and Dr Mervyn Fraser, together with Dr Janet Perry and Dr Mike Chilcott, two GPs from my surgery who also worked in the hospital, would all like to have a quiet word with me.

I guessed why. Susan was coming near to the end. Qh God, what would I do? How would I cope? Was I being selfish even thinking like that? No, no, of course not! I was still very much alive, and life had to go on even after Susan had... had...

The switchboard was buzzing again and I did not feel like answering any more calls that day. Not now, no, not now!

※

Just after 5.45 p.m. I left my small office, locking the door behind me. I kept a key to the office on my key ring, an arrangement that had been agreed with those above me in status, a long time ago. Before leaving that night, I chatted to the cleaning ladies for a while. There were four of them; Beryl Waydeson, Sue Garlick, Pauline Copley and Connie Jobling. All smashing women, all of them living close by on the streets that ran off Gunners Lane. Three of those women, Beryl Waydeson, Sue

Garlick and Pauline Copley, had teenage sons at the Gunners Lane Academy, or at the Sixth Form College. Connie Jobling had numerous grandsons there too. We chatted for a while then it was time for me to leave.

Chapter 7

I HAD ACQUIRED a new white cane from Wayne Clark, a black worker who liaised with all manner of workers for disabled people from his office on the third floor of our busy Family Support Unit. Wayne was in his twenties. He was a good bloke, and lived with his mum, Hesta, and several other family members in a three-bedroomed house on Harrison Street, which was the first street on the right off Gunners Lane. Wayne and I had become quite friendly over a period of time.

The evening was fine and warm. I unfurled my new white cane, a little longer than my other one, and strode quickly towards the top of Gunners Lane and the bus stop, which was not too far from the crossing. It was a stop for the bus going into town, and was slightly nearer than the other one. They proliferated in that area of Allerton, although I wished buses did, especially in the late evening. They were supposed to leave for town every 15 minutes, but sometimes the gap could be as long as 40 or 45 minutes at that time of night. I hoped it would be on time, or as near as dammit is to swearing, that night anyway, as I was hungry and wanted to get something to eat before I went up to the hospital.

I felt selfish thinking of eating when my lovely wife was lying up at the County Hospital dying of cancer, but I knew that she was receiving the best of all possible care, and that she would want me to face whatever they had to tell me feeling replete, comfortable and as happy as possible. That reminded me I would have to buy some more cigarettes that evening, and even as I thought of doing so, I felt a pang of guilt. Perhaps I ought to consider giving up smoking completely. Ah well! I would see.

I walked along, quickening my pace, towards the top of Gunners Lane and the bus shelter.

Chapter 8

Between the end of August, 1966, and mid-April, 1973, Susan had been pregnant seven times. On six occasions she miscarried early in each pregnancy. On the seventh occasion, she carried for almost the full term. We were both so excited and thrilled.

Nearly two weeks before her expected date of confinement, Sue was upstairs cleaning the bedrooms. I was out at work. She had been wishing to clean the dust from the light fittings, the pelmets and the tops of the wardrobes. She was standing on a chair when the legs gave way and the chair collapsed. Sue was lying on the .floor of the bedroom for some time before she could summon help using the telephone in the front bedroom where we slept.

At the time of the accident, Sue was cleaning in the rear bedroom, but she managed to crawl on all fours to ours, pick up the phone and summon the help of Jean Barradell, our near neighbour on The Circle. It was as she was speaking to Jean that Sue realised she was bleeding heavily between her legs. The child was stillborn later that evening—a little girl. Susan did not even see her. She did not wish to do so. We did not even give her a name.

Sue stayed in hospital for almost a month after the stillbirth, because they discovered the beginnings of cancer in her womb, and also found that her ovaries were diseased. They said we would never have been able to have a natural healthy child, but they were all very kind to both of us, seeing how upset we were about what had occurred, and the subsequent discovery of cancer. .

Susan underwent a complete hysterectomy, despite the fact that she was so young. They told us that if they had not performed the operation, then she would have died, and who were we to disagree with medical opinion? We both agreed that was the best course of action. Sue wanted to feel better. I just wanted her home again with me, and for her to feel as well as possible following the aftermath of the stillbirth of our unnamed daughter.

ĝ♥ঔ

The following September, Sue went back into hospital and had her left breast removed. They had found a lump there, and it was discovered to be cancerous. My poor darling Sue! Still, despite all, when she returned home, she endeavoured to remain cheerful and to keep herself busy. She was not the same woman, and our marriage was suffering, particularly in regard to our lovemaking!

At the beginning of 1975, we started sleeping in separate rooms, but we came back together again after some three or four months. It was good to feel her warm inviting body beside mine once more, and I was happy that we had come back together, but our lovemaking was never quite the same. Sue would only allow me to go so far, and I often ended up in the bathroom, masturbating and feeling angry and rejected by my wife, the person with whom I should have been able to enjoy the act of lovemaking. I was unaware of how poorly my wife really was, because she endeavoured to keep it from me.

Chapter 9

I N 1976, we decided to move from 48 The Circle and subsequently applied to the council for rehousing. On 27th August, 1976, our tenth wedding anniversary, we moved house, a very traumatic experience for both of us!

We had wonderful help from the network of people that had formed around us. They did everything bar carry us both over the threshold of the newly acquired house in Rutland Close. People really are wonderful, and the good far outweigh the bad—or at least they did there in that large North Midlands town. Most of the people who lived around there had very little, but what they had, they were prepared to share with you, especially if they took to you. We had been tremendously lucky. We had loads and loads of good friends, and Sue's family were very supportive, and we had needed their support in the past.

ຂ≫≼ງ

As I drew near to the bus shelter at the corner of Gunners Lane that evening, I knew well enough that I should be very glad of all the support I could get in the future, but for now, back to the present!

Such a noise greeted me as I turned the corner and walked briskly towards the bus shelter. There seemed to be loads of people waiting there that night. Were they all waiting for the bus? No, no, they were not! It very quickly became clear that they were boys and young men from the Academy and the Sixth Form College, and that they were all waiting for *me*! Oh, help!

I did not want a confrontation. I had a lot to think about. It had been a long and tiring day, and so much had happened. No, the last thing I needed was confrontation with those young people that night. There were literally crowds of them all around the bus shelter and quickly, quietly, excitedly, they gathered around me in such a vastness of numbers as I stood waiting for my bus to take me into town.

I pretended to ignore what was happening all around me, deeming that to be the best policy, but they would not allow me to do so. A tall, well-built young man came up beside me on my right and leaned his body heavily against mine.

"That's a fine cane you've got there, mate!" he said.

All around they giggled, then came a loud roar over my shoulders and from every direction.

"Yeh, yeh! That's a smasher, mate."

More pushing, more giggling, the sounds of even more running feet as greater and greater numbers of young people arrived on the scene. I felt hemmed in, trapped, totally overwhelmed by the strength and vastness of their numbers! I neither wanted to talk to them, nor did I want them to talk to me. I wished with all my heart that the bus would come and take me away from there, but there was no sign of a bus on the horizon as yet. They continue to push, shove, jostle and pack all around me, and to pile their bodies hard up against mine, as they pressed, struggled and literally fought to get near me.

It was all so embarrassing. On my left-hand side, a young person was standing very close up beside me. He pushed himself hard up against me and placed a hand on my left shoulder. I felt concern, concern that I was surrounded by so very, very many young people, concern that my personal privacy was being invaded by them, and in such numbers.

The young man on my left spoke.

"Aw'm called Jamie Ash, everyone calls me Smokey. Aw wor

43

one o' t'lads as pushed yo' into t'road an' in front o' that truck this mornin' an'… an' aw'm sorry, mate!"

He then seemed to kneel down at my feet.

"Sorry, mate. Sorry aw wor so stupid!" he said, kneeling before me.

Now it was my turn to feel stupid. Suddenly they were kneeling all around me, kneeling down on the ground all around me, where I stood, waiting for my bus to come and take me out of that totally bizarre situation.

"Sorry!"

"Sorry, mate!"

"Aw wor responsible, too!"

"We wor stupid, an' we are sorry, mate!"

"So sorry!"

"We behaved abominably this mornin', an' we all feel desperate abaht it!"

"Sorry, mate!"

"Sorry, pal!"

It went on and on and on as more and more, and even more arrived from everywhere, or so it seemed to me, standing there among them all. I was so dreadfully embarrassed!

"On your feet, lads," I said. "I understand! You did behave very stupidly this morning, but we can forget about it now. I am sure you've all been ticked off by your headteacher and other members of staff, and I am all right, so… so as far as I am concerned it's all over and forgotten. No more to be said. Please, get back onto your feet now, lads, no more grovelling, come on, on your feet, gents. This is silly! Come on, all of you, get back onto your feet, lads, and lean up off me. Arms off my shoulders please, lads! Please, gents!"

I had said much more than I intended to say, and it seemed to be having the desired effect. The bloke who was leaning heavily against me on my right then said:

"Aw'm Carl Pick. Aw wor the one who broke your white cane this mornin', an' aw wanted to say as 'ow aw'm sorry abaht that too, mate."

The volume of noise was growing all the time, but at least everyone seemed to be getting back onto their feet once again.

"It's okay, Carl" I said to the tall, hefty young man, leaning against me on my right. "I understand, it was just high spirits and ignorance and as far as I am concerned, it's all forgotten now."

A loud falsetto voice cried out from somewhere behind me.

"Here cum more of us, even more of us cummin'!"

I could hear the sounds of running feet as even more young people joined the vast numbers of those who were pushing, jostling, crowding all around me. Oh, help! How could I get out of that situation?

From two different directions, help came. From somewhere on my right, I heard feet running on the other side of the road then suddenly he was over on our side. Suddenly he was pushing in beside me. It was Tony Barradell, the eldest son of Jean and Terry, who used to be our near neighbours on The Circle.

"Yo' aal reet, Boyzie?" he asked anxiously, an arm around me.

I was shaking. At the same moment, from my left, I heard more running feet. That time it was PC Joe Capper, the young policeman who had come to Hay Street to talk to me that morning after the incident outside Gunners Lane Academy and Sixth Form College. He stood close in on my left. I was still shaking!

"I-I think so. These lads w-were just apologising for what happened this morning. There's nothing wrong. Everything's fine. I'm all right, thanks."

Quite suddenly everyone started talking at once—complete pandemonium. I just stood there letting it all wash over me, and in the midst of it all my bus arrived. Tony Barradell and PC Joe Capper helped me aboard, and there was a great and lusty roar from all the lads.

"Cheers, mate, you're a gud un, see yo' tomorrer, mate!"

As I settled myself into the corner on the right by the window, up towards the rear of the vehicle, I had no doubt at all that they mean it. I thanked Tony and Joe Capper for helping me and they both dismounted from the bus, which then started rolling on its way towards town. Ah well, that could have been a lot more traumatic than it turned out to be. I was sure the arrival of two blokes who knew me had prevented that situation from turning out much worse for me than it had done, and I was very grateful to both of them.

Now I sat back and concentrated on what was ahead of me that evening. I was dreading the meeting with the doctors at the hospital because I was almost sure I already knew most of what they were going to tell me. I resolved to have something to eat at the Laughing Cow then I would be ready to go to the County Hospital and learn my Susan's fate.

Chapter 10

THE NEWS summary had been read. Craig, my engineer, had just played my jingle. I opened up the mike.

"Hi! It's me, Rick Dee, and I'm here with you for the next 80 hours on the music marathon that will take us into a brand new decade—the last one of this twentieth century. Are you ready for the nineties?"

Rick Dee was my chosen name as a presenter on Sunny Gold Radio. I had worked full time for Sunny Gold Radio, a commercial radio station in the North Midlands, since June of the past year. That followed my return to Gaynsford from Harts Hill. I usually presented the 'Night Shift' between midnight and 6 a.m. six days per week, and 'Afternoon Delight' on Sundays between 2 p.m. and 6 p.m., but thatwas a special. I had been chosen to be the one to undertake that very special broadcast.

I went into my first section of the programme—a section I had named, 'Getting Started'—nine songs one after the other, all from the seventies. I started with 'That's the Way I Like it'. Now the first record was in progress, Craig knew what to do for the next several minutes, so I could relax again. I took a long pull from the can I had beside me, and lay back in the comfortable swivel chair in front of the mike. The mike was now closed, and Craig needed no instructions from me. It was time for more thinking back to that Wednesday evening at the beginning of May 1978…

Chapter 11

ARRIVING IN town, I went straight to the Laughing Cow, a very popular venue for eating and drinking, especially with truckers and bikers, and it was one of my favourite cafes in the town centre.

Rosie Turkington, an ex-neighbour of ours from The Circle, saw me at the door and quickly led me over to a table. Her son, Paul, went to the Gunners Lane Academy. Rosie was pleased to see me and she served me with a good meal; leak and potato soup, followed by liver and bacon casserole, and bread and butter pudding with lovely thick custard. All washed down with two mugs of hot chocolate. Wonderful!

Rosie was busy, but she had a few quick words with me. I told her that when I left the cafe I was going to the County Hospital to see Susan, and explained what had happened. Rosie expressed concern.

"Ah! Send her my love eh, Boyzie?"

I said I would.

Rosie was a large, loud, rather indolent woman, and her house was a tip, but like so many people in that North Midlands town, she had a heart as big as Texas. After my meal I ordered a taxi to take me to the County Hospital, and Rosie rang Phoenix Cars for me. Bob Douse, one of the four partners who owned and ran the outfit, arrived to drive me to the hospital himself.

Bob was in his late twenties, a big, well-made bloke, who originally came from Merseyside. He was ex-army. He was married to Carol, some four and a half years his junior, and they had one son, Steven. He was six years old, very mischievous and full of life, exactly as a boy of his age should be. Bob thought the world of him. Bob knew me as Boyzie, like so many other people who knew me well.

Boyzie is a nickname. It first occurred one day when I was very small and was hiding from Mum because I didn't want a bath. Doreen and Eric, my twin sister and brother, found me at the bottom of the garden by the chicken run. Together, they took me to the house and Mum, who was in process of baking and also running the bath for me, said distractedly:

"Come on, Boyzie! Come and have your bath!"

The nickname stuck, and from that day on I was known as Boyzie!

As we drove to the County Hospital, Bob chatted to me about all kinds of trivia. The match on Saturday was between Gaynsford and Glosport, on Merseyside, his home team, but he wouldn't be going down to Wembley. Instead, he was going down to the Gunners and then on to the Laughing Cow where they were having a luncheon party for whoever wanted to go, and then they would all get on coaches, or into cabs, and be driven down to the home ground. There they were planning to show the whole of the game on wide-screen TV, which they had recently acquired. He asked me if I wanted to go down with him and the lads.

"Aw cud fetch yo' from 'ome if yo' wanted to cum!" he said.

I thought about it! By rights, I ought to go and sit with Sue. I told him I would ring Phoenix Cars and leave a message if I wanted to go, and he agreed that would be fine!

When we arrived at the County Hospital, Bob walked with me to the porter's desk and left me there. I told him I would ring when I wanted to be picked up.

"Fine, aw'll probley cum back for yo' myself," he said.

I thanked him for his help that night and then stood waiting, waiting until someone would notice me! Eventually, a young fellow asked me whom I wanted. I told him where I needed to go, and he directed one of the porters to take me up to ward 20, women's surgical.

On the ward, Sister Wendy Smith greeted me. She took me to see Susan, who was very drowsy, but was, nevertheless, delighted to see me. I sat and held her hand and we tried to talk, but it was obvious that she was very sleepy due to the drugs that were being pumped into her body. Her understanding of what I was telling her and her responses were not very clear. This is how it will be from now on, I suppose, I thought. Ah well, we must try and make the best of it for the time we have left.

No!

No!

Stop thinking like that! That's defeatist! Stop it. You are here. You are with her for the moment, so enjoy it. Get the most out of it that you can, Boyzie, because... because... you'll need all the memories you can store—afterwards.

I steered the conversation around to the trivia of the day. I told her how Badger and Meggie were and that they were missing her. I tried to talk to her about how all the neighbours in Rutland Close were doing, and about how they were all asking after her, but her responses were very muted. Eventually she turned her head towards me, took my hand and gave it a little squeeze of recognition. Good. That's good isn't it? I said that I had seen Tony Barradell that day. She moved her head and spoke.

"Boyzie!"

"Well?" I said.

She lost interest then, and closed her eyes, but continued to keep hold of my hand. After a while, Sister Wendy Smith came over to me.

"She's fast off! Don't wake her, but take your hand away gently and I'll make her comfortable, then we'll go to my office. Dr Mervyn and Dr Mike are waiting to see us there!"

No Janet Perry? Ah well! Dr Mike Chilcot knew my wife and her situation as well as anyone in the practice, so it was not a problem, Janet not being there that night.

I gently let go of my lovely Susan's hand and Sister Wendy ensured that she was comfortable. She said something to a young nurse who was engaged in reading Susan's charts at the end of her bed then we walked together to her office. She ordered tea and biscuits for us all. Once those had arrived, the four of us sat around and chatted, or rather, three of them chatted to me!

I said very little because I was too stunned by what I was being told. Dr Mervyn Fraser began the discussion.

"As you know, Mr Dickson, your wife, Susan, is very ill! We feel we cannot really do any more to help her. All we can do now is to try and keep her as comfortable and happy as possible."

I nodded. I could feel the tears stinging my eyes. Mike Chilcot, the doctor from the practice where Sue and I had been patients for almost two years, sat close beside me. He was a pleasant, forthright, but nevertheless, kind and considerate Irishman, with a broad brogue and a very dry sense of humour. He was a couple of years older than me.

"It's been decided that we should move Susan tomorrow," Dr Merv was saying. "We are transferring her to the Mary Craigie Unit at the College Hospital, Lounds Hill."

I knew well enough what that meant! The Mary Craigie Unit was the cancer unit—the place where seriously ill cancer patients went to die!

No!

No!

Come on, Boyzie! You are not being fair. It's a lovely unit. You have seen it. You went to the opening of it along with Sue, and you both said how much you liked it. Yes, in all honesty, Mary Craigie is very pleasant and so peaceful. Susan will have her own room there, and she will be very well looked after by the dedicated staff. What more could anyone need?

I needed *her*! Oh, God, how I needed her at that moment. How I longed to reach out and hold her and never ever let her go again. Oh, Susan! Oh, my love, my fairest! How can I let you go? Yet...

and yet I must. I must, because you are suffering, and I cannot wish you to do that. You are going to a lovely place, and while you are in there, I'll be able to visit you plenty. We can spend precious time together, my love. Yes, yes we can.

I was saying all this to her in my mind, while the doctors droned on in my head. Sister Wendy gently shook me by the shoulder.

"Boyzie, *Mr Dickson*, your tea," she said.

"Oh, thanks, thanks very much," I said, almost mechanically.

I was staring, staring into nothingness, and my eyes were wet, wet with unshed tears, tears that would not come. They would not come until later, much later on that night, when I was at home, alone, except for my dogs. I sat and tried to drink from the mug of tea I had been offered, but I could not swallow the hot sweet liquid. It seemed to stick in my swollen throat.

I was listening to the plans to transfer Sue and her belongings over to the College Hospital at Lounds Hill, but if anyone had asked me what was being said, I would not have been able to tell them.

Sister Wendy Smith placed a cool hand on my forehead and spoke kindly.

"I know this is a lot for you to take in. We can go over things again when you come in tomorrow."

The inference appeared to be that I would go with Susan when she was moved. I eventually agreed to that, although a little half-heartedly at first, then I realised it would be good to help her settle into her new home—her last home. Yes, I might as well start getting used to that idea now, I thought. This will be her last resting place before...

Before!

At last the discussion was over. I was being escorted downstairs to the main entrance by a big, West Indian bloke called Oscar Henry. Oscar (Ossie) said he was the brother of Rue (Rupert) who worked as the barman at the Gunners. Rue was known to me! He had only been working at the Gunners in Allerton for about a month, and he worked evenings and weekends. He was a cabbie

Monday to Friday from 6 a.m. to 6 p.m., so he worked really hard! Like Ossie, Rue was a single bloke. The Henry family lived in one of the maze of streets that ran off Gunners Lane, and Ossie said he had seen me around!

We reached the main entrance of the County Hospital, and Ossie booked a taxi for me. I sat down in the foyer and waited for Bob Douse to drive me home. Now I could think, but I didn't want to think. My head was pounding. It was too full of thoughts whirling around like an endless kaleidoscope in my head, and it would not stop. Oh, God, *please*! Please make it stop!

When Bob came, he had to touch me on the shoulder to get a response. He spoke to me gently, not at all like himself. Bob was a big, rough Merseysider, but his manner towards me that night was gentle—like a 'gentle giant'.

"Boyzie! It's me, Bob. Cum on, mate. Aw've cum to tek' yo' 'ome nah!"

He and Ossie each put an arm around my shoulders, and helped me to my feet. As they did so, Ossie said:

"He's jus' 'ad some bad news."

"Yeh," Bob said.

We walked together outside and over to Bob's cab. They settled me in and then Bob drove me home. He was not inclined to leave me.

"Are you sure you'll be okay, Boyzie?" he asked anxiously.

"Yes, yes, I'll be fine, honest, thanks for all the help today."

I tried to pay him, but he would not take the money from me, and said he hoped to hear from me on Saturday. I had completely forgotten about the match, so important to the male population of that large, industrial North Midlands town, and of so little consequence in my life at that moment!

Bob shook my hand warmly at my front gate. He was still very concerned about me as he left. I was just about to close my front door and give myself up entirely to the rivers of tears welling up inside me, when I heard a shout from the house next door on the right.

"Hey, Boyzie!"

The three Williams brothers, Don, Dave and Dek, were on their way around to see me. Oh no not now, please, lads, not now! "Hello," I called out to them, hoping I might stall their attempt to come and visit me.

The Williams' family had been our next door neighbours ever since we moved into the house on Rutland Close, and excellent neighbours they had been to us. Vera, a lovely, jolly motherly woman, had really taken us under her wing. She loved to help Sue in any way she was able, and often did shopping, cleaning or other chores to assist us. Cyril, her husband, older than Vera by five years or so, was a good bloke. He had undertaken painting outside for us in the past and had helped me in the garden. He was a good man to have a drink with and to keep in with. Like his three sons, and his elder brother, Basil (Bas), who also lived with the family, Cyril was a six-footer.

All three of his sons, Donald (Don), David (Dave) and Derek (Dek) were tall, well-built young men in their twenties. All three were employed. Two of them worked at Webster's, the meat factory, and Dave worked in a warehouse, heaving and hauling goods around. All three were weighty, and all a little 'slow', not severely retarded, just a little slow. All three of them were dead keen on animals, and had loads of pets at home, and they also looked after my two dogs, Badger and Meggie, when I was at work etc. My shout of salutation did not prevent the three lads from coming around! They descended upon me altogether, all three talking at once.

I reluctantly let them in. They followed me into the lounge and distributed themselves around on the sofa and two chairs. I sat next to Dave on the sofa.

"I've literally just walked in, lads! I've come from the hospital and I'm very tired and hungry, so can we keep this short, please? Don't all talk together else I can't understand what you are telling me!"

I sounded sharp. I didn't mean to sound like that, but it passed over the heads of those three excitable and loud young men, who still told me what they had to say, speaking in unison.

"It's your Badger!"

Oh! Now what?

"Well?" I asked, puzzled.

Badger had seemed fine when I left him that morning, but then, to be fair, I had not really had a lot of time to devote to either of the dogs before I left home that day. Oh, what a long time ago that seemed now! I seemed to have lived a lifetime in one day that day, so much had happened, and now it seemed that it wasn't over yet.

Chapter 12

Badger, my old dog, was lying on a blanket on the kitchen floor at Vera's. The lads, speaking in unison, told me that they had taken both dogs for three long walks that day, and that, on the third of those walks, Badger's legs had seemed to give way, so one of them had carried him home to their house. Badger was lying very still. He kept gasping from time to time, and Vera said he had been moaning too. He had moved off the blanket twice, and had done everything under him, so Vera told me. She had coped in her usual accepting way.

As I have said, the family had loads of pets, including ferrets, fish, reptiles, birds, rodents, even stick-insects, but no dogs or cats, which was why the three lads took such a great interest in my two dogs and loved caring for them. Two of them had been on holiday that day as the meat factory was closed, and Dave had come home from the warehouse at 4 p.m. because he only worked part time on a Wednesday. They had been looking after Badger and Meggie all day for me, thank goodness!

Meggie, having been walked, brushed, fed, watered etc., was now in my conservatory, in her bed underneath the table, asleep probably. She would be all right until I got home. Now I would have to take poor old Badger down to the Parkside Veterinary Hospital. Ah well! Better get on with it. Cyril Williams said he would drive me down there. The three young men wanted to go with us, but Vera persuaded them not to do so, saying they would be too upset if anything bad happened to Badger, whom all three of them adored. They said their goodbyes to him, and Cyril carried him, wrapped in the blanket, out to the family's van.

It was a Morris Traveller van, quite elderly, but very well cared for, and still roadworthy after all those years. Badger was carefully and comfortably laid in the back of the van, and Cyril and I climbed into the seats at the front. We sped off towards the Parkside Veterinary Hospital. I had a very heavy heart. Badger had come to us as a tiny bundle of fur soon after our marriage. We had both adored him. Now, a few months before his twelfth birthday, it looked as though the old boy had had some kind of stroke, and if so, then I knew what I had to do. There was no way any animal belonging to me was going to be allowed to suffer unduly—not if it could be avoided.

The vet on duty that evening was Nicola Simms. She was young, brisk, but very thorough and extremely pleasant. She told me that she thought old Badger had had a stroke and that she might be able to get him back on his feet with tablets and plenty of tender loving care. By now, I was hardly able to keep the tears away. I told Nicola Simms that I had just come from the County Hospital, where my wife had been admitted that morning. I explained my situation, and she was very understanding. She told me gently, but firmly, that the decision was entirely mine, but that, if I wished it, she would put Badger gently and quietly to sleep.

After a few moments' consideration and after standing beside him making a fuss of the old boy, who had been the companion of me and my lovely Susan ever since about a week after our return from honeymoon, I decided that it was in everyone's best interests to let him go. Nicola did the job while I was there. I stood holding one of Badger's paws very gently whilst she injected him and he simply lay down and went off to sleep—as simple and as painless as that. As we travelled home to Rutland Close, I wished that they could treat human beings with as much dignity!

Cyril Williams dropped me off at the house. The three Williams brothers were all sitting together on my front garden wall, and when they saw us get out of the small Morris van without Badger, they gathered around us, all asking questions. Cyril silenced the three excitable young men, asked me if I would be all right, made sure my keys were returned to me by Don then led the three lads back into their own house, where he proposed to sit them down and quietly tell them what had occurred. I shook his hand, thanked him for his help that evening then gratefully took myself indoors to my house.

After removing my coat and shoes, checking on Meggie, letting her out into the big paved yard at the rear of the house, putting the kettle on for a hot drink etc., I flung myself down in my favourite armchair and wept profusely! The river of tears overwhelmed me and I gave myself up to it completely!

Chapter 13

I DON'T KNOW how long I sat there like that, but eventually, I, came to sufficiently to realise that Meggie was barking like mad in the yard, so I went and let her in. As I settled her down in her bed under the big table in the conservatory, which Sue had loved so much and in which she had kept so many plants, I kissed Meggie on the top of her head. She did something she had never done before; she licked my hand.

"It's just you and me now, Meggie!" I told her.

Having ensured that she was settled, I locked and secured the house, and went upstairs to bed. I stripped, showered and lay on top of the bed. The evening was warm, but not close. I lay there completely naked, stretched out on top of the counterpane, which I always kept pulled over the king-size bed I had shared with my lovely Susan. I lay there, but I did not sleep very well. I tossed and turned in fitful slumber all night long. I had dreams, strange dreams; dreams about Sue, dreams about Badger, dreams about being pushed into the middle of the road by the lads, dreams about marrying Alice May McNault, and the three Williams brothers were arguing about which of them was to be best man. All kinds of strange dreams invaded my sleep that night.

§☙❧§

At 5 a.m. the following morning, I awoke sweating, so decided to get up and have a bath. Afterwards, I went downstairs in my dressing gown and slippers. While Meggie ran in the yard and barked a hymn to the dawn, I made myself scrambled eggs, bacon and tomatoes, and buttered several slices of thick bread. I enjoyed a hearty breakfast, well washed down with several mugs of hot sweet tea. Afterwards I went upstairs again, made the bed and got ready for work.

Another day had begun!

Chapter 14

A T 1.15 p.m. that day, I left work and went into town on the bus. I had been given half a day off to go with Susan to the Mary Craigie Unit and see her settled in. I was also to have the whole of the following day off so I could spend the entire day with her down at the unit. I had decided not to tell Sue about dear old Badger. I knew how much his death would upset her.

I had had no dinner, so I went to the Laughing Cow and purchased some sandwiches and a can of fizzy orange, plus a packet of smoky bacon crisps and a Kit Kat. I popped those into my shoulder bag and then went to the bus stop and caught a bus up to County Hospital. I arrived there at around 2.25 p.m. I went straight up to ward twenty. Ossie, the porter, took me up there.

Sister Thornhill was on duty and so was Staff Nurse Christine Johnson, whom I knew. She was a lovely, lively West Indian lady, who always greeted me warmly.

"So, they are movin' your wife den, Boyzie?" she said brightly as I walked with her to Sister Thornhill's office.

"Yes," I said, "she's going to Mary Craigie at the College Hospital."

"Aw, she'll be very comfortable there, you know," said Staff Nurse Johnson, and she gave my hand a little squeeze as she left me at the door of Sister Jean Thornhill's office.

Jean Thornhill greeted me, made me a mug of hot sweet tea and I ate my sandwiches while she and Staff Nurse Johnson prepared Susan for her journey to the College Hospital and the Mary Craigie Unit. At 4.10 p.m. we set off in an ambulance, driven by Andy Lee, another bloke whom I knew. He had picked Sue up the day before from our house and taken her into hospital. Andy was in his early twenties, married with four young children. He drove us over to the Mary Craigie Unit.

§•~•§

Once Sue was settled in her room, they brought us both a drink; a big mug of hot chocolate for me, a pot of tea for Sue. We sat together in her room and drank while we chatted. She was tired, but in good spirits, and delighted with her beautiful room, which had en suite facilities being a shower and toilet, and a wash basin with a big mirror above.

"It's gorgeous, don't you think so, love?"

I agreed it was, but in my heart of hearts, I would rather have had her come home to me, even if it was only for a few weeks. Still, I had to admit, she was about to receive the very best of care there and that I would not have been able to match it if she had returned home.

"I'm happy you like it, me lady," I joked, putting on my butler's voice.

"Oh, it's luverlee, darlin'!" she said in a silly pseudo-cockney whine, which she hadn't adopted for ages.

We both laughed.

§•~•§

Later, while she ate her supper and we talked just before I went home, we became more serious.

"Boyzie?"

"Well?" I said.

"When I've gone, will you marry again?"

I was taken aback! We'd never talked like that before.

"Er... I... I don't know! Why do you ask, love?"

She took my hand, which was lying on the arm of her chair, and squeezed it.

"I want you to get married again, love. I don't want you to be on your own!"

I laughed.

"But I've got lots of friends, then I've got my family, and your relatives are very good to me. No! I don't reckon I'm in any hurry to marry again! Anyway… no, *no*!"

"Don't say that!" she said quite firmly and rather fiercely. "I really mean it, Boyzie, I hope you will remarry."

༄

After I left her and was on the way back to Rutland Close, I thought about what she had said. I would have to wait and see. One could never tell how life would turn out. I had never dreamed, for example, that I would shortly be a widower. Not until a few days before, anyway, when I realised how ill my darling really was! I know it's crazy, well, but you always hope, don't you? I had held on to my hopes right up until the previous day, when they had been gently, but firmly, shattered into nothingness by the disclosure that there was nothing else anyone could do for Sue except to keep her happy and comfortable. Ah well…

I could ensure that she was kept happy by my regular visits, and even when she did not wish to talk to me because she felt too tired, I would sit with her, talk quietly to her, generally keep up the lines of communication between us. When the final moment came to part, I would try to ensure that we parted with dignity. Yes, I wanted our parting to be dignified. Fool that I was, I did not think how hard it was really going to be! I did not realise how soon we would have to part either, otherwise I might have felt more emotional at that time than I did as we drove home from Lounds Hill that night.

Barry Barnet, another of Bob's drivers, drove me home. He was a pleasant young man in his mid-twenties, single, and greatly looking forward to the match on Saturday.

"We'll slaughter 'em eh, Boyzie?" he said as he left me at my gate.

"Ay, we likely will," I said, and walked quickly down my front garden path to let myself into my house.

Chapter 15

On the Friday morning I overslept. It was well after 8 a.m. when I awoke, and only then because I felt Meggie's rough tongue licking my face. She had slept on the bottom of the bed the previous night, guarding my feet. I laughed as I came awake and felt her licking my face all over.

"Oh well, I've had a wash now, I shan't need to do that when I get up in a minute!"

Meggie settled down again and started to snore.

"Come on, lady. Up we come!" I told her as I heaved myself off the bed.

Meggie jumped down and went padding downstairs to wait for me at the bottom. I put on my dressing gown and slippers, and went after her.

ॐ

At 9.15 a.m. I knocked on Vera's front door. She answered it, closely followed by her three sons, none of whom were at work that day.

"More holidays?" I asked.

"Ay, we're all off together today, Boyzie!" exclaimed the three brothers, speaking in unison.

"Good," I said. "You might want to look after our Meggie then?"

"Aw yeh," they all said, speaking together.

Vera took the keys from me.

"They'll all be back at work Monday, love, but *I* can look out for her if you need me to do so."

"Thanks, Vera, I appreciate it," I told her.

Simon Potts's red Volvo pulled up outside. I made sure my place was secured, then waved goodbye to the Williams family, who promised faithfully to look after Meggie all day, and then, sitting beside Simon Potts, I set off to spend the day with my Susan at the Mary Craigie Unit.

Chapter 16

I T WAS a cold, raw morning at 6 a.m. on Friday, 29th December, 1989.

The news jingle had just kicked in and there were three minutes of news before I started again—just time for a hot drink. Bill Grundy, the radio station manager at Sunny Gold Radio, had just walked into the studio where I was based. He had brought me a mug of hot chocolate.

"Thanks, Bill," I said, and I meant it, as you could work up a thirst and a half doing that job.

Bill placed the mug on the ops desk, where the mike and the switches were to connect me with Craig and to ensure I was going out to the general public. He took hold of my right hand in order to show me where he had placed the mug.

Good for Bill Grundy! He had remembered his training, the training I had given him and all members of the station staff when I first started working there. That was back in June of that year when I was offered the full-time placement as presenter of the 'Night Shift' and 'Afternoon Delight' programmes. By rights, I should have finished my show and should have been getting ready to go home at that time, but not that day. It was a special, and one I'd wanted to do ever since I had first arrived there. I would be the only one on air for the whole of the day, yes, and for all of the next day as well! In fact, I was the only one on air until 8 a.m. on Monday morning. I was just over six hours into an 80-hour music marathon.

The news was over, and I was three-quarters of the way down my large mug of hot chocolate. I heard my jingle and pressed the control on the mike that stood before me on the ops desk.

"Hi, it's still me, Rick Dee. I'm here with you all day today and into the New Year on this 80-hour music marathon. I hope you are going to join me and show your support for what we are doing here at Sunny Gold Radio, the best songs, all year long."

Again, I went into a music melange of non-stop eighties oldies, and once again I settled down to thinking.

Chapter 17

Simon Potts was 28 years old, single, a six-footer, weighed around 16 and a half stone, a smoker and he liked his pint. He enjoyed going to the Laughing Cow for dinner, and that was where we first met. We had become firm friends over a period of years. Simon drove freelance. He was a cabbie, but did not work for a recognised firm, preferring to work for himself. He reckoned to make quite a good living out of it.

"Goin' te the match temorrer," he announced as we drove along together. "Me an' my bruwers, we're all goin' dahn on a coach, startin' early in the mornin', so I ain't workin' late tenight!"

"I hope you enjoy yourselves," I said.

"Aw'm sure we will, Boyzie!" he said with gusto. "How're yo' spendin' the day temorrer?"

I smiled. The next day would be a red-letter day in the mind of almost every bloke in that town—the day when Gaynsford United took on the world! Everyone would remember for years afterwards where he was at the very moment the winning goal was scored, but for me it meant very little.

"I shall probably be over here with my wife," I replied, after a moment's silence between us.

Simon escorted me into the foyer of the Mary Craigie Unit and I stood waiting for someone to take me to Susan's room.

೬•ﻭ

We spent a very long day together, but it was a lovely day; the last really wonderful day we had together, as it transpired. At the

70

time I was unaware that it was going to be our last really optimistic day together. Sue was so positive that day and so full of life, it was hard to realise that she was so very, very ill. We chatted and laughed. We went out into the grounds and sat under the trees, Sue in a wheelchair, me on a bench with her beside me. We held hands, kissed, joked and chatted while we ate lunch together underneath the cooling shade of the beautiful trees in the almost silent gardens at Mary Craigie. There were only eight patients in the unit, and six of them were bedridden, so we had the gardens all to ourselves—it was bliss!

The staff made us a wonderful picnic lunch and later, a high tea, which we also ate in the garden. At 9.30 p.m. when I left her, Suzy was very tired, but we were both blissfully happy after a lovely day spent together, a day that I would remember for a long time, long after the inevitable occurrence, which was to take place much sooner than either of us envisaged.

That evening Suzy repeated her request for me to marry again. I said I would see then I laughed. She laughed too, but said again that she was serious and very much wanted me to marry again once she had gone. She said it with no rancour, no malice. She did not even seem afraid of what was to come, probably because she felt comfortable that day. She seemed to be in little pain and I was thankful for that.

We talked together about the following day. She said that Trudy was going in at around midday to stay with her for the afternoon because Mick and Dave were going down to Wembley. Dave had got the tickets as a surprise for Mick. Later in the afternoon, her mum and Aunt Annie were going. She said she was quite happy for me to spend the day with the lads watching the match if I wished to do so, and we could have the whole of Sunday together. She said they did a very good roast there at the unit, and she would book me in for dinner and tea. I said I would certainly go at around 10.30 a.m. and would stay until around 6 p.m., so I would have dinner with her, but said I might go over to Trudy and Mick's for tea. She said yes, that would be fine. She would be tired by then, and ready to settle down for the evening in front of the TV before going to bed. So that was the arrangement.

৳৯৯

When I got home that night, I rang Trudy to check out everything with her. She said, yes, she was going shopping in the morning then she would go to the hospital after returning home to put all her shopping away. She was booked in for dinner, she told me. Later in the afternoon, Mum (Lizzie) and Annie were going over, so Trudy would go home. I thanked Trudy for all they were doing, and she said the lads were both in bed, but she would give them my best regards and my good wishes for the following day.

Before I went to bed, I rang Bob Douse. I asked him if he would take me shopping in the morning and then said we could go onto the Gunners afterwards. Bob sounded tired, but nevertheless, pleased to hear from me. Bob told me he would see me at around 9 a.m. We would go to Cresta Dairies and then to Blume's, and also Wise Buys and Gregson's. We could get in all the shopping I needed, go to the Gunners afterwards and then on to the Laughing Cow for dinner, and we could spend the rest of the afternoon down at the home ground with loads and loads of other people, mostly lads and blokes, watching *the* match.

After speaking to Bob, I secured the house then Meggie and I went upstairs. I showered, cleaned my teeth then, naked, I climbed into bed. Meggie curled herself up at my feet and we were both soon fast off.

That night, I had a very strange and rather disturbing dream!

Chapter 18

I DREAMED I arrived home on a raw, cold midwinter evening. It was very close to Christmas and the town had been thronged with people doing their last-minute Christmas shopping. I had to squeeze onto a bus, which broke down halfway home, so I had to wait for another, and almost missed that one due to the numbers of people waiting at the stop, and the jostling when the vehicle arrived. Eventually, feeling very tired and jaded, I arrived home.

I dreamed I still lived in Rutland Close, although Sue had long gone and it was several years hence. In my dream, Meggie was about 11 years old, and she was still my only pet, my trusted companion, my ally in times of need! I dreamed I removed my coat and shoes then fed Meggie, went upstairs, made my bed, I usually did that in the mornings before leaving for work, then I bathed and changed into my dressing gown and slippers. I ate a substantial supper and then sat in my favourite armchair in the dining room, before a roaring fire, Meggie sprawled at my feet. I felt warm, replete and contented.

Outside a gale was blowing, and the rain was lashing the windows. I felt happy in my abode, safe from the storm, but found myself thinking about all the people who were out on the streets on a night like that. In the dream, my thoughts began to turn to all those who would not be with families and friends during the coming Christmas season. I began to feel sad. I started thinking about Susan, my family and her remaining relations. Again, I found myself thinking of all those without anyone to call their own, who would be in hostels or walking the streets on Christmas

Day. As I sat there, I thought I heard a sound like the shuffling and scuffling of many feet on my driveway, but perhaps it wasn't. Meggie moved, raised her head and commenced growling ominously, and, as I bent down to reassure her, the doorbell rang.

I was shocked! I was not expecting anyone. It was late. Who could be calling on me at that time of night? Someone started banging on the kitchen window then on the lounge window, and the doorbell rang again!

Meggie barked loudly! I arose and moved into the hallway, shouting:

"Okay, just a minute! I'll be there in a minute!"

I was very puzzled, and rather afraid. Who could possibly be at my door at that time of the night, and what was so desperately urgent that they had to bang on my windows as well as ring my doorbell? I could hear voices then, and the definite scuffling and shuffling as more and more people seemed to be arriving! What was going on?

In my dream I slowly and carefully opened the front door. I turned on the porch light as I did so and there I stood, revealed to all in my dressing gown and slippers. As I opened the door, the wind caught it and flung it wide. A terrific wall of sound greeted me, and, together with the strength of the wind, almost knocked me flat on my back in the doorway. The sound was like a great, tumultuous, ear-splitting, earth-shattering roar, deep, resonant and resounding for miles and miles all around, and topped by a shrill cacophony of falsetto voices, which sounded like hosts of demons as they reached a head-busting, brain-scrambling crescendo!

What a noise! It sounded as though each and every single individual was calling

out to me.

"Boyzie, help me!"

I shivered and shook with real and uncontrolled fear! I could not see, but was

convinced that the presence outside my house was phenomenal. I could sense miles and miles, masses and masses of boys, young men, older men, women and girls, masses and masses of young children. Many of the children were crying. Each and every single individual was standing there packed tightly together, swaying with the vast and seemingly endless throng—barefoot, ragged, scarred, both physically and mentally. They were cold, wet, hungry, starved of affection, in need of love and protection; the homeless, the inadequate, the rootless, the hapless and the hopeless, the misfits—the lowest forms of life!

As we stood facing one another, their number was increasing rapidly with every passing second. A huge Irish navvy moved towards me. He pushed his five beer bellies hard up against me! He swayed drunkenly on his huge filthy feet. His great hands were all over me. His breath stank of booze and his huge body reeked of sweat. He leaned his whole weight against me.

"Take me in, Boyzie!" he roared in my right ear.

His plea was taken up by all who were packed, stacked, swaying together on their feet for miles and miles and miles all around me.

"Take me in, take me in, please, Boyzie!"

Above the cries of their impassioned pleading, I heard the sounds of even more feet, pounding, on, on, on towards me.

"Take me in, take me in and help me, please, Boyzie!"

All the time, as this scene became even more bizarre, the large oval moon, the night's queen, smiled mockingly down from her throne in the night sky, the mad, mocking, oval moon—aftermath.

Chapter 19

I AWOKE FROM the dream, sweating profusely. I lay for a while, the sounds of their impassioned pleas and their mighty roars ringing and dinning through my head. Above those sounds I heard the pounding of bare and stockinged feet as even more rushed from everywhere to swell their ever-increasing numbers.

I pulled the bedclothes up tighter around me and lay very still until the nightmare and its memories would pass. My heart was thumping. I was still sweating and my head was pounding. My mouth felt very dry and my tongue felt swollen. I heaved myself up in the bed and sat a while because I felt dizzy. My feet went down to the bottom of the king-size bed.

Meggie had moved from her position where she had lain guarding my feet, and had transferred to the rug in front of the gas fire. I was extremely thirsty. I arose from the bed and looked at my watch—4 a.m. Quietly, so as not to disturb Meggie, I went downstairs, but she awoke and followed me. I unlocked the back door and let Meggie out into the yard then I poured myself a large glass full of ice-cold orange juice, followed by a second. After the second, my thirst had been somewhat assuaged. I let Meggie back in and she decided to go to her bed in the conservatory. I settled her and secured the downstairs of the house before returning to my bed.

I tossed and turned fitfully for another hour and a half before I got up again, showered, scrubbed myself from head to foot and cleaned my teeth twice because my mouth felt so horrible. I made the bed, dressed casually, but smartly, and went downstairs, releasing Meggie and then putting on the kettle for the inevitable 'pot that cheers'.

It was a fine morning, if rather cool to start, so I opened windows and doors, and let the sunlight in. I turned on the local BBC radio station to hear all the morning's activities from the start.

In Gaynsford, that vast, busy, North Midlands town, it was a red-letter day, and I wanted to be a part of it. Meggie was rubbing herself around my legs. I gave her a warm drink of milk and water, and decided to cook myself a large breakfast. Whilst so engaged, I listened intently to the radio, having now turned the one in the kitchen on as well. The first coaches were setting off from Gaynsford Bus Station at around 6 a.m., packed with blokes on their way to Wembley, and I was busy making more tea, frying bacon, scrambling eggs and toasting bread in my well-appointed council dwelling on Rutland Close.

Later that morning, Bob or one of the other drivers from Phoenix Cars, formerly Allerton Cars, would call and I would go shopping in Allerton. I loved Allerton. It was a rundown overpopulated area teeming with kids, dogs etc., but the people, although ragged and poor, were friendly, and it always felt like home to me. There were some wonderful shops there and a brilliant, busy market, and that day it would be even more packed because of the 'big match' in the afternoon, which no self-respecting male person living in Gaynsford would want to miss!

As I ate my substantial breakfast of scrambled eggs, bacon, tomatoes, fried bread and several mugs of tea, I said to myself, you must surely know that you deserve one day off! Thus, I consoled myself and rid myself of any feelings of guilt that I might have harboured. Yes, I was tired; I should be allowed one day off, and it wasn't as though she wouldn't have visitors that day. Trudy was going, and Mum and Auntie Annie later on, so I should go off and enjoy myself, and not think any more about it!

When we got well into the parkland, I released Meggie. She went tearing off at a great rate of knots, and I laughed to see and hear her running so fast. She loved a good free run, and the Williams boys took her most evenings, but I liked to take her out as and when I was able, which was why I had decided to do so that morning. I stood and waited until Meggie would return to me.

The morning was warming up nicely, the birds were singing and all seemed right with the world. What a pity there was so much sorrow when the birds sang so beautifully! I knew that from her room, if the window was open, Sue would be able to hear them too, and she would love that. On Sunday, if it was pleasant and warm in the afternoon, after we had had our dinner, we would go and sit in the gardens under the shady trees as we had the day before. That had been such a lovely day. I hoped we would be able to spend many more together before the inevitable day when... when... but I steeled myself not think of that.

I stood, waiting patiently for Meggie to return to my side. As I stood there, I heard the sounds of voices coming towards me: Soon I found myself surrounded by a group of boys and young men. Six, eight, a dozen or so, I was not sure how many, and they had several dogs with them; one or two sounding quite large and ferocious. They were barking, whining and growling! The boys and young men gathered close in around me were all talking excitedly, and they simultaneously let their dogs off the leads! They all went rushing headlong into the centre of the dogs' play area. I was now very concerned about Meggie, and also somewhat worried about my own personal safety! Those lads seemed to be gathered very closely around me. I stood where I was, hoping desperately that my Meggie would soon come back to me.

I had heard there were Gypsies living in caravans on the parkland, and wondered if those lads were from the camp. They were all chattering away amongst themselves and their accent and language was quite strange. They sounded, and smelled, like Irish tinkers. I shivered! It reminded me of my dream the night before. Could you dream something one night and make it come true on the following morning? I did not think so. One of the lads moved right up beside me and put his elbows on my shoulders, standing directly behind me.

"Aw'm Cornelius Maughan, Sir! Aw live in one o' the vans on the park here, wi' ma famly. These lads are sum o' ma reltiffs, brothers, cousins, nephews. Aw've got loads o' kids o' ma awn, Sir, an' naw munny! Hev yo' got ony munny yo' cud lend us, please, Sir?"

He leaned himself up against me, and the others crowded in even closer.

"Please! We'd be 'ver so thankful, Sir!" they chorused.

I felt trapped!

"I-I am sorry, gents," I said. "I haven't any money on me I'm afraid."

They still remained crowding around me, and Cornelius remained leaning against me.

"Aw, hev yo' not?" he said, in a voice that told me he did not believe me.

"Aw!" sighed all the others, crowding in even more closely around me.

Now I was becoming really afraid. One of the lads prodded me in the ribs.

"Are ye blind?" he asked me.

"Yes," I said.

Cornelius Maughan leaned up from his position, removing his elbows from my shoulders.

"Aw! Aw'm awful sorry, mucker!" he said.

He put out a huge hand and gripped my right one in his. He had a vice-like grip and I almost fell to my knees. Others were rubbing my shoulders and patting me on the back.

"Sorry, mucker!' they all chorused. "Wae didna mean ony harm."

I accepted their apologies, but still felt very shaky and uncertain in their company. Suddenly the dogs were tearing back towards us, and Meggie was with them! I called out her name, and she ran straight to me and rolled over, playing 'dead' at my feet. The Gypsies were rounding up their dogs and putting them back on their string and rope leads. They wished me 'good mornin'' as they trouped off back to their caravans.

I put Meggie's lead back on and set off for our house, grateful to be out of that situation, a situation that could have turned very nasty indeed if young Richie Feighan had not asked me if I was blind!

On arrival home, both Meggie and I had a large and well-deserved drink! Warm milk and water for her, hot chocolate for me!

Chapter 20

8.25 a.m.

TRUDY RANG. She was back at home, having driven the lads, Mick, Dave and two of Mick's mates, to the bus station so they could catch the 8 a.m. coach to Wembley! She had just walked in the door, she said. We chatted for a while. She told me she was going shopping and would then go on to the Mary Craigie Unit. She was booked in for dinner at the unit, and if the weather stayed fine she and Sue would sit outside in the beautiful gardens that afternoon.

Later on, Sue's mother, Lizzie and her Aunt Annie were going to the unit and they would stay until early evening, when Trudy would drive them home and then go home herself. The lads would probably be in about 10 p.m. that night after their day at Wembley, and they would bring fish and chip suppers in for the three of them, she said.

I told her about my day, or as much as I knew, and she asked me if I was going over to their house for tea the following day after I had been to visit Sue. I said yes, and she told me that was fine, Dave would come over and fetch me, as he had now passed his driving test. I said I would save the congratulations for when I saw him.

Dave was my only nephew on Susan's side of the family. He was

81

tall, slim, fair-haired and blue-eyed. He was 17 years old. A great youngster with a keen sense of humour and a great sense of adventure, and he thought the world of me!

9.15 a.m.

I had just been around to the Williams's household and left the keys with Vera so the lads could look after Meggie while I was away, when Ralph Davies arrived in his brand new Mercedes cab. Ralph Davies was 48 years old. He was five feet five inches tall in his stockinged feet, with a short, close-cropped haircut and a head of granite rock. He was as tough and as hard as they come. Ralph was ex-army. He attained the rank of corporal, and was known as 'Corporal Ralph' or 'The Little Corporal' by his mates on the fleet, i.e. Allerton Cars, or Phoenix Cars as it would shortly be called. Phoenix Cars would include more of the London-style taxis in its extended fleet. They had already purchased two Volvos and two Mercedes, and they were planning to buy others in the near future to enlarge their already fairly substantial fleet of vehicles. The objective was to become the largest fleet of cabs in the area.

Ralph waited in the posh new Mercedes outside my house until I emerged with shopping bags etc.

"Your carriage awaits, Boyzie!" he said as I climbed aboard, then we were off to Allerton.

⇛•⇚

I will now admit two things that most members of the male sex, if they are being honest, would not admit to readily! First, I greatly enjoy a good soap opera! I still listen to 'The Archers' on BBC Radio 4, usually the omnibus edition on a Sunday morning, and I also listen to 'Waggoner's Walk' on BBC Radio 2, which is on every weekday, twice a day, and I really enjoy both!

I do 'watch' some of the soaps on television when I have the time, and again, I often enjoy them. There now, there's an admission, and here is another one—I love shopping! I mean, I really love it. Yes, even shopping for mundane things like food and household commodities. Why? Well, I guess it goes back to my early childhood, when I used to go out shopping with my mum or the neighbour, Mrs Pellat, whom we used to call, well, at least, *I* used to call her, Nannie Pellat. She was a lovely woman. Died when she was in her eighties, but she had come to my wedding in Gaynsford. I insisted that she and her husband should be there, but Mum and Dad would have invited them anyway because they were very close to our family. That was when we lived in South-East London.

In 1957 we moved to Thamesford, but we still kept in regular contact with May and Alfie Pellat. We visited them often, Mum and me! May (Nannie) used to make us wonderful teas whenever we visited her. They were happy times. Now both May and Alfie are dead, but, like my Granny Annie, I still have wonderful memories of them both, and they can't take those away from me, but back to my original topic of shopping.

Dad (George) was as bad as me when it came to fairs, markets, arcades etc., and Mum shared my great love of shopping and soaps. It's funny what one inherits from one's parents!

I was looking forward to my shopping expedition that morning, and was glad Ralph was with me, because we got on really well. As I said, Ralph was 48 years old. He was first married at the age of 19, while he was still in the army. During the previous 29 years, Ralph had been married seven times! His latest wife, Pauline, was West Indian. She was a good deal younger than him, and had one daughter, Bethanne, who was 14 years old. Ralph had several children, and I believe he was also a grandad!

We were now heading towards Allerton, but the traffic coming the other way, towards the motorway and London, was very heavy. Ralph was full of the day's events, and greatly looking forward to the match that afternoon. Even I was beginning to feel excited about the prospect of 'watching' the game with loads of my mates and acquaintances.

We parked in the multi-storey on Highland Road, and walked down towards the shops. Allerton, the bustling suburb of Gaynsford, was already teeming with life on that bright and very special Saturday morning. Ralph, on whose left elbow I placed my right hand, walked alongside me as much as he was able, but in tight situations he always walked one step ahead of me, and I moved close in behind him. Thus, we could pass through tight spaces much more easily. I was teaching the skill of how to guide me to most of the cabbies who worked for the outfit currently known as Allerton Cars and would endeavour to do the same for any new drivers with whom I came into contact now that the firm was expanding and changing. The changeover was due to become statutory some time over the next couple of weeks, I was told. Bob, Ralph and four other blokes were to be the main partners within the newly formed company. All other drivers and employees were to be encouraged to become shareholders within the company..

Inevitably, while engaged in shopping within that area, I met lots of people whom I knew. As I have said, Sue and I lived on The Circle, Mount Carmel Estate, when we were first married, and certainly, most of the neighbours we knew then still lived in that part of Allerton, and most of them seemed to be out shopping that morning, so progress along our route was rather slower than I had bargained for. However, we were making good headway by 10.30 a.m., and had already visited Cresta Dairies, James Blume's, the bakery, Trotters, the butcher's, Mcguigan's, the home-made pie shop and Fine Foods, where they sold a lot of packs of food for the freezer.

We had made two journeys back to the car, and were now heading for the street market. There I bought potatoes and other vegetables, and ordered flowers from a stall who undertook to send them via InterFlora, and said they would ensure they sent them off to the Mary Craigie Unit at the College Hospital by midday that day. Next I went to Lacey's music stall and bought half a dozen albums I had ordered, plus a dozen or so music cassettes. Richie Lacey, the eldest of the Lacey brothers, who ran the stall, had become something of a friend. He and his brother, Rod, told me they would be at the home ground that afternoon, watching the match, but first, they were lunching at the Laughing Cow, so maybe they would see me there. The market was closing down at 1 p.m., they said. Well, all the shops in Allerton would be closed. There would be no one out shopping in Gaynsford *that* afternoon.

Later, we went to the off-licence and I bought two bottles of wine and a dozen cans of lager, plus a bottle of Scotch whisky, then we went to Wise Buys to look for bargains. We ended up at Gregson's, the big superstore on the fringes of Allerton and Osleston, and we drove there and parked in Gregson's car park area. I bought quite a lot of canned food there, plus three jars of jam, two of thick cut marmalade, two of lemon curd and two big jars of pickled onions, plus two of the big squeezy bottles of red sauce and four two pint bottles of vinegar. Well loaded, we staggered back to the car then drove home after an exhausting shopping expedition.

Once we arrived home I would put everything away, then we could go off to the Gunners for a couple of pints before adjourning to the Laughing Cow for a substantial lunch. We would later go on to the home ground, where the match was to be shown on big screens, and I would be able to wear a headset and listen to the commentary direct from Wembley. I was looking forward to it very much now, and I had thoroughly enjoyed my morning's shopping in the bustling crowds around Allerton and Osleston.

When we got home, the three Williams brothers were sitting side by side on my front garden wall. As we got out of the cab, to start unloading the shopping, I perceived that some of the Gypsy lads were with them. They all hailed me, speaking together.

"Hey-up, Boyzie!"

I asked, quite casually, what they were all doing, sitting together on my front garden wall, and made it clear I was not happy about that. They apologised, but made no attempt to move. Ralph and I started to carry bags of shopping down to the front door, and immediately the three brothers got to their feet to help.

"No! That's okay," said Ralph. "We'll manage, lads!"

The Williams boys sat down again and they all started talking among themselves, lighting up cigarettes etc. When we had finished, and I had put all the shopping away, I let Meggie out into the yard, then ,once she had had a good run, I let her back into the conservatory where she lay down in her bed underneath the table.

I then ensured that the house was secure, and as we left to go to the Gunners, I asked Don to move the lads on, as I did not want them all hanging around my house that afternoon.

"We ain't causin' no trouble, Sir!" exclaimed Richie Feighan, the 16-year-old who had asked me if I was blind when I had stood on the parkland earlier that morning.

"I don't want you all sitting around here for the rest of today, so please would you move on?" I said, with a tone of authority.

Some brief discussion, then Don Williams said:

"Cum on, lads, let's move!"

They all stood as one man and marched off into the Williams's house, where apparently the Gypsy lads were to be welcomed that afternoon in order to watch the match. We waited until the front door of the house at number 25 Rutland Close had closed behind the last man before we drove off and headed for the Gunners.

Chapter 21

ON ARRIVING at the Gunners, we found the pub car park brimming over with vehicles and could not get ours in, so we had to leave it parked outside on the street. Ralph locked it and left the alarm on. It was a brand new vehicle, but we were pretty certain nobody would touch it until we got back there to collect it that night.

At 12.30 p.m., a fleet of buses would arrive at the pub and wait outside the Gunners in order to take us all down to the Laughing Cow, and after lunch there, the same buses would ferry everyone over to the home ground. We all had tickets as though we were going to Wembley; Bob Douse apparently had mine with him. As we entered the public bar of the Gunners, a great and glorious shout went up from the men already packed, swaying on their feet and swilling back the booze.

"Hey-up, Corporal, hey-up, Boyzie, how's it hangin', lads?"

We struggled our way through the jostling, swaying crowds and pressed our bellies up to the bar!

"Yo've got three pints in a'ready, Boyzie!" said a voice in my right ear.

It was Rob McCallasky. He had said he would probably see me there that day and there he was, right enough. With him were his brothers, Mitchell (Mitch) and Matthew (Matt), and also a cousin, just over from Ireland. His name was Martyn McCallasky, known to all the family as Marty the Priest, because he had just finished his training to be a priest. He was now over from Ireland, living with the McCallasky family in Allerton, in the hope of landing a position as one of the priests of Saint Jude's.

Father Dominic, the new young priest at Saint Jude's, was in the bar that morning, swilling back the ale. He was a great sportsman, loved his pint and was very well thought of among the young people of the area. Father Martyn would be working along with him.

Marty stood to my right and we chatted as we swilled down the pints. He seemed a pleasant young man. I also talked with Rob and his two younger brothers, and later, with others who spoke to me amongst the vast crowds of blokes pressed up against the bar of the Gunners, which was now swimming in beer and cider. As quickly as it became saturated, it was cleaned by Dennis Parkin, his son George or one of his three daughters, all of whom were involved in helping in the pub because it was so busy that day. Even young Celia, the youngest of Dennis's four children, was blithely doing her bit to assist her dad in serving pints etc. Lennie Bishop, who worked in the bar, and Rupert Henry were busily engaged in washing glasses, wiping down tables etc. We stood, packed in the three bars of the Gunners, literally wedged on our feet. I managed to swill four pints of Strongbow cider down my neck before the buses arrived and it was time to move on to our next venue, the Laughing Cow!

We piled into the buses, and had to wait while Dennis closed the pub down, then he, George, his son, together with Lennie Bishop and Rue Henry joined us, as did Mary and young Celia Parkin, two of Dennis's daughters. They were both mad keen soccer fans. That left Joan and their other daughter, Iris, to clear up at the pub, but most of it had been done anyway, so there would not be a great deal for them to do before putting up the shutters. The fleet of buses moved off towards the Laughing Cow.

When we arrived, we found the place all decked out with tables set and piled high with food. There were all kinds of sliced meat, hams, turkey, pork, bacon joints, chicken, corned beef, roast beef and cold sausages, together with loads and loads of potatoes, also all kinds of salad stuff, quiches, home-made meat and tatey pies, fruit pies, trifles, gateaux etc., and plenty to drink as well!

The Laughing Cow had obtained a special licence so they could have drink on the premises for the buffet that day. We piled in and made great inroads on the masses of food. The booze flowed and the chatter rose to an uproarious crescendo! Everyone was enjoying themselves! Rosie Turkington was one of the staff on duty and her son, Paul, only 16 years old, was coming along to the home ground later, and so was his mum. He came and stood beside me for a while and talked to me. He told me he was 'one o' the lads' who had been among the vast crowds of young people surrounding me at the bus stop the other day. He said loads of others would be there at the home ground that afternoon.

I was eating from my third or fourth plate full of food, and endeavouring to get another drink! Marty McCallasky came and acquired the drink for me, and held it because my plate was laden and I could not carry it and hold a drink as well.

"Thanks," I said.

"Not at all!" said Marty, and wedged himself in next to me.

We sat happily eating and chatting away together until it was time to move on to the home ground.

More buses arriving! Everyone piling out of the Laughing Cow, well fed and well oiled, ready for the match that afternoon. I was on the bus with Marty and Rob McCallasky, Ralph Davies, Arnie, Dicko, Gary Moxon, Gary Wilkinson, Bob Douse and his son, Steve, Den, George, Mary and Celia Parkin, Rose Turkington and her son, Paul, George Wyatt, his brother, and Les, who had recently returned from Australia. There was also Harry Darlington, who drove for Allerton Cars, several other cabbies, plus Tony, Paul, Kenny and Terry Barradell and their dad, also called Terry, Steve Larner, who was a neighbour of mine on The Circle, Ernie and Fred Allsop, who were both from The Circle and both truckers and, sitting beside me on the front seat, Oscar Henry, brother of Rue.

We were quite a lively bunch on the way to the home ground!

I thought of Mick and Dave, plus the Braun brothers and also Simon Potts, all of whom were now down at Wembley, and felt as though I was going there as well. It was tremendously exciting!

Chapter 22

THE BUSES at the front of the convoy were pulling up outside the home ground. By 2.54 p.m., we were off the vehicle on which we had travelled from the Laughing Cow, and immersed in the vast crowds waiting to pass through Gate B. I was with Oscar Henry, and Marty and Rob McCallasky. The Lacey brothers, Richie and Rod, were behind me, then came Ralph Davies, who had hardly left my side since he had picked me up at 9.15 a.m. that morning, and Rue Henry and Lennie Bishop.

The crowds around us were vast. Would we all get in in time to see the first kick? I still had to pick up my headset, but we were told at Gate B, as we passed into the home ground, that it would be brought to my seat as soon as we were settled and the stewards knew what number seat I was occupying. We turned left inside and walked along until we came to a flight of four steps. We mounted those and took our seats. I was sandwiched between Ossie and Marty.

Shortly after we sat down, they sang, 'Abide with me' and there was great cheering both from Wembley and the 40,000 plus who were packed into Gaynsford's home ground. The atmosphere was electric! The whole place was a cauldron of sound! It was fantastic to be there—quite as exciting as it would have been if I had been at Wembley—and I was not even a native of Gaynsford, although I had lived there for nigh on 12 years. I was, however, a staunch supporter of the town's soccer team, and I knew the names of all the players. Our goalie, Jim Pratt, Steve Clemmo, Dave Jordan, Mick Reilly, Micky O'Rawq, Danny Nightingale, George Deakin, Andy Peasley, Mick Harper, Sammy Wainwright and the great little legend, although he had only been at the club a short time, Les Greaves. What an exciting squad indeed; a squad of players who all played for one another. That was what made a team great—teamwork.

From the outset of the game I sat enthralled. The first half was full of chances for both sides, but there were no goals at its climax. Still, the atmosphere remained heady, with every one of the 40,000 plus crammed into the home ground 'stoned' on Gaynsford, and determined to thoroughly enjoy themselves! During the break a band played on the pitch and they sold hot dogs, ice creams, etc. The game had started late, at 3.20 p.m., but not because of any trouble. It was merely because there were so many people trying to get settled down in the ground, which at that time held over 100,000 people when full, and that day it would be crammed to absolute capacity, as indeed the home ground in Gaynsford was that afternoon. The first half did not finish until 4.10 p.m., with added time for the few stoppages that had occurred.

The second half duly commenced at 4.20 p.m. When Franco Morelli scored the first goal for the opposition within ten minutes of the commencement of the second half, heads went down a bit at the home ground. However, within three minutes we had responded with a cracker of a goal from Steve Clemmo! The entire place erupted into something akin to madness! I was hauled to my feet by Ossie and Marty, and together with all others, we swayed on our feet whilst chanting, roaring and shouting ourselves almost hoarse in support of our 'gracious team'. That was the only thrill of the whole of the second half, which culminated in a one all draw!

Until the end of the previous season that would have meant a replay early the following week, probably at the ground of a club such as Aston Villa or Manchester United, however, the new rules said that we were now entitled to 30 minutes' worth of extra time, 15 minutes per half, before the 'replay' rule came into being. Thus, on completion of the second half, we waited another ten minutes and then the first period of extra time commenced. It ended with no score on either side.

The heads were beginning to drop again at the home ground, the bastion of football and other sports on the fringes of Gaynsford town. For almost the last 15 minutes, the crowd of 40,000 plus had sat in virtual silence, their eyes fixed on the many wide screens that were displaying the game to us all. I had sat back in my seat, my ears attuned to the commentary, my hopes pinned on the key players in our magical squad, but all to no avail. Now we sat and hoped, crammed together into the home ground of Gaynsford United. We sat and hoped, and in the end all our hopes came to glorious fruition! In a most glorious and exciting finale to that peach of a game, during which there had been hardly any stoppages, and an atmosphere of cordiality had pervaded both teams and the crowds, both at Wembley and Gaynsford United Football Club's beloved home ground.

Glosport County, the top Merseyside team, was really proving a headache for our lads, a real tough nut for them to crack. Two minutes into the second part of extra time, their centre forward, Frank McCartny, scored their second goal, and the entire home ground was stunned into complete silence! Not for long, though! In the seventh minute of the second part of extra time, young Les Greaves equalised for our side, and once more the home ground erupted into total mayhem, so much so that we almost missed the follow-up goal—a truly marvellous one by any standards—scored by Les Greaves two minutes later! Now we were winning, three goals to two. Less than five minutes later, literally in the last 90 seconds of the game, young Les Greaves, the darling of the hour, the hero of the day, Gaynsford born and bred, scored his hat-trick. We had won the FA League Cup by four goals to two, and the entire home ground went absolutely bananas!

Nobody heard the final whistle from Wembley! Nobody within the confines of the home ground cared about that because, as far as we were concerned, young Les Greaves, 'Super Brat', at the age of 19 years, had won the game for us with three cracking goals in the last period of extra time. That was the signal for the whole of the North Midlands town to go completely crazy—and we did!

The following day the team would ride in glory on an open top vehicle through the town to the council offices, where they would be royally and regally entertained in the Mayor's Banqueting Suite! Later on during the week, there would be interviews, photo calls and the parading of the FA League Champions' Cup before as many fans as were able to attend at the home ground! Little Les Greaves would probably be granted the 'freedom of the town'.

That night belonged to the people of Gaynsford, and it was one that none of us would forget in a hurry! It all began in that vast, excited, almost hysterical crowd, swaying on their feet at the home ground.

Before the final whistle had blown at Wembley, we were pulling off our shoes and flooding onto the hallowed turf in our stock-inged feet. The police, who were there in force, were doing nothing to stop us, rather, many of them were joining in—the crowd was good-humoured! Everyone was ecstatic! We were the league champions! Nobody was going to cause any trouble, so the police were pulling off their boots too and lining up with all of us on the hallowed turf, and I was right in the very centre of it all. Yes, there we were, boys, men, some women, all ages, all types, from all walks of life. All shapes, all sizes, blokes of every height, weight and build standing jammed, crammed, packed tight together, swaying altogether as we stood on our stockinged feet covering every inch of the hallowed turf that was the pitch at our beloved home ground.

As we all swayed together, our arms wrapped around one an-other's waists, our heads buried in each other's shoulders, many of us showing great emotion, we sang, chanted, whooped, yelled and roared out altogether into the aether:

"Champions! Champions! Champions!"

We moved over so that even more could cram onto the pitch. Almost 40,000 people, jammed, crammed, packed close together, swaying on their stockinged feet. Little kids, wide-eyed, standing on their fathers' shoulders! Everyone ecstatic, everyone blissfully happy, swaying, roaring out, singing and chanting altogether:

"Champions! Champions! Champions!"

That went on for ages and ages, but nobody cared. It seemed that people wanted it to go on and on and never end. No one in that vast, swaying, highly emotional and ecstatically happy crowd at the home ground that evening wanted to go home, so we stayed on, altogether, getting as much as we could from the ecstasy of having been there on the hallowed ground when 'ahr team' won the FA League Cup on Saturday, 6th May, 1978.

⁂

It was well after 6.30 p.m. when we boarded our buses to ride back into town, and it was well after 7.45 p.m. by the time we arrived back in the Cornmarket, as the traffic was so heavy, and everyone was hanging out of the windows of vehicles, shouting, gesticulating, singing, pointing, waving etc. The town had gone 'football crazy'. That night, every pub, every club in Gaynsford would be crammed, jammed full to capacity with revellers, and many of them would be able to say in years to come to anyone who might care to listen:

"I remember that day. I was there at the home ground when Gaynsford United won the FA League Challenge Cup and the League Championship!"

I would be one of them!

As I got down from the vehicle in the Cornmarket and Ralph joined me to take me over to Ryan's Bar where we were to have a few drinks before I departed for home, I thought of my lovely Susan. How I would enjoy relating to her the events of that day when we met up the following day at the Mary Craigie Unit. I was booked in for dinner there, which was why I could not, *must* not, be out too late, or else I would never get there in time to spend the day with her, and I was greatly looking forward to that.

We walked from the Cornmarket over to the Gunners at Allerton. It took us around 50 minutes, even walking at our pace. People kept stopping us, wanting to shake hands, pat us on the back etc., and progress was slow! We arrived at the Gunners at about 8.40 p.m., and managed to get a couple of pints down our necks. At 9.20 p.m., we were driving in the posh new Mercedes back into town, and towards Ryan's Bar. They were having a sin-galong there and the place was literally heaving! I drank down a pint of cider, then I climbed up onto the stage and there, in the heavy, boozy, smoky atmosphere of that packed and heaving bar, I sang, 'Black Velvet Band', which has always been one of my favourites among my repertoire of Irish songs:

"Her eyes they shone like diamonds,
I thought her the queen of the land!
And her hair it hung over her shoulders,
Tied up with a black velvet band!"

Everyone joined in, heartily, lustily, and when I came down from the stage, there were two more pints lined up on the bar! I was surrounded by crowds of people who wanted to shake my hand, pat me on the back and buy me drinks!

§◦∞◦§

It was well after 11 p.m. before I left the bar on that wonderful, outrageously happy night. As we drove home, me and Bob Douse, who was as happy as anyone that Gaynsford had won, we had all the windows down and listened to everyone singing, applaud-ing, shouting, dancing in the streets in joy at having been present in the town on such a marvellous day—the day when Gaynsford won the FA League Challenge Cup Final!

Again, travelling home, progress was slow. We spotted the Crest of a Wave fish bar, still open and doing good business apparently. When we eventually reached the counter, I bought haddock and chips twice, four fishcakes and a large carton of baked beans! I would settle Meggie then go upstairs and put that lot out on the bedroom floor on newspapers! I would then strip down to my underpants and socks, and crawl on the floor, eating my huge supper, drinking ice-cold 'rough' cider from a quart bottle I had in the fridge—fabulous!

Bob dropped me off at home at around 11.50 p.m. I shook his hand and thanked him very much for all his help that day, plus that of others who worked for Allerton Cars.

"Aw shucks!" he said, a little embarrassed, "Glad you 'ad a gud day!"

By a few minutes after midnight, I was upstairs, Meggie now settled in the conservatory and my large supper, still piping hot, spread at my feet on newspapers! The quart bottle of cider was beside me as I knelt on the carpeted floor. I was in ecstasy, thoroughly enjoying myself, oblivious to the world!

The radio was on in the background playing pop music, and I was eating a hearty supper and quenching a seemingly almost unquenchable thirst. I waded through the quart bottle and my enormous supper, and finally, at around 1 a.m., I heaved myself into bed, still clad in my underpants and socks!

My last thoughts before going to sleep were of the day I had so very much enjoyed, and of my darling Susan. The following day I would see her again, and I would have so much to tell her. With that passing thought, I drifted off happily and comfortably into the land of nod, and slept the sleep of the dead until around 8.15 a.m. the following morning.

Chapter 23

ON THE Sunday morning it was bright, warm and sunny. I was glad; I would be able to sit outside with my beloved Susan after we had had dinner at the unit, and I was greatly looking forward to my day with her as I climbed into the taxi and set off for Mary Craigie and the College Hospital at around 10 a.m.

The Williams boys were happy to have Meggie for the day. They were going to pack up a picnic and loads of pop, crisps and chocolate, and take her up the park, they said. I daresay they would see the Gypsy lads up there. They seemed to be very friendly with those young men at that time. I was sure Vera and Cyril must have been concerned about the friendship between their sons and those wild, young Gypsy lads!

Sam Doherty drove me to the College Hospital that day. Sam was in his late twenties. A single bloke, he was one of a very large family who lived on The Circle, who were near neighbours of ours when Sue and I lived there. He was still at home and so were seven of his brothers, plus a sister and her two young children, and a couple of younger sisters. What a tribe! Ira Doherty, their mother, always seemed a pleasant enough woman, although rather loud. I never saw much of her husband, Gerry, although he had done some work for me once at 48 The Circle. Gerry was a foundry worker, and did some decorating 'on the side' for mates of his. That was how he came to work for me. He did a good job and was very polite to both Sue and myself, but he never became a regular mate like so many of the blokes up on the Mount Carmel Estate.

Sam was chatting to me and said he had been at the home ground the day before. We talked of what an exciting day it had been and how much we had both enjoyed all the events. Apparently all the clubs had been turning people away because they were so busy, even the newest ones in the town like Annie's Room, which had not long been open, and Shades Disco, where I was told the police eventually had to clear the place because there were too many people dancing inside and it had become dangerous! That was apparently at about 2 a.m. that morning.

As we talked, Sam drove on towards the College Hospital. We arrived at around 10.25 a.m., and Sam left me just inside, waiting by reception. Almost immediately, an inner door opened and Staff Nurse Lesley Peters came to me.

"Ah, Boyzie, can you come with me please?" she said.

Staff Nurse Lesley Ellen Peters was in her early thirties. She was about five feet five inches tall, slim, with long brown hair and deep-set brown eyes; quite an attractive young female, who was the daughter of Chris and Lennie Peters who lived on The Circle. She knew me very well. She came to me and guided me through into a large lounge at the end of a lengthy corridor. I sat down in one of the armchairs and she sat down alongside me.

"Susan had a lovely day yesterday with members of her family," she began, and I smiled with pleasure.

However, Staff Nurse Lesley Peters went on to tell me that that morning, around breakfast time, Susan had had a serious fit, and was now resting. Dr Mervyn Fraser had been to see her and said she must be kept as quiet as possible, and had also suggested that she remained in bed.

I was shocked! Lesley could see that her news had been a shock to me and she asked if I would like a drink. I said, yes please. She left me and went to make a pot of tea. She was soon back and I took the proffered mug of tea from her with shaking hands. Was this it? Was this the beginning of the end? Oh, God, oh, my good

God! Please, not yet, not yet!

As I drank the hot sweet tea, Lesley and another young woman called Penny Dwyer talked quietly to me. They told me Sue was happy and very comfortable, and Penny, who had just been with her, said she was greatly looking forward to my visit. They told me they would serve my meal in Susan's room, and that she would probably take a little soup and perhaps some lightly grilled fish and mash, and maybe a small portion of rice pudding. I could have the full roast dinner if I wished to do so, but somehow I did not feel hungry any more.

I finished my tea and was taken to Susan's room. She lay in bed, pale, restless, not really very sure of whether she wanted me there or not. When she was properly awake I was able to talk to her, but for most of the day she lay in a sort of half-wakeful, half-slumbering state, and I was unsure whether she heard half of what I was telling her. Nevertheless, I sat with her and talked to her from around 11.15 a.m. until well into the early hours of the evening, stopping sometimes because I knew she was well asleep.

When she slept I sat beside the bed and held her hand. She seemed very comfortable and I was glad of that. I did not have anything to eat at lunchtime, but I did have several drinks during the course of what seemed a very long day. At 6.45 p.m., one of the staff members came to me and told me she was going to book a taxi to take me home.

"She's very tired, Boyzie, and I can see you are out on your feet!" she told me.

I was extremely fatigued, and I was very, very upset! What I had believed would be a lovely day with Sue, following my happiness the day before, had proved to be just the opposite! I knew that Sue's illness was growing progressively worse, so I felt angry, desperately unhappy and utterly helpless! The combination of those feelings was really bringing me down.

৪৯৫৩

Harry Ash drove me home. He was a small, stocky bloke in his mid-fifties. He was the grandad of Jamie Ash, 'Smokey', the tall, red-headed lad who had been involved in the incident with me outside of Gunners Lane Boys' School the previous Wednesday. It was around 8.40 p.m. when I arrived home. As I stepped out of the taxi, I remembered I was supposed to have gone over to Trudy and Mick's for my tea. I asked Harry to wait at the door while I ran into the house. I quickly rang Mick's house, and Dave answered.

"Oh, Boyzie! There you are, we were wondering abaht you."

I apologised for not having gone over to tea as planned. I explained that I was supposed to phone from the unit.

"Yeh, I was going to come an' fetch you."

He asked where I was now. I told him I was at home, and had a taxi waiting outside.

"Let 'im go, Boyzie, aw'll cum ower an' fetch you nah. There's plenty o' stuff left, an' Gran and Aunt Annie are here," Dave said

I told Dave I would see him in a few minutes. I went outside, paid Harry Ash and apologised for keeping him waiting, then I went around to the Williams's household and collected Meggie.

The Williams's house was crammed full of people. Vera was there, with Cyril, Basil and her three, tall stout sons. Her sister, Rose, was there with her husband, Kenny, and their son, Tommy. Several of the young Gypsy lads were there, including Cornelias Maughan and Richie Feighan. The television was on and the three parakeets and three budgerigars were all squawking and whistling like mad! Meggie came to me and seemed glad to see me. I asked Vera to step outside with me for a few moments, and she did so. I explained the situation to her, and asked if she would take my keys and keep a set for me until I came home. I said I was going to ask my brother-in-law if I could stay with them for a few days, as I did not want to be on my own.

Vera put an arm around me and held me close to her. She was a big comfortable woman, very motherly and had always been a superb neighbour to Sue and me. She was very fond of my lovely Susan and was most distressed to hear how poorly she was.

"Dawn't yo' worry, lad, aw'll mek' sure as 'ow your ahse is safe an' kept clean an' tidy fr yo', lad."

Thanking her, I left the chaos of that household and returned to my own peaceful domain. There I packed two holdall-type bags and a big shopping bag with items I might, or might not, require; clothes, a toilet bag, my razor, slippers, shoes, pyjamas, smoking jacket, a radio, an alarm clock, my Walkman and a dozen cassettes, tablets of soap, two or three flannels, a couple of hand towels, a couple of thick bath towels, plus toys, feeding bowls, tins of meat and a bag of biscuits for Meggie, whom I had definitely decided to take along with me. There were already four dogs at Trudy and Mick's, but I was sure they would not mind the presence of my Meggie. I did not want to leave her to the tender mercies of the Williams boys, because I had no idea how long I would be gone.

Dave arrived, and he had Mick along with him. I started to ask them if I could stay over for a few days, but Mick interrupted and said that he was going to ask me to do so and that all the arrangements concerning beds etc., were currently in hand. All I had to do was come with them and relax. Everything would be taken care of by the family. As I secured the house and Dave carried the last bag to the vehicle, Mick held Meggie's lead, she was jumping about, and becoming quite excited, and I felt an enormous weight had been lifted from my shoulders.

§◦◦§

On arrival at Trudy and Mick's, I was given a huge plateful of sandwiches, sausage rolls, salad, pork pie etc., and was told there were trifle and cakes to follow. In between huge forays into that mountain of food, I released Meggie, who joined the other animals in a rough and tumble, and I relayed the information to the family about the day I had spent with Susan. Everyone was very concerned.

It was after midnight when Lizzie and Annie were dispatched home in a taxi then we locked up the house and went up to bed.

Dave slept on the put-you-up sofa in the lounge. Trudy had moved into Dave's room. I slept with Mick in case I should need to get up in the night, or should require anything. Michael Smith was Susan's only brother. He was nine and a half years older than her, a thickset guy, standing about five feet ten inches tall in his stockinged feet, with brown hair and brown eyes. Mick was a trucker's mate and worked at Webster's, the meat factory.

As we climbed into bed that night, both having showered, I lay close beside Mick, my brother-in-law, in the comfortable double bed with its crisp clean sheets and high piled pillows. He soon slept, breathing heavily as he lay tight beside me, but I lay awake—I could not sleep. I was thinking, thinking of Susan. Now I was with her family I knew they would take a lot of the load off my shoulders. Again, that was like another part of the 'network' that seemed to surround me and hold me up—a network of support, which always seemed to be there for me. Yes, in that way, I was very lucky!

With that thought in my head, I did manage to drop off into slumber at last, but my slumber was fitful, and I kept waking up and wondering where I was, why I was there etc., and then reflecting on what was to come. Whenever I awoke it seemed that beside me Mick awoke as well, and was there to console me, to assuage my fears of the future and to be my guide if I needed to leave the bedroom for any reason.

The following night, he would sleep on the put-you-up in the lounge, and young Dave would sleep in the double bed beside me. They had planned it and worked it out like that, so that there was always one or other of them 'on duty' as it were, to look out for me. As I said, I was very lucky in many ways, but they couldn't grant me my greatest and dearest wish.

Nobody could do that.

Chapter 21

ON THE Monday morning at 6 a.m., Mick got up to go to
work. I arose at about 7.15 a.m., and on my way back to
my room from the bathroom I met up with Trudy at the
top of the stairs, and told her that I thought I ought to go into
the office. She was on her way downstairs to the lounge to arouse
Dave, who was on a fortnight's holiday starting that day then she
would cook breakfast for us all.

I was just walking back into Trudy and Mick's room to dress
when the telephone rang. It was Staff Nurse Jenny McGregor from
the Mary Craigie Unit. She spoke first to Trudy then to me. She
told me that Susan had taken a turn for the worse again in the
night, and that Dr Mervyn Fraser was very concerned about her.
She asked if I could get down to the unit that morning. By now,
Dave was downstairs, standing alongside me. I said yes, of course,
if it was necessary. Trudy insisted that I ate a large breakfast and
had another mug of hot sweet tea before Dave was allowed to take
me down to Mary Craigie.

On arrival I was first taken to the lounge where I had sat the
previous morning. Dr Mervyn Fraser came in and sat beside me.
He said he would take me to Susan's room, but that she was very
drowsy due to the extra drugs they had given her to quell the
pain. I said I was very sorry to know she was in so much pain.

I sat with her until midday, but I don't think she knew I was
there, then I went and phoned Trudy. She said Dave would go and
fetch Mick from the factory and bring him over to the unit. She
would go and pick up Mum and Aunt Annie, and bring them over
then we would all be together.

Afterwards I went back into Susan's room. Flowers had arrived.

I had ordered them from the florist on Saturday. They made the room smell lovely. The windows were all open and a new clean bedspread adorned Sue's bed. She was out and sitting in a chair with her head back. She was on a drip. As I walked back into the room, she smiled.

"Hello, Boyzie!" she said.

I went and sat beside her, taking the hand that did not have the drip needle in a vein. I held it and kissed it, and again, Sue smiled! I could feel tears welling up into my eyes.

"Shh!" she told me. "Don't cry. I'm comfortable, I'm happy, please be happy for me, Boyzie!"

She then closed her eyes, her grip on my hand relaxed and she seemed to lose consciousness.

CONCLUSION

AT AROUND 2 p.m., they came and lifted her back into her bed. It was all newly made up for her. They made her very comfortable. They took the drip out, and told me they would give her a very deep injection in about an hour and a half. I sat beside the bed, holding her hand tightly in mine, and talking to her.

Lizzie and Annie came in for a while, but were both very upset and left. Trudy and Dave both came in, then Mick came into the room and sat on the other side of Sue's bed. He tenderly took her other hand. We both sat there in complete silence—the brother and the husband—each one clinging on helplessly to one of her hands!

She lay there almost completely oblivious to everything that was happening, although occasionally it seemed that her eyelids fluttered, but only for a second or two.

ईॐई

At around 3.45 p.m., they came and told us that tea was being served in the lounge. We were both reluctant to leave, but felt perhaps we should go and spend some time with the rest of the family. Mick got up and walked around to my side of the bed. As I arose to my feet, Staff Nurse Lesley Peters came in and told me that she was going to give Susan an injection to 'help her'. I smiled, guessing what she meant!

Mick and I walked down to the lounge arm in arm and we had tea, sandwiches and cake with the rest of the clan. Later, each of us went into Susan's room. We all knew the end was coming without anyone having to tell us, but why? Why so soon? It wasn't fair! Oh God, it wasn't bloody fair!

I was sitting in her room with her hand still in mine, and Mick was on the other side of the bed. It was 5.35 p.m. on Monday, 8th May, a warm and pleasant afternoon, with the sun still shining through the open windows, and my dear, darling Susan, the joy of my heart, passed quietly and easily away into eternity.

Before we left her room, Mick and I both kissed Susan and pressed her hands. We thanked the staff nurse on duty and other staff members, including Dr Mervyn Fraser. He stood beside me for some time, and when he shook my hand, he seemed sad. I am sure Staff Nurse Peters was crying as I embraced her.

The windows of the room were all still open and the sun came flooding in. The scent of the flowers still pervaded the small room in which my darling had been so comfortable for such a short period of time—the room in which she had eventually died!

§≈≈§

They moved her into the mortuary at the College Hospital, and said she would remain there until the necessary arrangements were made. I promised everything would be put in hand, and that I would endeavour to commence making all necessary arrangements for her funeral as soon as I felt able to tackle the task. In the event, we commenced making the arrangements on the following morning.

After a few more words of thanks, Mick and I, our arms around one another's shoulders, walked back to the lounge where the rest of the family were still waiting. We were all offered mugs of tea, and I gratefully accepted. As I sat there in the lounge among Susan's grieving relations, I could not get her last words out of my head.

"Shh, don't cry! I'm comfortable! I'm happy! Please be happy for me, Boyzie!"

How could I be happy? How could I ever smile again? Now all the light had gone out of my world, and I was completely enveloped in *darkness*, or at least that was how it felt, but even as I sat there, with my two shaking hands gripping the large brown mug of hot sweet tea that I had been given, I knew that some day

I would once more emerge from the darkness into the light, but before that day, there was a long dark road to travel. I knew that all the way along the long dark thoroughfare, I would have plenty of guides to help me. I knew that the 'network' would continue to surround me and offer me support. What good was all that without the main bread of life, my own special light? The jewel in my crown, my own, lovely darling Susan!

I lifted the mug of tea to my parched lips and took a long, hard painful swallow.

Book Two

Starting Over

PROLOGUE

SUNNY GOLD Radio! The best sounds around! The greatest songs, all year long!

I was 20 hours into my 80-hour marathon broadcast, to welcome in a new year and a new decade, and so far it was going very well. No hitches, well, none to speak of anyway. No rigours, no real traumas, everyone seemed very pleased. Yes, so far it was going well, thanks to someone 'up there' plus all those who were supporting me and looking after me down there.

Starting over!

Chapter 1

Friday, 29th December, 1989.

A COLD, RAW winter's night outside, but where I was, ensconced in the studio at Sunny Gold Radio in the town centre of Gaynsford, it was lovely and warm. Bill Grundy had just been in with a huge plate of fish and chips for me, plus another mug of hot chocolate. As I enjoyed the meal, and as yet another musical melange played on to fill yet more time, I was still reflecting on the time that had passed, on the year of 1978 and what had followed after the death of my lovely wife, Susan.

Whitney Houston was singing, 'Saving all my Love for You'.
How very appropriate!

Chapter 2

Saturday, 12 August, 1978.

I WAS SITTING in seat 5, coach D, of the 11.20 a.m. train from Gaynsford Parkway to London King's Cross. It was 11.10 a.m. approximately. The station was bustling with people craning their necks to see when their trains were due to arrive or depart, and porters and other station staff from customer services were rushing all over the place with cases, passengers, or information about delays to services. Doors slammed. Announcers made comments over loudspeakers that nobody could interpret clearly! Young children cried or yelled out excitedly. People crowded together and then started pushing and jostling as the train came into the platform. I sat there and listened to all that was going on around me.

I was lucky that day. Barry Barnet of Phoenix Cars, which was now up and running, and quite the largest and busiest cab firm in Gaynsford, drove me down to Gaynsford Parkway Railway Station at 10.35 a.m. that morning, and I was taken by him to the customer assistance office, which was just to the left of platform one. From there I was taken to the train I was to board for my journey down to the south-east and the metropolis!

I would have liked a drink before leaving, but was told I would be able to purchase one after the train got going, so I had decided to wait. I was thirsty. Well, it was my own fault, of course! I had eaten two bacon and sausage 'toasted doorsteps' for my breakfast! I felt as though I ought to have a substantial breakfast before travelling, then I would not need to take sandwiches with me. I could buy something to eat and drink on the train on the way down, and I knew I would get a good meal once I arrived at Mum and Dad's, for that is where I was going to stay, at least for the first part of my month away. I had been planning that for some time, almost from the day of her funeral, and now, at last, it was coming to fruition.

As the whistle blew and the last of the carriage doors banged shut, the train began to move away from platform four of Gaynsford Parkway and I sat back and looked forward to the lengthy journey ahead. A time to think, a time to go over past events!

The train was picking up speed on its way towards London and the Home Counties. We had been going ten minutes and I had just had a can of ice-cold fizzy orange and some chocolate, and was feeling much more replete. Now, once again, I could relax, and as the train speeded up and I lounged back in my comfortable seat with my bags piled on the seat beside me, and my mind went rolling back over the events of the past three months.

Chapter 3

TUESDAY, 16TH May, was the date of her funeral. It took place at the same church where we were married. The same vicar, the Reverend John Lammie, said many very kind and wonderful things about my Susan, and talked about the happy day when he had married the two of us—that wonderfully happy day in August 1966. After the service and blessings, including four hymns, the funeral procession drove very slowly through town to the crematorium right on the outskirts of Gaynsford. There, my darling Susan was finally put to rest. The Co-op had made all the arrangements. Dave, Mick and I had gone there on the Tuesday afternoon, 9th May. The two people to whom we had spoken were both very kind and extremely tolerant and helpful. In very little time, all arrangements had been made.

I had returned home with Trudy, Mick and Dave on the evening of Monday, 8th May. I had gone to bed early that evening, after I had endeavoured to do justice to the substantial supper that Trudy had set before me. Mick helped me to bed, and he slept alongside me again that night in the double bed that he usually shared with his wife. Both Mick and I were distraught; he had lost a beloved sister, I had lost an adored and revered wife. That night, as we lay in bed side by side, we sought consolation from one another.

Trudy was very solicitous to both of us during that time of sorrow. Dave was a tower of strength. Nothing seemed too much trouble for that lively, still rather 'gawky' 17 year old. He drove us here and there, carried messages for me, took me down to Bread Street to sort things out there, ie, how much leave I would be allowed to take etc.

Pat Lenham sat with us in her office and told me I must take all the leave I required. Chris Braun put a comforting arm around my shoulders, he seemed unable to speak! Jacky Paternoster brought me hot drinks and patted my shoulder. She was very kind to me. Mandy Moss, Sandra Couchman and young Tina Jobling all cried, but they all came to her funeral.

Fourteen members of my own family came to her funeral. My parents (Mary and George) drove up from Thamesford, Essex. With them came a long-standing friend of our family in the person of Eleanor Newman. Eleanor was 60 years of age. She was a health visitor, who worked for the local area health authority in a very large and busy health centre in Thamesford. Eleanor would have retired at the age of 60, but during the previous three years she had had her own share of tragedies. First, her husband, Lionel, to whom she had only been married for eight years, died of cancer, then her only sister, Letitia, also died suddenly after suffering a massive stroke, so Eleanor went on working. She had been a friend of our family for many years and was someone of whom I had always been very fond. That feeling was reciprocated, hence her presence at Susan's funeral.

My Auntie Joyce and Uncle Len had driven up from their home in South-East London. They had a second-floor flat on a vast council estate, which they shared with their two sons, 25-year-old Gary and 23-year-old Terry. I had not seen either of my cousins for several years. Neither of them attended Susan's funeral with their parents. They were still both single and both still lived at home with my aunt and uncle. Joyce was the second eldest of the four daughters of my late and still lamented Granny Annie.

My Auntie Batty and Uncle Bill drove up from Thamesford. They lived about ten minutes from Mum and Dad. Mum and Dad, and Betty and Bill regularly saw one another. They usually got together on one or other day of every weekend. They had often spent holidays together. Betty was the third of the four daughters of Granny Annie. She was small in stature, slim, with brown hair and eyes, and a wonderful, if somewhat quirky, sense of humour. That last named attribute appealed to me! Mine was weird as well, and Betty and I had always got on very well together! Betty and Bill Gurney had three children; Mike, their only son, was 22 years old, single and still lived at home, although he did try living in a flat with four mates for a short while, only to return home to his parents, dejected and disgusted with life. Susan, their eldest daughter, was 21 years old, married, and had two small children—twin girls! Susan's husband, Andreas Sava, known to all as Andy, came from a Greek family.

Neither Betty nor Bill was mad about the marriage, but they had accepted it because of the presence of the two babies. They tolerated Andy, who was a grand young man, tall, athletic, handsome, and very polite and charming. I had only met him a couple of times, and had never seen the children, twins Lilly and Lucy. Their youngest child was Anne. She was nearly nine years old, and was born on 25th September, 1969, almost 12 years from the date of Susan's birth. Anne was a most attractive girl, always laughing. She had not been spoiled and, although she was slightly overweight, she was nevertheless a popular little girl at her school and a most delightful child, with her mother's sense of humour. I was very fond of Anne Sava.

Nelly and Alf Sunley came up from Seaport. With them came my Uncle Sid. Nelly was the fourth of the four daughters, and Mum's youngest sister. Alf was her husband, and they had Uncle Sid with them. He was the only son of that family—G ranny Annie's pride and joy! Sid was well over six feet in height, well built, with the characteristic dark brown hair and brown eyes. He was just 39 years of age. He had never married, but for the past 22 years, he had been 'wed to the navy'. 'Sailor Sid', with his rolling gait and broad shoulders, his huge feet and slow way of talking, his ready wit and fount of daft jokes and japes, was now home from the sea for good, he said. He had come ashore in June and, since then, had been living down in Seaport. I had not seen him for ages, and it was great to see him again, even in such sad circumstances.

Yvonne and Eric had travelled up from Cambridgeshire. I was surprised about that. Eric, my brother, and I had never been all that close. I guess the closest we ever came to one another was the time just before he was married in the summer of 1965. We spent quite a bit of time getting to know one another then. I was home from school for good, and Eric, whenever he was not visiting Yvonne's home, which was quite a frequent occurrence, involved me in his activities as much as he was able. We went out drinking with his mates! He had some good pals, with whom I got along very well, in fact, Johnny Day, Mick Harmer and several others used to come around to our house regularly on a Friday and Saturday night, even after Eric was married to Yvonne, to see if I fancied 'goin' aht for a few jars'. In essence, they became my mates, and Johnny Day and his 'twin' brother, Jimmy, came to my wedding... but going back to Eric.

As I said, that was the closest we had ever been to one another. Once he was married, I used to go over for a weekend say, a couple of times a month, and then, of course, I moved to Gaynsford in the March of 1966 and subsequently married Sue, but Yvonne and Eric were both there at Sue's funeral. They were married in the October of 1965, and had one son, Michael, who was born in 1968. Eric's 'twin' sister, Doreen, along with her husband, Fred Dingle, arrived from North Yorkshire.

The funeral was at 10.35 a.m. at least that was when the service took place. They arrived at the church at around 10.15 a.m. They had a new car, a big Volvo. Mum and Dad, who had very little to do with them, were both profoundly shocked. Mum spoke quietly to Doreen and totally ignored her husband, Fred. Dad initially ignored both of them, but later he had a drink with Fred and gave Doreen some money for the kids, although she would not accept it, apparently, or so I learned later on from Fred, when we were talking together at the bar. At least they afforded me the courtesy of not having a family row on the day of my late wife's funeral, and there so easily could have been a full-scale family row. I was very grateful that did not occur!

With so many of my relations arriving, it made Sue's family look a poor little group with just her mother, Lizzie, Lizzie's elder sister, Aunt Annie, plus Trudy, Mick and Dave. We all introduced ourselves to one another outside the church before walking in behind the coffin.

I had paid for an oak coffin and it was certainly beautiful. There were flowers, two wreaths, laid on the top of it, one from Mum, Aunt Annie, Trudy, Mick and Dave, and one from me. Mine had pride of place, of course, but both wreaths were beautiful. The church was packed with people for her funeral. We sang four hymns; 'Jerusalem', 'Praise my Soul, the King of Heaven' and 'Lead us, Heavenly Father'. The last one was by special request of Sue, her favourite hymn in all the world, 'I vow to Thee my Country, all Earthly Things Above'! The vicar gave two lovely readings, and I read a poem that I had written especially for Sue at the time we were married. It was a lovely service and took around 50 minutes.

The cremation was at exactly midday, and only the family went along to that, as well as one or two especially invited people, like Janet Perry, Dr Merv, Jean and Terry Barradell, Vera and Cyril Williams and the matron from The Mary Craigie Unit, Margaret McKenzie.

Twenty-four of us went back to the Oak Room at the Co-op. That included all the members of both families, plus the Barradells and the Williamses, whom I had especially invited, and me, of course. In the Oak Room, on the second floor, towards the back of the Co-op, the staff waited upon us very courteously and efficiently. They had prepared a large and very substantial buffet for us, and there was a bar just across the way if we wanted drinks. Everyone had a drink, except for Lizzie and Annie, who got a bit upset about all the drinks my family were having. I had to tell them quite forcefully, but quietly, that it was also a celebration of Susan's life and not merely a 'wake'. Annie seemed reasonably accepting of that, but Lizzie was not very happy.

At the buffet, everyone came to talk to me. Lizzie and Annie asked if I was okay. Both women kissed me. Mick stood beside me and squeezed my hand. He was so very, very distressed. That night he would sleep with me once again and we would spend another night consoling each other. Dave, our rock, was solicitous and helpful, running between the families to see if everything was all right and to ask if there was anything he could do for anyone. Trudy kept in the background, but she had quite a chat with my sister, Doreen. Mum and Dad wanted me to go back home with them. I quietly played that down, saying I would visit, but not at the moment. Yvonne and Eric both asked me to go and stay with them. I found that quite heartening considering we did not really get on. I thanked them both for coming, and said, yes, I would visit them soon. During that holiday, I intended to do so. All the aunts and uncles came to speak to me and talked quietly about the future. I did not even want to contemplate the future or what it might hold! It was all far too painful at that time. However, I bore up bravely, because, as I had said to Sue's mother and aunt, it was not just a funeral to say goodbye to my lovely late wife, it was a celebration of her life and the love we had shared together.

We drank, we ate and we laughed, and Lizzie and Aunt Annie grew more and more restless. Eventually Trudy agreed to drive them back to their respective homes. I think I was supposed to apologise to Lizzie for my behaviour during that afternoon, but frankly, I could see nothing for which to apologise. I had hurt no one as I could see. Even Mick, who was so distressed about the loss of his only sister, was laughing with my Uncle Sid and others while he stood at the bar opposite the Oak Room and had a drink or two—and why not?

Sue was dead, but she would never leave me! I knew that, and neither would she have wished us all to be so melancholy. We all had to make efforts to try and cheer up and get on with our lives, but I knew none of that would mean much to Lizzie! Susan's mother, like her own parents, had always lived for drama. If she could make a drama out of a crisis, she would do so, her one failing, I am afraid.

After they had gone, Mick and Dave stayed on with my family and the Barradells. The Williamses had departed fairly swiftly after getting plenty of food and one or two drinks down their necks, but they had both been very civil and polite to my family, especially to my parents and to Lizzie and Annie. Jean and Terry Barradell were collected by their son, Tony, who shook my hand and wished me well, then there was only family.

I stood at the bar with Mick, Dave and my Uncle Sid. Fred Dingle came to join us and Sid and Fred stood each side of me. They had been introduced, and had had quite a lot to say to one another. Fred, a massive Yorkshireman, had a very pronounced accent, as had my Uncle Sid, who was a cockney 'froo an' froo', so I didn't really know how much of what they said to one another each man really understood. However, with me in the middle to interpret, they got along very well together, those two big blokes— Sid, the ex-sailor and Fred, the pig man! Each put a hand on one of my shoulders and both bought me drinks. Dave came and stood behind me with Mick. Fred Dingle, always friendly and affable, bought them a drink apiece, and there we stood, altogether, propping up the bar opposite the Oak Room at the Co-op.

"It's gud to see yo' again, mate!" said Sid, leaning on my right shoulder.

"Are you glad to be home?" I asked.

"Not 'arf!" he exclaimed, taking a good long pull at his fifth or sixth pint.

"Wot ye' plannin' te do nah that yo' are 'ome f'r gud?" asked Fred.

Sid was silent for a moment or two.

"Aw reckon as 'ow aw might try an' start up a transport business!" he said.

We all wished him luck with his venture.

"An' when yo' cummin' dahn to see us in Seaport then, Boyzie?" asked Sid.

I smiled, and took another pull at my pint of rough cider.

"As soon as I feel up to it," I said.

Sid slapped me on the shoulder and said he hoped he would see me again very soon. He then moved away.

Doreen came and stood beside me. Doreen and Fred already had a very large family, and she was heavily pregnant again. It was grand to see both her and Fred Dingle at Sue's funeral that day. Fred bought his wife a mineral water and she put her arm around me. Both she and Fred made me promise I would visit them soon. During that holiday, the latter half, I intended to honour that promise, which I made on the day of my late and loved wife's funeral.

§☙❧§

I was going to be quite busy during the time I was away from Gaynsford. On 12th August, I was travelling down to stay with Mum and Dad, who would be there to meet me once the train arrived at King's Cross. That night we were going out with Betty and Bill, and also with Mike and his latest girlfriend, Marilyn. She was supposed to be a very nice girl, according to Mum and Aunt Betty, both of whom telephoned me regularly.

Mum and Dad rang me at least twice a week, and all the aunts and uncles, including Sid, phoned me at least once a fortnight. Doreen and Fred had taken to telephoning me, say, once a week, on a Sunday evening as a rule, and if I was not at home then one or other of them would call me on the Monday evening.

I rarely went out in the week, except perhaps to the pub. By the time I had got home, been shopping, cooked a meal or whatever, there was not a lot of time left. I had to take Meggie out to the park most evenings. She was becoming quite a tie, although I still loved her, and the place would have seemed very empty without her. Trudy and Mick were looking after her while I was away.

The Williams boys had wished to do so, but they were still friends with the Gypsy lads and I was afraid to leave Meggie too long in their care. The Williams brothers, although big strong lads who looked tough were actually very gullible! They adored

Meggie, and would never mean to let anything happen to her, but still, I was unsure about leaving her in their care those days. As soon as I had decided I was definitely having a long break away from Gaynsford, I asked Trudy and Mick to take her over to their house. As they already had four dogs, they readily agreed to do so.

The train was slowing up at Melton Junction, the first stop en route to London and the south-east.

Chapter 4

I T WAS almost midnight again on Friday, 29th December, 1989. It had not seemed such a long day as I had anticipated. The 24 hours during which I had been undertaking the music marathon had gone fairly quickly thus far. I suppose it was because I had been busy, and when I hadn't been sorting out music, discussing plans with my engineer or taking phone calls, which had been numerous from people listening in, I had used the time to think. Now I was playing a long medley of music before the midnight news.

I had had another good meal and spent time having a wash and brush up and I had also had another change of clothes. I felt fresh and full, clean and not too tired. So long as I never left the studio for longer than the allotted time, I could wash, change, clean my teeth, use the usual facilities etc., but I normally ate in there, despite the fact that space was at a minimum. There had been no major accidents as yet! I had had so many people wishing me well; it was still a tremendous challenge, and I was endeavouring to make the broadcast as exciting as possible. It was coming up towards midnight and the 'wee small hours' of the morning might prove somewhat lonely. However, I reverted to my thoughts.

Certainly, the time I was spending on my own in the studio, and the challenge of undertaking the broadcast for 80 hours was proving to be good character building for me. Does that seem a strange thing to say? When life has dealt you a few hard knocks, you get so that you don't trust your own judgement any more. I was beginning to lose confidence in myself, but the exercise was proving not only to be extremely enjoyable, but also I felt sure it was increasing my self-confidence and my belief in my own strengths!

It was midnight. The news jingle had just finished; I had another drink, opened the mike and spoke.

"Hi, it's still me, Rick Dee here on Sunny Gold Radio, the sounds of summer all year long! We're continuing with our 80-hour music marathon to ring out the old and ring in the new. I hope to be here with you on your radio until well into the first day of 1990, so don't you move that dial, you hear? I need you with me, to give me your support, like you have been doing all day. Bless you and thank you for that!"

I closed the mike and brought in the Sunny Gold Radio jingle then I began a series of nine records in which each song told a story, starting with some Harry Chapin. Now, I could relax, and my mind went back over the years, back to the August of 1978 and the long holiday I had spent away from Gaynsford soon after my late wife's funeral.

Chapter 5

AT AROUND midday, as the train rattled on its way from Melton Junction down to Southborough, I bought myself a can of still orange and some sandwiches. I enjoyed those; I appeared to have got my appetite back again! After Sue's funeral, I was not eating very well for about a month, and then, one morning, I just got up and decided to cook myself a huge breakfast. Amazingly enough I ate every last scrap of it, which pleased me.

Life without Susan had not been easy! The neighbours were very good, but I didn't want to let too many of them into my life as we had done once when we lived on The Circle. It was very nice to have lots of friends, but one had to be a little bit selective as to whom one let into one's life. I mean, I didn't want my most intimate secrets known to all in the area, and if the wrong people came into my home to help me, then that could well be the result. One had to be tactful as to how to turn someone away in a polite and pleasant way, a way that said, 'Thanks very much for your offer. I don't need your help right now, but it was kind of you and maybe in the future, I'll welcome your help. Thanks again! Okay?' If you can do that, with a smile on your face, then people do not take umbrage. Well, that's what I have found anyway!

Chapter 6

I STAYED WITH Trudy and Mick until the Sunday after Sue's funeral. After tea on the Sunday evening, Dave drove me home. I was intending to go back to work again on the Monday morning. Dave had made sure that the house was warm and comfortable for me on my return, and Trudy had been in to clean up for me on the Saturday. Vera had bought shopping and stocked up the fridge for me according to my instructions.

Now, as he left me on my front driveway, Dave warmly shook my hand and said he and his parents would see me at the weekend, and that, if I needed or wanted anything prior to that time, then all I had to do was telephone. I squeezed Dave's big hand, and thanked him very much for everything then I unlocked my front door, carried my two bags over the threshold, again thanked my nephew for everything, and closed the front door as he departed down the driveway and set off for his parents' home.

I duly unpacked, made myself a hot drink, fed Meggie, let her out into the yard and made myself a plate of sandwiches. I sat in the dining room with Meggie, and ate and drank my fill, realising that now we were really on our own. How would we fare? Well, it was up really to me now. One thing I knew for certain, I could not and would not rely on Sue's mum to cook, clean etc., for me. She lived too far away and besides, it wasn't fair. Trudy and Mick would take me shopping once a fortnight, which would be on a Saturday morning, whenever they could do so. I would then get a taxi into Allerton. I could make sandwiches, do fry-ups etc., for myself, so I wasn't that troubled about food, but the cleaning, polishing, washing, ironing and the baking, who was going to do all that for me now?

As I secured the house that night and went up to bed, followed by Meggie, who wanted to sleep at my feet again, and whom I was glad to have around me for the first few nights at home anyway, I was thinking about my situation. I drifted off to sleep still pondering about it.

{❧}

I almost overslept on the Monday morning. It was Meggie's rough tongue licking my face that woke me. I had forgotten to set the alarm clock. Great, and that was only the beginning of my time alone, ah well! If I wanted breakfast, I would have to get up and make it.

I heaved myself out of bed, and Meggie jumped up off the rug and followed me downstairs. I let her out, put the kettle on, opened several windows, put the radio on and set about preparing breakfast. I gave Meggie a drink and put four Weetabix into a bowl. I boiled some milk and poured that onto the cereal, then put two eggs into the same saucepan with some water and set them to boil. When I had eaten my large bowl full of cereal and warm milk, I put the bowl into the sink to be washed and then buttered five small rounds of wholemeal bread to go with my two hard-boiled eggs. A good, substantial breakfast indeed! I washed up after breakfast, cleaned around the kitchen then let Meggie out into the yard again for the second time that morning.

While she ran, barked etc., I went upstairs, showered, shaved and dressed. I packed myself up some sandwiches, they were ham that day, and took my front door key around to Vera's. She said she would pop in and see to Meggie, and might give the house a 'good clean rahnd' if I didn't mind. I said, no, I didn't mind, and thanked her profusely then I was running to catch my bus.

It was the first day back at work since her decease. It was going to be very strange, very strange indeed, but I had no idea of the events that were to take place later on that day.

Chapter 7

WE HAD now pulled into Southborough, which was a large town on the borders of Bedfordshire and South Lincolnshire. We were awaiting the arrival of a connecting train. It was around 1.10 p.m., roughly another hour and 50 minutes before we arrive into London King's Cross.

I was looking forward with great anticipation to seeing Mum and Dad again, and to getting home. I understood they had recently decorated my bedroom, the bedroom I had called mine from the day that Doreen, my sister, had left home. I believed they had also bought me a new bed and had purchased a whole lot of new bed linen for my return. I knew we would dine very well that night; we always did at Mum's. Good old Mum! She always was a fantastic cook, just like her mum, my Granny Annie. Granny Annie was the best cook in the whole darned world, and no substitute. That's my opinion anyway. Biased? Yes, perhaps I am, just a little bit, anyway!

I was sure Mum had been cooking and preparing for my visit all week. That was the kind of mum I had. She loved to have me home; well, they both did really, but I knew Mum loved it most. She was so sure that, when I left school in 1965, the September of that year, I was home for good, but it was not to be. I knew that when I left to move to Gaynsford to marry Sue it hurt her very deeply, but Mum would never tell me so, because she only thought of my happiness. That was the title of the first song I ever sang, at least, that's what Mum and Dad told me. It's strange, the things that stay in one's mind!

The train was pulling away from the platform in Southborough, and I was lying back, relaxing in my seat, my bags beside me, contemplating the future. I was sure it would be a good holiday, it certainly promised to be a very busy one. I knew that that evening, after we had eaten dinner, we were going to the Florida Club, and we would meet Betty, Bill, Mike and his lady friend, Marilyn, down there. I daresay Susan would have Anne for the night. We would remain at the Florida until well after midnight, and would then drive home. I thought we would have a bit of supper when we got back home and it would be at least two in the morning before we got to bed.

The following day, after breakfast, I knew we were driving up to South-East London to Joyce and Len's. Apparently Sid was living up there now, having moved from Seaport, and he had been driving his own minicab for a mate of his who was in the navy with him and who now owned a minicab business in the Lewisham area. Sid might well buy into it and become 'partners' with the bloke, at least, so Mum said. There would be ten of us for dinner; Mum, Dad and me, Uncle Sid, Gary and Terry and their girlfriends, Karen and Tricia, plus Joyce and Len. Later, Betty, Bill and all their family were coming over for tea.

On Monday, Mum and I would go shopping in Thamesford while Dad was working, then in the late afternoon Eleanor Newman was coming over to have tea with us. On Tuesday, Dad would be at work again and Mum would be busy packing because on the following day we were driving down to Seaport to stay with Nelly, Alf and family in their guest house. I was greatly looking forward to that.

Nelly and Alf had seven children, and on the Saturday while we were down there, their eldest daughter, Queenie, aged 18 years, was getting married. That was a week away. She was marrying a bloke called Matt, who was 24 years old and a market gardener. I was glad for her. Queenie was a nice girl, very outspoken, like me, but a real smasher and a half! I had not yet met Matt, but I was sure he would be a credit to her and would look after her well. That was the kind of bloke she deserved.

Betty, Bill and all the family were coming down to Seaport on the Friday and staying until the Sunday. We were staying over until the following Wednesday when we would drive home to Thamesford. On the Thursday after dinner, Eric was coming over to take me back with him to Cherry Wootton to spend a long weekend with him, Yvonne and Micky. On the Sunday morning, after breakfast, Eric would drive me to the bus station at Southborough, so that I could get on the coach that would take me all the way up north to Briggthorpe, where Fred Dingle would meet me and take me back to Harts Hill. There, I would stay with Doreen, Fred and their large and chaotic family, for almost a fortnight. That was the part of the holiday I was looking forward to most of all; my sojourn in North Yorkshire with the Dingle family.

Chapter 8

O N THAT first Monday I went back to work after Sue's funeral, I caught my usual bus, the 7.50 a.m. I saw Dean Sadler delivering his papers and he wished me good morning. I told him I was going back to work for the first time that day since the funeral, and he wished me well. On the bus I sat with Steve Lambert. We chatted easily and amiably. All the neighbours had been very kind since Susan died, and many of them were at her funeral on 16th May. We caught the 8.35 a.m. bus to Allerton, and I alighted outside James Blume's, the baker's.

As I stepped off the bus, I heard a great roar.

"He's here, he's here, lads, it's Boyzie!"

They were swarming around me then, pushing, jostling, trying desperately to get near me. Everyone wanted to press my hands or pat me on the back or on the shoulders. There were so many of them!

We walked along towards the crossing at the junction of Hyland Road and Gunners Lane, which was situated almost directly outside the gates of the Gunners Lane School and Community College. As we walked, their numbers seemed to be increasing all the while. I was not frightened, I was not even embarrassed, but I was very touched! Feelings were running high in me, and I was very emotional about the vast numbers of boys and youths surrounding me and the fact that they all cared enough about me to want to be with me that morning!

I had had a communication by telephone from Jacky Paternoster while I was away and she had told me that on two recent occasions there had been huge crowds of young lads and youths amassed at

133

the end of the driveway outside the Family Support Centre, and now they were literally swarming all around me as I endeavoured to walk towards the junction and the audible level crossing.

"Boyzie, Boyzie, Boyzie, where yo' bin, Boyzie? We've all missed yo', mate! We're glad to see yo' back again, Boyzie! Boyzie! Boyzie! He's here, come on, come ovver 'ere, lads, he's here. Boyzie! Boyzie! Boyzie!"

So it went on and it was now becoming a struggle to walk along. As we neared the crossing and the junction of the two main roads, they seemed to be packed around it, waiting for us to arrive. We crossed the road—a massive column moving in front, a mighty army moving in close behind, with me in the middle, surrounded by umpteen willing escorts, each with a hand on my back, my chest or my shoulders. When we reached the other side of the crossing and commenced our walk along towards Bread Street it seemed they swarmed out of every side street to left and right.

"Boyzie, Boyzie, Boyzie, it's gud to see yo' again, mate! Where yo' bin, mate?"

I could not speak. I merely tried to keep walking, as they pressed and pushed and 'jockeyed' for positions all around me!

"Boyzie, Boyzie, Boyzie!"

Eventually, after what seemed an eternity, we reached the end of the driveway leading up to the Family Support Centre. There, we paused, and they literally packed themselves around me, everyone talking, such a cacophony of sound, such a deep, full-throated roar, such a loud, shrill clamour of falsetto voices. So many, so very, very many young people pushing, shoving and jostling all around me. The vast crowd was like the crowd at the home ground on that wonderful afternoon when we won the FA League Challenge Cup. Everyone was shouting out my name, swaying altogether on their feet.

"Boyzie, Boyzie, Boyzie!"

I was hemmed in, utterly surrounded on all sides by excited, chattering schoolboys and youths of all types, shapes, colours, sizes and sorts, but it was good to hear them.

"Boyzie, Boyzie, Boyzie!"

A big youth leaned on my right shoulder.

"Where yo' bin, Boyzie? We've all missed yo' arrahnd 'ere, mate!"

Thomas Paul Copley, only son of Pauline Copley, was 15 years old, stood over six feet three inches tall in his stockinged feet and weighed a stone for every year of his age. He pushed himself hard up against me and again, asked casually:

"Cum on, where yo' bin, mate?"

The roar was taken up by all around.

"Where yo' bin? Where yo' bin? Where yo' bin?"

I hung my head! I could feel tears welling up inside me as the emotions I was struggling to keep in check fought to be released. Oh God! How could I begin to tell those young people all about my lovely late wife and what had happened to her? How could I expect them to understand the profound effect her decease had had upon me?

"Where yo' bin! Where you bin! Where yo' bin, Boyzie?"

The noise was getting greater and greater with every second that passed. I was becoming embarrassed by the presence of so many young people around me. I struggled to compose myself then held up my two hands in a gesture that I hoped would evoke silence amongst them. My hopes were realised.

Once silence had fallen upon the amassed crowds still swaying altogether on their feet, I raised my head.

"I've… I've been off for a while. My… my wife!"

I was struggling! A friendly hand was placed on my right shoulder and Thomas Paul Copley pushed his body hard up against mine.

"Easy, mate, we're all 'ere an' we're all listenin'. Jus' tek your time, eh mate, an' tell us where yo' bin!"

"Yeh! Tell us where yo' bin, Boyzie," came the great, tumultuous roar from all around.

I held my head erect and spoke, trying to sound casual.

"My wife, sh-she died a few days ago, and... and I've been off because of that. You know lads, seeing to all that needed to be done with regard to her funeral and that, b-but I'm back at work now, so I'll be seeing you most days I expect!"

There was complete silence after I had stopped speaking. Everyone seemed to have his eyes riveted upon me. I could feel their eyes boring into me as we all stood together at the end of the driveway leading up to the Family Support Centre. Carlo Santin, a dark-skinned, swarthy Italian youth, was the first to break the silence.

"Aw'm very sorry, Boyzie," he said, and patted my left shoulder.

The tears came then, flowing unchecked from my swollen eyes. I hung my head down and looked at my feet. I rocked on my feet, and cried as though my heart would break, and they packed in tighter, tighter, even more tightly around me, each individual wishing to comfort and console me in some way, if he were able to do so.

For a long while after that, nobody spoke and nobody moved, then Thomas Paul Copley, still leaning on my right shoulder, spoke gently.

"We'll all look after yo', mate."

That was taken up by everyone all around.

"Yeh, we'll look after yo', Boyzie. We're your new mates, we'll help yo', mate. We reckon you are a gud bloke, we'll help yo', Boyzie. We'll look after yo', pal..." and so on, and so forth!

They were then pushing, jostling, shoving, almost fighting on their feet to get near me, everyone offering me a hand to shake, everyone trying desperately to get as close to me as possible, so he could shake my hand, pat me on the back, rub my shoulders etc., etc.

"We'll look after yo', Boyzie, dun't yo' worry, mate, we're all your new friends, we'll look aht f'r yo', Boyzie!"

Eventually they made a way through for me, and I was able to get onto the driveway and walk slowly up to my office. As I went through the doorway leading into the porch that fronted the

building, I heard them roar all together:
"See yo' tonight, mate, see yo' tonight, Boyzie!"

Chapter 9

THE TRAIN was fairly speeding down towards Haddingham in North Bedfordshire, and I was relaxing, still thinking about the past and contemplating the future. A refreshment trolley was pushed past and I ignored it, not wishing for anything else to drink or eat at that time. I knew very well the size of the meal I would get when I arrived home with Mum and Dad that afternoon.

*

That first day back at work following Susan's decease seemed a very long one. When I walked into the office, everyone was there to greet me. Chris shook my hand warmly. Pat greeted me and said how pleased everyone was to see me back again. Jacky Paternoster kissed me. Mandy Moss brought me a steaming mug of hot chocolate. Tina and Sandra both came to speak to me and told me how pleased they were to see me back.

After a while I settled back into the routine again. We were certainly very busy that day, and there were loads of tapes for me to type, lots of calls for me to answer on the switchboard and plenty of people coming in and out of reception. I did not have much time to think. As the day wore on, I felt rather tired; I suppose I was still feeling very emotional and that in itself was fairly tiring.

I went to lunch at the Gunners, and saw Rob McCallasky and his cousin, Marty. They both appeared pleased to see me and we chatted amiably over a good lunch; big 'toasted doorsteps' containing bacon and sausage, and a big bowl of chips. Three pints of cider for me, each one ice-cold—lovely!

"Aw've missed yo', mate!" said Rob, who, along with other members of his family had attended Sue's funeral.

We talked easily, and Rob and Marty invited me out with them the following Saturday afternoon. They were going on their bikes, Marty had just acquired one apparently, and they were going on a long ride. Rob asked if I wanted to go on the back of his. I thought for a few moments.

"Yeh, why not?" I said.

"Aw gud, aw'll call f'r you abaht 1 p.m. then, okay?"

I said that would be fine, all things being equal. I would have to go shopping in the morning, but after that, the day was my own. As we parted, the lads reminded me of their phone numbers. Rob was living back at home again, and said if anything went wrong I should ring them there to let them know not to call for me. I undertook to do so, but said I would be there and that I was already looking forward to it.

I knew that certain people, especially Sue's mum, would not be pleased about me 'throwing myself back into life' in that way, but felt it was the only way. She would not expect me to sit around moping! Life was too short; hadn't that just been made obvious to me? So I would not, and if anyone didn't like it, well then, they would just have to lump it!

❧

Haddingham was passed and then we were heading pell-mell for Drayton in Hertfordshire. That was the last stop before London King's Cross. I had bought another can of orange, because it was warm and I was thirsty. I sat knocking it back and still thinking about the past few months, and the train rattled on its way towards London. I would soon be seeing Mum and Dad again.

I was feeling quite excited, like a young lad going home from school. I remembered how thrilled I always used to feel whenever I went home from boarding-school, thrilled and delighted at the prospect of going home. That was until that summer of 1960, and after that summer, everything seemed to change.

Chapter 10

A T THE end of that first day back at work following Susan's funeral, I left the office at around 5.50 p.m. I chatted to the cleaning ladies for a while, and then walked on towards the end of the driveway, and there they were; hundreds and hundreds of them, waiting in virtual silence for me to get to them.

Once I had arrived in their midst they immediately surrounded me—once more in virtual silence—and we began our slow walk towards the junction of Gunners Lane and Hyland Road, all walking along slowly together, and, as we walked along, I quickly realised I was the only one with shoes on my feet. Everyone else had removed their shoes or boots and were carrying them.

We moved in a vast and seemingly endless procession towards the junction of the two main roads and the bus stop. As we walked along, they poured out of every side street. The word went around.

"Shh, shoes off, shoes off, lads!"

We continued to shuffle along altogether, me walking in the very midst of that vast and growing stockinged-foot army of boys, youths and young men. The vast and ever-increasing network of young people surrounded me protectively on all sides, and each night since then, they surrounded me and walked home with me, packing in on all sides, walking altogether in their stockinged feet. They had looked after me as they promised they would.

There were usually 12 of them packed close in around me, in the very midst of that vast stockinged-foot brigade. The other lads referred to these 12 as the 'Apostles'. The 'Apostles' were Thomas Paul Copley, 15 years old and very tall for his age. He weighed a stone for every one of h is 15 and a half years. Carlo Santin, 16 years, a dark swarthy Italian, good-looking, hot-headed and very protective of me. Paul Turkington, 14 years, small, wiry, dark-haired and quick on his feet. Paul was the only son of his single mum, Rosie Turkington. Steven Grubb, 16 years, best mate of Paul Copley. Jamie Ash, 'Smokey'. Carl Pick, the one responsible for taking and breaking my white cane on that fateful day when I was pushed into the middle of the road. Now he pushed his great weight hard up against me and was very protective of me. Barry Briggs, 16 years, tall and slightly built, but nevertheless, as tough as ten! Barry was the son of a builder. Dan Waydeson, only son of Beryl Waydeson. Dan was only 14 years old, small for his age, sturdy and tough! His voice has still not quite broken, and sometimes he piped up in a high 'falsetto' while, at other times, he croaked like a bullfrog! The other lads called him by that nickname, poor Dan the Bullfrog! Little Dan Waydeson was one of my loyalist followers and protectors. George Berry, 13 years, another hothead, who was fiercely protective of me and would do anything on earth for me! He thought the world of me as indeed did all those lads. George was the son of a policeman.

There was Jim Brady, 14 years, son of a cabbie, who was well known to me. Melvyn Potter, the eldest at 17 years, a big, well-made black lad, and Will Garlick, about five feet seven inches tall. He was 13 years old, and he pushed his body hard up against mine. Will was always poorly dressed, and often completely without shoes, having to wear pumps or sandals even on really cold days! The Garlick family, which was very large, and was overseen by a single-mum, who was one of the cleaners at the Family Support Centre was very poor! They were the 12 'Apostles' and always seemed to be surrounding me the most closely as we walked from my office back to the end of Rutland Close each evening.

There, the vast and mighty army stopped, and the 'Apostles' walked with me to my front gate. Sometimes, they sat on my front garden wall for a few moments, and sometimes, when we reached the wall, it was already occupied by the three Williams brothers and a large number of the Gypsy lads. They were usually led by Richie Feighan. There had never been any trouble between the opposing factions, indeed, they rarely acknowledged one another. They would sit there talking together in their groups, but not even noticing one another's existence. It was a very strange concept.

The 'Apostles' would gather together, put their shoes on and walk back to the end of my close, where they would meet up again with the rest of the vast clan and begin their long walk back to Allerton and Osleston. The Gypsies would put out their fags, drop their cans and rise to their feet. They nodded to the Williams boys, said a friendly and courteous, 'Gudnight' to me, all speaking together, and walked off towards the park and their caravans. The Williams boys would gather up the cans then make their way into their own house.

They still looked after Meggie for me, but not as much as they once used to do. I did not like leaving her with them so much those days because of their close ties with those Gypsy lads. Vera, their mum, still cooked for me and sometimes she cleaned through the house. I decided that when I got back from my holiday, I must actively look for a cleaner-cum-housekeeper.

Chapter 11

WE WERE pulling into Drayton Station. Once we left there we'd be in London King's Cross within half an hour, and a long journey would be at an end for me. I was sure of a warm homecoming that day! Not like that summer—that summer 18 years before in 1960.

My mind roamed back again to that July when I had arrived home for the long summer holiday. It was a Wednesday in mid-July—a blazing hot summer's day. In the evening, after a high tea, while we were listening to music on the tape recorder, Mum and Dad told me of the death of Uncle Stan. Stan Vardy had been my Granny Annie's lodger for many years, and they had been very close, especially since the death of my granddad, Walter, in 1948. It was said by some of the neighbours that Stan Vardy was in fact the father of my Uncle Sid, but I didn't believe that.

Stan had been like a granddad to me and the twins, and we called him Uncle Stan and adored him because he was a lovely guy and very kind to us, always cheerful and ready for 'fun an' games' whenever we went over to Granny's house in South-East London. Uncle Stan had been ill for a while, so perhaps it was not such a shock, but he was not old, only in his late sixties, or early seventies, when he died. Granny Annie was devastated. As I said, they had been very close and had thought the world of one another.

We had all gone to South-East London for the funeral. We were living in Thamesford by then. Almost as soon as I arrived home on that never-to-be-forgotten day, I was aware of an atmosphere within the family, but I had no idea of all that had occurred in order to cause it. Right from the start everyone had always sought to keep bad things from me. Whenever I went home for the holidays it was a sort of unwritten rule within the family that everything should always be made to appear as though it was all right. I was not often home, and when I was everything had to be made to appear okay so that I would enjoy my holiday. Quite naturally, that situation could not be sustained by everyone for the duration of, say, an eight-week break from school, and thus it was that I discovered, as though I hadn't already guessed, that my family were actually completely normal human beings with human failings, and not the 'perfect' nuclear family unit that my parents had wished me to believe they were. To be honest, the discovery was something of a relief to me, as I no longer had to pretend either!

To begin with, I discovered that both my parents were involved in affairs. Dad with a woman called Betty Cox, a blonde bombshell Brummie. She was 30 years old, married with three young daughters and worked as a clippie on the back of the bus that Dad drove at that time. Betty was five feet three inches tall, plump, but still very attractive. She had long blonde hair and baby-blue eyes. She was friendly enough on the two occasions when I met her.

The first time I ever met Betty Cox, my mum and I were walking together towards the depot to meet Dad, who was about to finish work. We were going shopping in town. It was near the end of a school holiday and I was about to move up to senior school. I knew that Dad and that woman were fond of one another by that time, but as yet, I had never encountered her. Suddenly, there she was, ice-cool, stepping from the bus and approaching us. She did not speak to Mum, but made a great play of taking my hand in both of hers.

"Hello, Ian," she said in a broad Brummie accent. "Aw've heerd a lot about yo' an' it's noice to meet yo' at last!"

I politely made some comment or other, believing that was expected of me. She squeezed both my hands in hers and said:

"Oooogh! You'm noice an' warm, jus' loike your Dad, yo' are! Noice an' warm!" She then added, as an afterthought, "Aw! Oi shuddn't talk loike this in frunt of your mom, shud oi?"

Still, she made no attempt to speak to Mum, and I could feel how angry my mother was. It's funny how you can tell. As we parted, I again made what I hoped was an appropriate comment. As we got into the car to go shopping, you could have cut the atmosphere between Mum and Dad with an axe! So that was Betty Cox!

Mum was having an affair with a bloke called Ken Stratton. Ken, pushing 40, was tall, lean and angular, with a good strong jaw, hair that was turning white, a rather serious profile, but Mum said he had a very keen sense of humour, although it was somewhat 'dry' apparently. Ken Stratton was a businessman, the owner of a factory specialising in making and exporting toys. He spent a lot of his time abroad, but whenever he was home, he and Mum had 'meetings'. One night, soon after I arrived home for the long summer holiday in 1960, he actually came to our house on a Friday evening at about eight o'clock.

I will never forget that night, the night when Ken Stratton came into my life, the night when I discovered that my mother—my sainted mother—was really a 'human being' and that she had a woman's needs! I had always believed that Dad satisfied those needs, but it seemed I was wrong!

Doreen was upstairs washing her hair, Eric was out with his mates and Dad was at work. Mum and I had been out for a walk and were having our tea; bread and jam, a sponge cake that she had made earlier in the day, and hot sweet tea. There was a knock on the front door.

When Ken Stratton entered the lounge-cum-dining room of our house in Bellingham Road, Thamesford, Mum didn't know how to introduce him to me! Ken made it easy for her by explaining that he was, 'your Mother's cousin'. I thought I had met all Mum's relations, but I knew I had never met that bloke before, so I did not believe him when he explained who he was, and I did not like him! I did not like him any more than I liked Dad's 'paramour', Mrs Betty Cox! I did not like either of them for breaking up our nuclear family unit, which I had always believed had been such a happy one.

Oh, how little I knew or understood at that time, but how much more I was going to understand before the end of that long summer break!

Chapter 12

WE WERE about 15 to 20 minutes out of London King's Cross. I was feeling great anticipation welling up inside me. It was real excitement, excitement that I always felt when I was going home. Although I lived up north in those days that is how I always thought of London and the southeast. Not so our Doreen. I didn't know all the ins and outs of it, but for a long time Doreen had been very unhappy at home with my parents. She and Eric had never got on particularly well, but I put that down to Eric, who, to be frank, never got on with any of us all that well, believing himself, I suppose, to be better than any of us. I don't know why, but Doreen, who shared my sense of humour and was usually very easy-going, seemed to have taken great umbrage at both my parents over their respective affairs.

One night I heard Mum crying. That was about a fortnight after I had gone home for the summer break in 1960. I had gone up to bed and Doreen was downstairs with Mum. Dad was out at work on late turns. Both Mum and Doreen had been upset, and then I heard raised voices. The next thing I remember was a loud shout from Mum, then a noise like a smack, and a scream from Doreen. Next I heard her running upstairs to her room, and Mum followed, shouting something I couldn't catch.

In the early hours of the following morning I thought I heard sounds of someone moving around. I reckoned it was probably Dad using the bathroom or getting up to undertake an early shift because it was holiday time and lots of the staff were off. It turned out to be neither of those. Later I discovered that what I had heard was Doreen packing her bags and preparing to leave home!

On that day in August, 1960, Doreen, who was not yet 15 years old, left Thamesford, Essex, and travelled up to North Yorkshire. There she lived with our Aunt Muriel and Uncle Jack Dabbs. Muriel was Dad's only sister and she was almost ten years younger. She had married Jack Dabbs, a farm labourer, in 1954, and they had two sons, Ronnie and Bobby. Muriel and Dad had always had something of an uneasy truce between them, but all that ended when our Doreen moved up to Yorkshire to live, and steadfastly and resolutely refused to return to live in Essex and finish her schooling!

She took a job on the farm, and later, when she could not stand that any longer, became a tea girl working in a factory, then later worked as a waitress and sandwich maker etc., in a cafe bar in the town of Briggthorpe, North Yorkshire. The cafe bar was called Loui's.

Mum and Dad were very upset about Doreen leaving home, but decided they would not force her to return against her wishes. However, they more or less cut her off from the rest of us and that was certainly true after 1963, when she met, and subsequently married, David Frederick Dingle.

Chapter 13

THE TRAIN was pulling into London King's Cross. I was being helped from the train and my parents were coming down the platform to meet me. Dad's first comment was: "What you need to bring all them bags for?"

"It's all stuff I need to have with me" I replied.

Dad took two of them from me and I kept the other one around my shoulders. Mum's first words to me were:

"You've lost a bit of weight, boy! Oh, you've had your hair cut, you look very smart, son!"

Dear old Mum, she was so steeped in her ways. She could not bear anyone not to look his or her best, especially in public. That probably explains why she could not cope very well with Doreen, Fred and their large and unruly brood of kids, to say nothing of all the animals they kept at their house up in North Yorkshire! I would see them later during the course of that holiday.

I was walking quickly towards the place where Mum and Dad had parked their car, and soon we would be on our way home to Thamesford. The excitement was welling up inside me. I felt just as though I had come home from school again, like I used to feel in the old days, and when I think about it, those days were not so very far away!

੬੭

In the car on the way home, Dad was concentrating hard on driving, while Mum, seated in the back with me and holding my left hand, was chattering away nineteen to the dozen. She was so thrilled and happy to have me home again, and when I saw her like that I felt a little guilty. I knew that was daft. One can never know everything that will happen during one's life, but one thing Mum was almost certain of was that, when I came home from boarding-school, I would be staying with her for several years to come, if not for good. I went and spoiled it all by telling her and Dad that I wanted to marry Susan and, when they objected, by saying I *was* going to marry her, no matter what anyone said or thought, so that was that and all about it, as Granny Annie would have said!

From then on, both Mum and Dad accepted that was what would occur. Dad was always fairly easy-going about it, but I knew it had affected Mum very deeply. She was happy enough that I had met someone, that I had fallen in love and that I wished to be with that person, but somehow she felt betrayed. I know that sounds strange, but I am sure that's how it was. Mum had been very reluctant to allow me to go away to boarding school in the first place. However, faced with no alternative, and having been told quite firmly that in order to receive an education of any sort, I would have to go away from home, and that that applied no matter where in the country we lived, she reluctantly accepted the inevitable—but she had never liked it.

⊱•⊰

Again my mind went back over the years, back to days when I had to leave home and go away to school. The inevitable day would dawn and I would come downstairs, bleary-eyed from sleep and probably from crying! Mum would try to get me to eat a hearty breakfast, but I never seemed to want anything to eat because I was feeling so full of emotions. Eventually, to please her, I would endeavour to do justice to the substantial meal she had prepared for me—the last meal before leaving home for around three months because I did not go home for weekends.

Once every six weeks my parents were allowed to visit, and usually they managed to come over and spend the day with me. Even then, some kids went off with their parents for the .evening, either to their own homes if they lived near enough or else to hotels, but I never did! I suppose on Dad's wages he could not really afford to pay for the three or maybe the five of us to stay in a hotel. At the end of that perfect day we would usually spend together once a term, everyone went home at about 6 p.m. or 8 p.m., if it was the summer term. I always went to bed feeling totally miserable and somewhat rejected!

Going back to the days when I used to have to travel to school. After breakfast I would wash then go upstairs and change. Mum would come up and we would finish packing my bags, then Dad or Eric would take them all downstairs. Later, Dad would drive to the station with Mum and me, and then we would travel into London by train. Usually they came all the way to the school with me. Sometimes Mum would help me to unpack and put everything away where I could find it easily! There would be other mums in the dormitory, helping their sons to do the same thing. The banter and chat among us all was good, and that often helped to settle me into the regime—the inevitable and all-embracing school regime. It was like being in the army! When the time came for Mum and Dad to leave me, well, that was always hard, and both Mum and I usually cried!

৪৯৫

Mum was still chattering on, telling me what we were passing en route home, talking about the meal she would prepare when we arrived back at Bellingham Road, telling me about things we might do while I was home for a few days. Most of this I already knew! We had discussed it on the phone before I left home to go down to Thamesford, but it was good to hear Mum talking about it all with such enthusiasm. It was good to be sitting there in the back of Dad's car, travelling with him and Mum towards Bellingham Road, Thamesford, and the house I had called home since moving there with my family in the spring of 1957.

Chapter 14

I T WAS 4 p.m. on Saturday, 30th December, 1989. I had been involved in the music marathon for 40 hours and I had received loads of cards wishing me well, and lots of telephone calls from listeners spurring me on. The studio manager, Bill Grundy, was very thrilled with the way it was all going. I had also received flowers—we had a studio full of them—a magnum of champagne and a huge box of Cadbury's Dairy Milk chocolates.

Those were all from the same person, Johnnie Friscoe! So, she was out and about again. Johnnie, Johnquel Amelia Friscoe, was tall, brunette and very attractive with big, deep-set 'come to bed' eyes! A dusky Oceanian beauty, who hailed from New Zealand. She had always fancied me since the first time we met. She was gorgeous! She was devious, manipulative and a psychopath!

Chapter 15

THE FIRST part of my holiday with Mum and Dad in August 1978 had gone supremely well.

First of all, the weather had been very kind. On the Saturday when they met me and drove me home to Thamesford, it was rather cloudy, but we had our dinner, which, as I had suspected, was huge, and afterwards we sat and had our tea and cake out in the back garden. The dinner consisted of turkey and all the trimmings. Mum had made the stuffing with sausage meat, just the way I loved it. She had cooked roasted potatoes, jacket potatoes and loads of different vegetables, and had even made a huge Yorkshire pudding!

"She's gone over the top, as usual!" said George, my Dad, but he was smiling as he said it.

"Of course I have! I don't have my little boy home all that often, do I?" said Mary, my proud mum, and I laughed.

After dinner, as we sat in the garden, Mum brought out the tray of tea and two sponge cakes, from which she cut liberal slices for me and smaller ones for herself and Dad. We sat and chatted and laughed, and later we had baths and then got ready to go to the Florida Club, a dance club in the town of Thamesford.

The Florida Club was a very popular venue for people of all ages. There were three bars and a big dance floor. A band played and there were 15-minute breaks between sessions, so that you could go and get more drinks or else go to the buffet and help yourselves to food. There was always a huge buffet on at the Florida Club on a Saturday night.

Later we were joined by Betty, Bill and Anne. She loved to go along on those Saturday nights, and was very thrilled to think I would be there that night. Anne was nine years old, or at least she was almost nine years old. She was a lively little girl, very sharp and extremely 'with it'. She was always laughing. Betty ought to have been really proud of her, but she didn't seem to be. She always appeared to be finding fault with the little girl, but Anne seemed to take it all in her stride. I knew it worried my mum. Dad adored Anne and took the mickey out of her! She really seemed to love that. She danced with all the men, with her dad, with me, with my dad, George, and she loved it all. It almost seemed as though Betty was jealous of all the attention her pretty young daughter was receiving that night. Strange! Very strange indeed!

We went home late, as I knew we would. We did not have any supper when we got in, only a hot drink, but we did sit up chatting until around 2.30 a.m.

ĝ≈∞ĝ

On the Sunday, after a hearty breakfast, we all got ready and went over to Joyce and Len's flat in South-East London. On arrival we were greeted by Joyce, Len and their two sons, who were there with their girlfriends. Gary and Terry, my two cousins, were both six-footers. Gary was tall and slim with fair hair and blue-grey eyes. Terry was chunkier and had brown hair and brown eyes. He was two years younger than Gary. I had not seen either of them for some considerable time.

All us blokes went down to the Bricklayer's Arms, where we met up with Sid. He was very happy driving his cab for a living. He worked with an old army chum of his, and they apparently had quite a thriving minicab business. We stayed down the pub for about an hour and a quarter; me, Dad, Len, Gary, Terry and their girlfriends, and Sid. That left Joyce and my mum at home to finish preparing the meal and to have a good old natter, which we all knew they would enjoy.

All four sisters got on pretty well together really, although they did not see as much of young Nelly as they would wish. She was always very busy, what with the guest house down in Seaport and all her children. Alf was not a lot of help to Nelly, preferring to spend his time in the betting shop and at the bar in the Jug and Glass, which was just down the road from their guest house.

Later in the afternoon, Betty and Bill arrived with Anne, Mike, Marilyn and Susan, Andre and their twin girls. It was good to see them all again, and we had a splendid tea altogether.

It was an excellent weekend in all, and I went to bed on Sunday night, just before midnight, feeling very tired, but extremely happy.

Chapter 16

JOHNNIE FRISCOE. I shivered! The last thing I wanted was another altercation with her. Johnnie Friscoe could be a very dangerous adversary, as she had proved in the past. As I started the next musical sequence following the 4 p.m. news on that Saturday afternoon, I was concerned about Johnnie and the fact that she might come to the studio during the next 40 hours!

Bill Grundy came into the ops room with Tony Bonetti and Rob Wilde, the two security guards. Tony had his dog with him, a 16-month-old Rottweiler bitch called Carla. They all found space to sit down, and we had a 'council of war'.

"Aw fink wae shud call the police!" said Bill Grundy.

He was a tall, slim young man, who always looks sloppily dressed because most of the time he wore jeans, sweatshirts and canvas shoes with no socks, but he was a bright, alert young fellow, and he ran the radio station very well indeed. He was fair-minded and kept his staff involved in everything that was happening. I could tell he was very concerned about the latest episode with regard to Johnnie Friscoe, who had already made two attacks upon me in the past!

She had been detained for the previous six months at Broadlands Psychiatric Hospital in a secure unit following the last attack on me, when she got into the studios while I was undertaking the night shift during my second week of broadcasting. She was wielding a knife on that occasion! The first time she had endeavoured to attack me was at my own home, when she had broken in and tried to set fire to the house while I lay upstairs in bed!

She was very determined and a very dangerous female was Johnquel Amelia Friscoe!

Chapter 17

MONDAY, 14 August, dawned bright and sunny in Thamesford. After breakfast, Mum suggested we should go out to town. I agreed, thinking that would be great. It was ages since I had been shopping in Thamesford with Mum.

Mondays and Thursdays were always market days there, so the town would be exceptionally busy. There would be plenty of people about and plenty going on. I was really looking forward to it. We started out from home at about 11 a.m. and caught the bus into town. I sat beside a large Geordie lady who came from North Yorkshire. She said she knew Harts Hill very well. We almost missed the stop because we were so busy chatting!

Once in town, we went everywhere, my shopaholic mother and me. She loved to treat me whenever I went home, thus, she went on a buying spree for me. At the end of a very busy day, we had purchased a new anorak with two inside pockets and a zip-up pocket on the outside, six new sets of underwear, four new T-shirts in various colours, two beautiful new sweatshirts, four pairs of trousers, two pairs of shoes, six pairs of short sports socks, a smashing fisherman's jumper for the winter, another new shoulder bag, which was bigger than the one I had taken down with me, a load of new music cassettes and a new set of headphones for my radio cassette player. We were loaded, and we were ecstatically happy!

We caught the bus home, and on arrival back at Bellingham Road we had tea. We sat in the garden and had our tea with Eleanor Newman, who had promised to come over to see me while I was at home. It was good to see Eleanor again and to hear her chattering away nineteen to the dozen. Eleanor and I had always got along really well together; she had a wonderful sense of humour. She used to have me over to stay for days when I was on my school holidays, even when I was a teenager. We had some tremendous japes, me, Eleanor and her lovely sister, Letitia. 'Tishie' as I called her, is now deceased. She died of cancer and is sorely missed by everyone who knew her.

Eleanor was still working, and she always had stories to tell us about some of the characters whom she encountered during the course of her work as a health visitor. She would work now until she is 65 years old and maybe beyond, she said, if she had the opportunity to do so. Eleanor stayed until at least 8 p.m. that evening, and after she went, we sat together, Mum, Dad and I, watching a drama on the television. Dad suggested we got some of the photos out and looked at the films he had made up.

Dad had always been interested in photography and he had had a projector and all the cine equipment for ages. He enjoyed taking shots and piecing them altogether to make anthologies of family life. We enjoyed doing that until at least midnight and slightly beyond, fuelled by drinks of hot chocolate. Again, that night I went to bed feeling very tired, but utterly fulfilled. It had been a smashing day!

Chapter 18

O N THE Tuesday morning, Mum was busy, washing, ironing, cleaning through and preparing to pack stuff for our
journey to Seaport the following day. She said she would
pack a bag for me, so I decided to let her do so. I sat in the garden
for a while then decided to go out visiting old neighbours. I had a
wonderful morning. Many of the people who lived in Bellingham
Road, Thamesford, had lived there as long as my family. One or
two even moved in at around the same time as we did.

I visited the Newmans, the Taylors, the Masons, the Fishers,
the Grants and the O'Goremans. I had a wonderful time, chatting, drinking cups of hot chocolate and trying different cakes,
pies etc., that the women had prepared. It was all great.

Later, Mum and I went out for a long walk to Hill Farm Park.
They had a pets' corner there, and we looked around that for some
time. The weather was very kind again that day. The sun shone
down brightly from a clear sky, and it was very warm and dry, so
it was not unpleasant.

On Wednesday we drove down to Seaport. We set off at about
1 p.m., and arrived in the town of Seaport at around 3.45 p.m. We
drove onto the front first and had a walk, before driving to Nelly
and Alf's guest house on Fowley Road. We received a warm welcome indeed, and the six children of the family were delighted to
see us. Again, I had not seen my cousins in Seaport, West Sussex,
for some considerable time.

Later, Queenie came home with her 'fella'. Matt was a six-footer,
as broad as he was tall. He was 24 years old, and a market gardener, apparently in business on his own account. Queenie was

three months pregnant by Matt, but they were very much in love, and were greatly looking forward to Saturday and their forthcoming wedding. Nelly talked gaily about the wedding and seemed genuinely fond of Matt. Alf, a quiet bloke, small and chunky in stature, who liked his pint, his smokes and his bet on the horses and the dogs, had little to say about it, but in private to Dad and me over a drink at the Jug that first Wednesday night when we arrived in Seaport, he professed to us that he was not keen on the lad, but reckoned if he said so, he'd be shouted down by the women, so he kept his own counsel. Alf tended to take little part in family life and was only minimally interested in the running of the guest house. Thus, everything seemed to land upon the shoulders of Nelly.

Nelly was a happy-go-lucky sort of woman, who just got on with her life and didn't ask anything of anyone. She was making a great success of running the guest house, and she hadn't done a bad job of bringing up her large family either.

Chapter 19

THE WEDDING between Queenie and Matt took place at 11.30 a.m. on Saturday, 19 August, and was a tremendous occasion, and very well attended. The pre-wedding party at the Seaways Guest House on Fowley Road was attended by all Mum's family, and that was a great success too.

The booze flowed freely and the food was plentiful. Sid played on the old Joanna, there was a piano in the lounge at Seaways, and we sang all the good old favourites, plus a few of the more modern songs as well for the youngsters. I thoroughly enjoyed it, in fact, we all did. Anne, Betty and Bill's youngest all did a turn; she recited a very long monologue, which went down very well with all the family. Gary and Terry sang, 'I put my Finger in the Woodpecker's Hole!' and everyone fell about laughing! I sang, 'Black Velvet Band', and everyone applauded.

Eve and Eric did not come to the wedding, nor did anyone from North Yorkshire, but they were not expected to do so. Susan and Andre came, but did not bring the twins, and they only stayed the one night. Apparently Andy's mum had the twins. Mike, Betty and Bill's eldest came with his girlfriend, Marilyn. She was a very nice girl, and it seemed that they were considering becoming engaged. Marilyn was small, where her consort was tall! She had one of those baby-doll faces, with twinkling blue eyes that always seemed to be laughing. She was slim, with fair hair that lay in tresses on her shoulders. She was, to all intents and purposes, a most attractive young woman. Gary and Terry brought their girlfriends, Kas and Trish, who were both rather loud; pleasant enough, with broad South London accents, but loud! Still, they made me laugh, with their South London humour!

I enjoyed seeing all the family again under those circumstances, and made sure I had plenty to eat and drink. I was very impressed with Cathy, the 16-year-old sister of Queenie. Cathy, second eldest of the seven children of Nelly and Alf Sunley, had never really impressed me before. She was a tall, willowy girl, not at all unattractive, with brown hair and flashing eyes. Her eyes seemed to flash pleasure and fun, and she was a very jolly and friendly young woman, who made a great deal of me. This was another cousin whom I had not seen much of before, and to be honest, had never really taken a lot of interest in whenever I had seen her in the past. I suppose I merely accepted her as one of the children of Aunt Nel and Uncle Alf, but that day, on the wedding day of her elder sister, I saw Cathy in a completely different light!

The week in Seaport passed only too quickly, and suddenly it was time to return to Thamesford. For me, the return would be short-lived, for the following day, Thursday, I would be travelling up to Cherry Wootton in Cambridgeshire to stay with my brother, Eric, his wife, Eve, and their son, Micky.

Chapter 20

IT WAS just gone 2 a.m. on Sunday, 31st December, 1989, the very last day of the eighties, the end of a decade. For the past few hours, since about 9.30 p.m. on Saturday night, I had shared the studio in which I had been broadcasting since midnight on Thursday, with two police constables. DC Joe Capper and DC Andy Mullins, who were there to help to protect me if, or rather, *when*, Johnnie Friscoe decided to show her trump card. I was desperately attempting to carry on and not to think about what might occur in the imminent future!

I had been remembering happier times during the past 48 hours or so. Now, my mind wandered back to the time when I first met Johnnie and fell for her pleasant, smooth, easy-going style. She could certainly charm the ducks off the water, as my Uncle Stan used to say! Oh yes, Johnquel Amelia Friscoe could certainly be most charming! She had beauty, poise, elegance and a sharp tongue, also a wicked mind and a long, flashing switchblade! I shivered!

The telephone rang. I answered it almost mechanically, without thinking.

"Hi there, it's me, Rick Dee, on the Sunny Gold Radio 80-hour music marathon. Who's on the other end of the line?"

For a moment the line was silent.

"Hello, Boyzie!"

I knew that velvety voice, and the slow, steady drawl of her accent.

"Hi… hi, Johnnie!" I said into the receiver of the instrument. "What can I do for you on this long winter's night?"

Almost immediately, Joe Capper signed to Andy Mullins, 'Get a trace, get a trace on the call if you can'. Joe Capper was the young police constable who had picked me up off the road on that never-to-be-forgotten day when the lads pushed me right into the middle of the junction of Hyland Road and Gunners Lane. He had made the grade of detective constable, and I was grateful to have him around, plus Andy Mullins, a big swarthy lad, who was a rugger player, and a damned good, super-fit cop! Both DCs worked out of Bread Street Police Station.

Johnnie's smooth velvety voice was coming down the line again.

"You know what to do for me, Boyzie, you can play, 'Crazy' for me! Yeh?"

"Yeh," I said, "I'll play it for you with my love and best wishes!"

I was trying to keep her sweet. She laughed a strange mirthless laugh.

"O-ho! You'll send me all your love and best wishes will you, Boyzie?"

"Yeh, surely will!" I told her.

"Aw, thanks, darling," she drawled in that slow Oceanic manner of hers. "I'll be listening. Do it in about an hour, yeh?"

"Yeh," I said.

"And wish me goodnight, eh, mister?"

"Yeh," I rejoined, beginning to feel more easy in my mind now that we had spoken again after all that time!

"Okay! Cheers, I'll be waiting to hear you!"

"Cheers, Johnnie!" I said, and the line went dead.

20

On the Thursday morning, 24th August, I lay in until just after nine o'clock. Mum wanted to bring me breakfast in bed, but I went downstairs. I had cereal, cornflakes with cold milk, three poached eggs, four large Irish sausages, four rashers of bacon, two large grilled tomatoes, plenty of button mushrooms, three large fried potatoes, a small piece of black pudding and half a tin of

baked beans—a truly wonderful breakfast! Mum put a plate of
bread and butter on the table, and I liberally helped myself to that.
Afterwards, I had four slices, or rather half-slices, of toast with
orange marmalade and another mug of hot sweet tea, my fourth
since rising.

I showered, shaved and dressed after breakfast, and several of
the neighbours came around to say goodbye to me. One brought
me half a cherry cake, another fetched a tin of shortbread, another,
half a newly baked apple pie! Mum packed all that up carefully so
I could get it into my bags. By the time I had packed all my belongings, including all the new stuff Mum and I had bought, my
three big bags, plus my smaller shoulder bag, were all bulging!

At 1.30 p.m., we had a good dinner. Mum had made a big meat
pie and a trifle. Dad said 'cheerio' to me at about 3.30 p.m., as he
was on a late turn that day. Dad was an inspector on the buses
and did different shifts. He claimed he quite enjoyed his job, and
was pleased to be 'elevated to the heights' in 1970. He had enjoyed
driving, but that job carried more clout, and he appeared to be
very happy with his present position. There were only four in-
spectors in the whole of the area.

At around 4.15 p.m., Eric arrived. He had a cup of tea with Mum
and me, then helped me take all my bulging bags downstairs and
stowed them in his car. By 5.30 p.m. we were off, and left Mum
standing on the pathway by the front garden gate. We had hugged
and kissed each other a good deal before I left. Now, although
she had called out gaily as the car drove out of Bellingham Road,
I knew she was crying. I daresay one or two of the neighbours
would be around in a while, giving her a bit of consolation following my departure. Poor Mum! We had had such a lovely time and
now I had to go yet again. Would she ever get used to it?

Chapter 21

A NDY MULLINS could not get a trace on the call made to the studios by Johnnie Friscoe, at least, not an accurate one. Joe Capper said she would undoubtedly ring again, and he wanted me to forget to play her request, so that she would be certain to call back. Andy Mullins did not think that a good idea and neither did I. Joe seemed to go back inside himself, and sat back on his chair, defeated. Andy was thinking, and so was I, but I was trying not to think about Johnnie Friscoe!

I was wading through a huge plate of sandwiches that had been sent into the studio for the three of us about an hour before. Neither of the cops seemed to want anything to eat, but I was ravenous! I was also very, very thirsty. Andy Mullins sent Joe out to get us all drinks. Tony, one of the two security guards, said he would make us all mugs of hot chocolate. Good, that would be great, just great!

I was into a sixties music sequence, and was quite enjoying it. The two cops had temporarily left the studio. It was becoming rather untidy. I was still eating my way through the mountain of sandwiches, and I was still thinking!

Chapter 22

THE LONG weekend with Eve and Eric was really a tremendous success. Eric and I drove up to Cherry Wootton from Thamesford on the Thursday evening. It took us around two and a quarter hours. When we arrived, Yvonne, my sister-in-law, showed me the bedroom that would be mine during my stay with them. It was pleasant, spacious and seemed to have everything I could require, even en suite facilities.

Yvonne and Eric had a five-bedroomed detached house in Leaming Drive, Cherry Wootton. It was delightful. The rear garden was vast and led down to fields. The front drive had hard-standing for a car, and a large garage that could hold two sizeable cars within its portals. Yes, Eric, as an accountant, had done well for himself and his family, but in my secret heart I wondered was he happy? Was he, for example, as happy as Doreen, his twin sister, appeared to be with her pig man, their large brood of kids and their totally chaotic lifestyle? Was he even as happy as me? All things considered, now that I was adjusting to my new life without Susan, things could have certainly been be a lot worse for me!

I counted myself as happy and very, very lucky to have so many relations and wonderful friends back in Gaynsford to help me. Of course, I hadn't got over her. How could I? No, I would never, never get over her!

About a month after she died, and I had returned to my own home, I had a dream. She was there in my dream, mocking me with her laughter, telling me to get on with my life!

"You know what I said to you, Boyzie? You remember what I

said before I left you? I hope one day you will remarry. You are still alive, love! I'm dead, but I'm happy, and I want you to be happy too, Boyzie! So go on, get on with your life and let me rest in peace, eh?"

She laughed and kissed me, which felt very strange indeed, then left me.

When I awoke, I felt different; I cannot really describe how I felt, it was a strange feeling! It pervaded my whole day and has lasted since that weird dream. It is a feeling that I can still mourn, but I can also 'get on with it'. So that's what I am endeavouring to do, and the purpose of that month away was to assist that endeavour. Certainly, up to then, things had gone very well for me.

The long weekend spent in company with my brother Eric and his wife, Yvonne, known affectionately as Eve, and their son, Micky, a wild young scallywag with a mop of unruly fair hair and the most angelic eyes, was a most pleasant and enjoyable experience, quite the most pleasant time I had had with them for many a year!

It had always been a source of sorrow within the family how distant from everyone Eric always seemed. None of us could ever explain it, but it seemed that he always thought himself to be better than anyone else within the family. That was noted by aunts, uncles, even by cousins, and by Granny Annie and Uncle Stan; so it was not just the nuclear family who felt it. During that long weekend I spent with them, Eric and I got along splendidly, and Eve, not noted for being the 'hostess with the mostest', looked after me like a king. She cooked me a wonderful macaroni cheese on the Thursday evening. It was far too large, but Micky helped me out when I was really bloated and could not eat another mouthful, then she cut me a huge slice of jam tart she had baked, and poured me another mug of coffee.

Later, after Micky, protesting loudly and long, had been put to bed, Eve, Eric and I sat in the conservatory overlooking the vast rear garden that ran down to the woods and fields beyond. We had the radio on in the background, a local commercial music station. I had to admit that Eve and Eric lived in a glorious area. The summer was at its height. It was coming towards the end of August and very warm and pleasant. Cherry Wootton, with the onset of autumn, would be a very beautiful place, I felt certain— and it was so quiet!

I wondered what young Micky found to keep himself amused, and whether he had lots of friends around the area. I was assured that he did, and was told I would probably meet quite a few of them at the barbecue the following evening. I eagerly looked forward to that event.

Chapter 23

IT WAS 4 a.m. on the morning of Sunday, 31st December, 1989; another raw, cold morning. Craig Brown, who had been my engineer for the past 20 hours or so, was taking a well-earned rest. My new engineer was Bob Groves. Bob was in his mid-thirties, with a beard and receding hair. He was small, tough, wiry, quick on his feet, and never wore shoes when he was in the studio.

Bob was originally from Rhodesia, but his family were all over in our country then. He was noted for being rather finicky, but he knew my ways, and we got on very well together, most of the time anyway! Bob, like me, loved his music, and he certainly knew his stuff. Whenever I was broadcasting he enjoyed working with me, and we had a good professional relationship. He loved to twiddle the knobs etc., for me! Bob was a tough little cookie and could look after himself should the need arise. He was in the little room off the main studio in which I was currently seated. It was like the ops room of a ship; all the technical equipment was in there.

In the large reception area there was quite a gathering of persons present. Bill Grundy, the station manager, was there with his deputy, Alan Glazier, and the chairman of the company that owned Sunny Gold Radio, Mike Shepherd. With those three gentlemen were Detective Chief Inspector Nora Scott, from Gaynsford Central Police Headquarters in Bread Street, who was co-ordinating the whole case, Detective Sergeant Jane Bonnier, also from central police headquarters, Detective Constables Joe Capper and Andy Mullins, from Bread Street. Craig Brown, my other engineer, was also present, who must have been very tired by then, but held on because I did. Our security guards, Tony Bonnetti, with his dog, Carla, and Rob Wilde were there, also my driver, Simon Wallis. Quite an assortment and they were all talking tactics. Like me, they were all awaiting the next move by our friendly neighbourhood psychopath, Johnnie Friscoe!

The telephone rang in the studio! I reached forwards to answer it!

Chapter 24

WE SAT up well into the early hours of Friday morning, 25th August, drinking and chatting, watching videos of 'Derek and Clive Live' and also Billy Connolly. Eric and I had always shared a strange sense of humour. It was all that we had in common! So far, during the short time I had been staying with him and his wife, Eve, we had all got along very well indeed.

I went to bed at around 3 a.m. on the Friday, and awoke again at 8 a.m. or so. Yvonne brought me a mug of hot sweet tea, and then told me she would get me breakfast after she returned from the hairdresser's. She had an appointment at 9 a.m. that morning, and before that she would take Micky over to a friend of his. She asked if I minded if she left me on my own for an hour and a half or so.

"No, that's okay. I can sort myself out, so I'll be up and ready when you get home," I said.

She warned me about Libby. Libby was an eight-year-old West Highland terrier, not the friendliest of dogs! Libby, who was rather overweight and had been thoroughly spoiled by Eve, and even by Eric, who was not noted for his love of animals, was rather a mean creature! If she took against you, then brother, you had had it; a bit like Johnnie Friscoe in that regard! Yvonne said that if Libby and I encountered one another, it was best if I gave her a wide berth! I said, yes, I would do exactly that!

Later, Micky came dashing into the bedroom to wish me good morning and to tell me he was going out, but to say he would see me later on. I had quite a lot of time for Micky, my nephew. He was rather a wild kid, and I am afraid he got away with an awful lot, mostly because of his mum, who doted upon him, but nevertheless, he was growing into quite a decent youngster, notwithstanding he was rather cheeky and a little wayward at times.

I heard Eve's car going down the driveway and out of Leaming Drive. I lay in bed for a few more minutes then got up and went to have a shower, shave etc. It was another bright morning and the day seemed set fair for fine weather. I showered, shaved, dressed and went downstairs. I walked into the lounge. There I encountered Libby, who was lying on the rug beside the radiator. She growled at me, but made no attempt to come towards me. Eve and Eric also had three Burmese Blue cats, whom they had christened Pip, Squeak and Willum. They yowled and moaned a great deal—not my favourite 'mogs' those three cats. Mike had a hamster called Hammie and a budgie called Blue, and that was the sum total of the animals in that house.

I sat down on the sofa. The radio was on. Eve had told me where the kettle, the teapot etc., were in the kitchen. She had showed me the night before and had told me to help myself to anything I wanted. I had said I would wait and have breakfast with her when she returned from the hairdresser's. I sat back on the sofa with my head against a cushion. Radio Two was on.

I had a Braille book on my knee. I did not often read Braille in those days. It was what I was taught to read when I was at school, and for ages I read nothing else, but in those days I liked to listen to books on cassette. However, Eleanor Newman had bought me a two-volume Braille book. It was an abridged version of a novel I had wanted to read for some time, so I had been pleased to have it, and now sat reading the first volume. As I sat there reading, with the radio on in the background and doors and windows wide open to let in the summer air, Libby came sauntering over and lay at my feet. She put her head on my right foot and subsequently went to sleep, snoring loudly! I sat and read on. Libby and I spent a pleasant morning together, and at around 11 a.m., Eve came home. We had coffee and biscuits together then we went out in her car to Cambridge.

We went shopping. She wanted to look at some new furniture for the lounge, and I thoroughly enjoyed accompanying her on that window-shopping spree, because before purchasing anything she must first ask Eric. At least we could look and get some idea of what she liked.

We roved around Cambridge and looked at lounge suites for about an hour and a quarter, then Eve bought some new shoes and later we went and had dinner in a very pleasant restaurant near the river. Later we went to the cinema, and afterwards had a mug of chocolate in a truckers' cafe in town. It was all quite wonderful.

Micky would be staying with his friend that night and would come back after dinner on Sunday. He was spending the weekend with friends of his who lived about 20 miles from Eve and Eric. I had not realised that. Anyway, as we drove out of Cambridge, Eve said that I would see him later when we went to the barbecue that his friend's parents were holding that evening.

We arrived home at around 7 p.m., and I went upstairs almost immediately to wash, change etc. Eric was in from work, and he had bathed and was getting ready in their dressing room. We left for the home of Inga and Dave Saunders at around 8.15 p.m. We were there in less than 20 minutes.

Inga and Dave Saunders had four children. Their eldest son, Grant, was Micky's pal. Grant was 11 years old, and several inches taller than Micky. He and Micky were both at the barbecue, so were Grant's older sisters, Cindy, who was 14 years old, and Vickie, who was a year younger. David, the youngest of the four children at seven years, was allowed to stay up because it was Friday and the following day was the weekend.

Inga, who was Swedish, and her husband, Dave, a tall well-built fellow with a rather dry sense of humour, had gone to a lot of trouble to make that evening rather special. There was loads of food and the drink was positively flowing! There was lager, cider, beer, wine, soft drinks, even whisky. I was glad of a couple of glasses of La Fraig, which went down extremely well;

I do love my whisky!

There were plenty of people at the barbecue. Many of them would be at Brawnstone, Northants, the following day, as there was racing, and we were due to travel down there in the morning. Eric had a Shevron, a low-slung sporty model, and he loved racing the car around a good, fast racetrack. That was his main hobby. He had two good mechanics who worked along with him and, together, they formed a hard-working team. The team would be 'showing out' at Brawnstone the day after, and hoping to win all three races in which Eric was entered. The whole event promised to be most exciting, and I was looking forward to it very much.

§⊶⊰§

As the night wore on, I moved out of the crowds and sat under some trees in the large garden of the home that belonged to Inga and Dave Saunders. Micky, Grant Saunders and half a dozen of their mates had found me, and were chattering to me as I sat and drank another glass of La Fraig. It was going down a treat, that lovely smooth whisky. Micky had excitedly introduced me to all his pals as his 'Uncle Ian, known as Boyzie, who came from the north'. They were all very polite and friendly, and chatted away to me nineteen to the dozen.

As we talked, I was conscious of someone standing close beside me on my right. As I finished the contents of my glass, Micky offered to take it and get it refilled for me.

"I know Gaynsford, I used to live and work there," said a voice close beside me.

"Oh!" I said, looking to my right from where the voice had come.

"That's right, Boyzie," she said gaily.

I laughed; so, she had heard the lads say my name.

"Whereabouts did you live and work then?" I asked her.

The young female sat down beside me on the grass, beneath the trees on that warm beautiful evening. She sat very close to me and I could smell her exotic and heady perfume!

"I lived in Osleston and worked at the Moorside Children's Hospital in Gaynsford Broadway," she told me.

She had a very strong accent.

"So," I said, "you *do* know it well, don't you?"

"I sure do, Boyzie," she said.

I laughed again. She seemed very pleasant.

"ı'll go and get us both .another drink, and some more food, yeh?" she said. "Oh, I hope you don't mind if I join you?"

"No, absolutely not, it's a pleasure," I told her.

She laughed.

"Good, don't you go anywhere, mister! I'll soon be back with the loot!"

I laughed again and she went off to get more provisions for us. She was soon back with me, bearing two loaded plates of food and two full bottles with two glasses, one of Martel brandy, one of La Fraig whisky. She poured us generous glasses and we made great inroads into the food and drink.

"What made you move down this way?" I asked her.

"Oh, I work for the Peter Pan Children's Homes now, but... but I don't really like it. I think I might be on the move again soon."

We sat drinking, eating and chatting, and we laughed, we really laughed! It was great.

"What brings you down here then, Boyzie?" she asked me.

"I'm the brother of Eric Dickson," I told her.

"Oh, I see," she said.

"But you have the advantage of me," I told her. "You already know my name, but I don't know who you are!"

She moved closer to me. Her perfume really was quite overpowering.

"I'm Johnnie," she told me, "Johnquel Amelia Friscoe!"

That was my first meeting with her, and how I wished with all my heart and soul that it had been my last, but it was not. It was only the first of many, which was to lead ultimately to near disaster for me! At the time I did not know that, and I did not have a clue as to the type of person Johnquel Amelia Friscoe might be.

She impressed as a very pleasant, friendly, jovial and lively young woman. She came on to me so that I was really taken in by her charm, poise, elegance, beauty, fun-loving nature, friendliness, her jovial personality and her easy-going style. Oh yes! I was really taken in by Johnnie Friscoe!

As time went on, I began to fall hopelessly in love with her, but that was her whole plan, and I fell for it hook, line and sinker! How could I ever have been so gullible, so naïve, so crass? As I sit here now and think about how it started, I guess my only excuse was that I was lonely!

It was nice when I was back in Gaynsford, having all the lads around me. It was good having such smashing neighbours and so many friends. It was marvellous to have my family, both nuclear and extended, and to know they would always be there for me, no matter what. Susan's family were all very kind to me as well, and looked after me like a king when I was back home.

That night it had been fun sitting under the trees at the home of Inga and Dave Saunders listening to the chatter of Micky and his mates as they surrounded me, but it was absolutely *great* to have a smart, pleasant, friendly, lively young woman like Johnnie Friscoe sitting beside me, chatting, laughing and obviously enjoying my company! For her to be sitting so close to me was wonderful; I was literally breathing in her perfume, and it was very heady! Combined with the whisky, the wonderful scents of the garden and the balmy evening, it was all going straight to my head—and I was loving it, every last second of it! Johnnie knew it; she was fully aware of the spell she was weaving all around me! She knew very well the effect her presence was having upon me. Oh yes!

As I sat there in the early hours of that last Sunday morning of a decade, I could see clearly that that was her whole plan—to entrance me and then to ensnare me within her web, like the spider and the fly syndrome. She was the spider, and I, quite willingly, was the fly. Yes, I was more than happy to enter her web, and to become thoroughly and very deeply ensnared!

Oh, what a fool, what a bloody crass fool! As I have said though,

I was lonely, wasn't I?

ই৯৶৽ও

It had turned midnight, and we were still sitting under the trees at the bottom of Inga and Dave's long garden. We were several drinks to the good. We had consumed great quantities of food between us. We had kissed and cuddled, and generally enjoyed ourselves in the seclusion of our private tree shelter. Nobody had discovered us! I had enjoyed it, oh God, how I had enjoyed it all!

I was reluctant to break away from her, the more so in case I never encountered her again. Idiot, stupid, pathetic idiot, but I was falling in love, wasn't I? At least, I believed I was, and the night, the moonlight, the drink, her heady perfume and the general atmosphere were all combining and causing me to believe I was falling even deeper in love. She seemed to be reciprocating! We held each other tight and we kissed passionately—again and again and again! We clasped each other wildly as we kissed.

"Ooh!" I breathed, "ooh! This is wonderful!"

Johnnie's body was so responsive. Again and again our lips found one another's, and we kissed, our tongues almost going down one another's throats, so hungry and so passionate were our kisses!

"Boyzie," she gasped.

"Shh!" I said. "Don't talk!"

As we lay side by side on the grass, under the trees, with the moon shining down from her lofty heights above, Johnnie was holding my head in her lap and stroking my hair gently.

"Are you coming racing tomorrow, Boyzie?" she asked quietly.

"Yeh," I said, "are you?"

"I'm driving in three," she told me proudly.

"Great," I said. "The same races as my brother, Eric?"

"I think so," she rejoined, and continued stroking my hair out of my eyes.

Later, as we walked together back to the house, she said:

"Tell you what? Why don't I call for you tomorrow morning,

and then I could drive you over there, if you wanted to come with me? What say, Boyzie?"

I thought about it for a moment or two.

"Yes, yes, why not?"

Eve and Eric were waiting for us back at the house.

"We were wondering where you were!" exclaimed Eric. "We're ready to go now, are you?"

I said I was, then, as an afterthought, introduced them to Johnnie and told them she had offered to drive me over to Brawnstone the following day. Eve and Eric seemed okay about it and Johnnie said she would collect me from their house at around 9.30 a.m. Eve and Eric were setting off at about 10 a.m., and Eric's first race was at midday, the same race in which Johnnie would be driving, and I hoped she would win. Was that disloyal of me? Well, I was falling in love with her, wasn't I?

Eve and Eric said they would have to wait for their mechanics to arrive with their families in their caravans. They would help Eric load the Shevron onto the trailer, and they would then drive to Brawnstone in convoy. Everyone was happy, and so it was agreed that I would drive over to the racetrack at Brawnstone with Johnnie on the following morning. We parted, and Eric drove Eve and me back home in the early hours of a Saturday morning. It was true that he was several drinks to the good, but then, so were we all! Micky stayed at Grant's house, but they would all see us at Brawnstone racetrack later that day.

Chapter 25

DESPITE IT being the early hours of the morning on Saturday before I was in bed, I was up and in the bathroom at Eve and Eric's by 7.45 a.m. and feeling none the worse for it. True, my head ached a bit, but that was nothing. I showered, shaved, washed my face, cleaned my teeth twice, then returned to my room with a glass of water and took two aspirin to alleviate the pain in my head. That would soon be gone—it was self-inflicted! I should have laid off the whisky.

I quickly dressed casually and then made my way downstairs. I found my way to the lounge, where I encountered not only Libby, but also Pip, Squeak and Willem, the three Burmese Blue cats. They all three yowled a 'good morning' at me, and came around my legs for a fuss. I bent down and caressed each of them in turn, although with little pleasure, because they were not my favourite animals. They all three stalked me to the kitchen. I found three saucers and went to the fridge to get a pint of milk so I could give each of them some milk and water. They lapped it up with relish, and looked around for more. Libby, the plump and lively West Highland terrier, jigged around me and barked playfully, quite delighted to see her new friend that morning; I was heartened that we were no longer enemies! I found a bowl and gave her a warm drink, which delighted her too. I then unlocked the back door, and all four animals went outside.

By then, Eve was downstairs and in the kitchen with me. She put eggs on to boil and fetched some cereal dishes out of the cupboard. She gave me three Weetabix with warm milk for starters and later, two boiled eggs with half a dozen slices of toast, liberally spread with butter. I washed it all down with three big breakfast mugs of hot sweet tea.

"Lookin' forrard to today, matey?" she asked me, slipping into her cockney accent!

"Yeh," I replied.

Eve sat down at the table and drank a mug of coffee with me.

"Boyzie," she said, a little guardedly I felt.

"Well, Sis?" I said, using an expression I often used when teasing her.

"I want to say something and… and you might not like it."

I steeled myself.

"Okay, say away, Sis!" I said.

Eve took another long drink from her large and rather ornate breakfast mug then said:

"I should beware of getting too involved with that young woman! What's her name? Johnnie?"

"Why?" I asked. "What do you know, Eve?"

She was quiet for a moment, bending down to make a fuss of one of the cats.

"It's not that I know anyfink," she said, still staying within her cockney way of speech. "I'm jus' warnin' yer! Be careful of her, Boyzie, she's dynamite!"

I was a little angry now, but I masked it with a laugh.

"She certainly is," I said.

Eve finished her coffee, asked me if I wanted more tea, and I said no thanks. I went upstairs and finished getting ready to go to Brawnstone. .

ৡৢৢৢ

At 9.15 a.m., Johnnie Friscoe arrived to collect me in a very snazzy sports car. It was white, 'low-slung' and very stylish.

"A winner!" she announced gaily as we drove away from Eve and Eric's house towards the village of Cherry Wootton.

Johnnie seemed in surprisingly good spirits and, like me, was obviously looking forward to the day ahead.

"I've packed us up a big picnic hamper," she said, putting her foot to the floor and revving the engine of her smart little Sprite, which was fairly whizzing along towards Brawnstone on an almost clear road, "and two humongous flasks, a cool box and two bottles of Jack Daniels!"

I laughed.

"It sounds like you've thought of everything," I said.

"I sure hope so, Boyzie," she rejoined, as we flew on towards the racing circuit at Brawnstone.

We were there in less than an hour. We found a good place to park beneath some trees. There were stalls and all kinds of things happening. Caravans were pulled onto the grass. There were tents, and they were setting up three marquees. One would certainly be a beer tent, but I did not know what the other two would be used for.

"It's going to be a carnival here all day!" exclaimed Johnnie with considerable satisfaction.

"Yeh, looks that way," I agreed, from all she had told me about what was going on.

I was feeling very excited, really quite exhilarated that day, and her company was one of the main reasons for that grand and glorious feeling surging up inside me. It was completely enveloping me, and it was lovely!

⁊⳺⳼⳽

The day was a rip-roaring success in every way. I spent most of it with Johnnie, and also with Eve, Eric, Micky, Grant and the rest of the Saunders clan, also Eric's two mechanics and their families. The two mechanics were from South-East London and had apparently been friends since their schooldays. They were both 27 years old. One was tall, heavily built and very fair, the other small, stocky and dark of hair and complexion. They were known as Butch and Peanuts. Butch was the more heavily built of the two. Tall and blond, with wavy hair and twinkling blue eyes, he was very good-looking, and he knew it! Peanuts was somewhat in the

183

shadow of Butch, or at least so it seemed to me. He was about five feet six inches tall, very stocky, with dark brown hair and brown eyes.

Butch was married to a young woman called Jan. They had no kids, but were possessed of an enormous Great Dane bitch that was about 14 months old and weighed in excess of 120 lbs. Her name was Abbie, and she was completely mental, but Abbie was Jan and Butch's pride and joy!

Peanuts was married to a girl called Lou. They had four children. Kirsty was seven years old, Robbie was six; Jamie was four and Mary was three years old, and grizzled constantly. Lou, their young mum, and the partner, not yet the wife, of Peanuts, looked like a Gypsy! They also had a dog, a mongrel-type called Rags. Abbie had little time, or love, for the mongrel. She kept knocking him over and looking as though she was about to devour him and everything else within reach that did not move quickly and adroitly out of her way. She really was a menace!

Johnnie and I sat a little away from the rest of them. She had certainly gone to town over the food preparation, and had packed us a fine picnic hamper. We dined on boiled eggs, tinned potatoes, pork pie, sliced cold meats of various types, loads of salad, pickled onions, fruit flan, various cakes and chocolate bars! There was also plenty to drink; a couple of two-litre flasks of iced tea, and two big bottles of pop, fizzy lemonade and Tizer, and also, for later, in the cool box were two bottles of Piersporter, a dry white wine that I had always loved. I was glad it was one of Johnnie's favourites too. She had bought a bottle of Jack Daniels especially for me. Bless her heart! What a smashing woman she really was. We found some shade, as the day was hot, and sat together, eating, drinking, talking, laughing etc.

We were blissfully happy until Abbie, the mentally retarded Great Dane, found us and blew our cover!

"Dratted dog!" exclaimed Johnnie heatedly, and she struck out viciously at Abbie, who ran away yowling.

Frankly, I was surprised by the venom with which Johnnie had struck out at the dog, who was playful and only looking for attention. However, I said nothing. We finished our picnic in peace after that incident and packed everything away before Johnnie had to go and register for her first race.

She was not in the same races as Eric. Her first one was 1.30 p.m. then another at 3.30 p.m., and finally, her last one at 5.15 p.m. that evening, the last race on the card. I was glad they were not to be rivals, as I wanted both of them to win their respective races. I knew it would make Eric happy, and hoped it would do the same for Johnnie.

"Do you want to race with me in the last one?" she asked me.

The adrenalin began to flow and I felt tremendously excited.

"Could I?" I asked her incredulously.

"Of course you can, if you would like to," she told me with authority.

We decided that I would go with her as her 'passenger' in the 80-lap race—the last one of the day. I would be strapped in beside her in the front, and would have to wear a helmet, but she said I would be completely safe and that she would try to give me a commentary on what was happening as we drove around the track. I told her to concentrate on her driving and not worry about that! She laughed! I knew that, if she could, she would manage to do both.

She certainly was a most extraordinary young woman, and I was growing more and more fond of her minute by minute! 'Come into my parlour,' said the spider to the fly! How willingly the fly acquiesced and entered the web of the cunning, sly, manipulative and cruel spider, with her wheedling ways, her soft caresses and her poisonous venom!

੬❧੭

The day wore on. Eric's first race had finished and he had won supremely; he was a very happy bloke. Peanuts and Butch, however, were not happy with the performance of the Shevron, and had to busy themselves, looking over and under, sideways and up and down its body and its machinery to ensure that in the next race it ran even sweeter. Eric wanted to be involved in all that too, thus, the women of the party and the children were left to their own devices.

I was still with Johnnie. We were together eating, drinking, laughing and generally enjoying ourselves in a shady glade. I guessed I was being antisocial and, to an extent, somewhat ungracious, so told my enthusiastic hostess that I must go and talk for a while to my sister-in-law and her friends.

"I'll come over with you, Boyzie," she said.

We walked together over to the caravans and chatted easily with Eve, the Saunders family and the partners of the two mechanics.

Jan had Abbie locked in the caravan because her behaviour was becoming totally impossible! She had knocked over several children and eaten half a loaf of sandwiches. There was loads of food, and just as well, since the children of Lou and Peanuts were little gannets! We had our own picnic hamper, so we were quite unruffled, and would have been prepared to share our spoils with the others, had they not had enough, however, that did not arise. Abbie's unfortunate mode of social behaviour certainly needed checking. Thus, to her consternation, she was shut in the caravan belonging to Jan and Butch. She was making plenty of noise about it, expressing her feelings for all to hear!

Eve was very thrilled about Eric's race, and I was pleased that Johnnie had come second in her first race of the day. She vowed and declared that she would win the next one and, of course, I was going to ride with her in the last race of the day. I was becoming somewhat concerned about that, but, naturally, would not say so. I did not want to appear 'chicken'. As I was thinking, I took a large, meaty chicken leg and began gnawing it—it was lovely. I had a plastic cup of white wine pushed into my other hand. It was cold and went down a treat. More food, more drink; I would not be fit to undertake the fast ride in Johnnie's sporty little car later that day! I had to ride with her or be considered a wimp, and I couldn't have that!

ဒ**ာ**ဒ္

At 6 p.m.

On that warm, beautiful Saturday evening in August I was sitting strapped into the front passenger seat of Johnnie Friscoe's sporty little car. She was going through the final stages of preparation for the last race of the day. She had come second in one race, the first one she had entered that morning—20 laps of the track—but she had only come fourth in the 40-lap race later on, and she was not pleased. No, she was not pleased at all with her performance, and vowed she would improve it and do a great deal better during the last race.

She had actually fared better on the day than poor Eric. He had only raced in one of the events, and he had won that. He had been delighted with his performance, but later, had expressed concerns over the running of the car, and Peanuts and Butch had worked on it long into the afternoon, so that he was unable to run in the 40-lap race, in which he had hoped very much to compete. Thus, he had also dropped out of the last race in which he was supposed to compete, and now he was 'guesting' in the same race in which Johnnie was taking part—the last race of the day; 80 laps of the track against the clock.

Eric was not pleased when he learned that I was to be a passenger in Johnnie's car during the length of the race. He thought it might be too much for me, he said. Johnnie had mocked him and openly laughed when he had expressed that thought.

"Boyzie said he wanted to race with me," she told Eric, "why do you think it will be too much for him?"

Eric said if I wanted to do it, it was up to me; he wouldn't try to tell me what I should do, but he was concerned that perhaps I was not thinking clearly and that I was being 'dragged along screaming' as he put it. Johnnie blazed!

"Ah! You don't know your own brother very well He's not the kind of bloke to do anything he doesn't want to do. So, mister, go screw yourself! Boyzie is coming along with me and we're gonna beat the pants off yer!"

Eve and Inga Saunders, who had both heard what Johnnie said, were shocked, and Eve wanted Eric to persuade me not to go with her, however, Eric, always shying away from trouble, would not discuss it any further, saying whatever I wanted to do was up to me. Anyway, he was more concerned with ensuring that his Shevron was up to the mark, so he could 'beat the pants' off Johnnie Friscoe!

§❧§

6.15 p.m.

Johnnie jovially climbed into the front seat and strapped herself in beside me.

"All ready, Boyzie, for the ride of your lifetime?" she asked me.

"As ready as I'll ever be," I said, feeling a tremendous sense of excitement.

"Okay! Eyes down! Look in! Here we go!" she cried, and the engine of her sporty little vehicle roared into life.

The flag went down, and we were off to race around 80 laps of the track against the clock.

I will never ever forget that race; I still have dreams about it, especially the last ten laps of the track, which we must have completed in record time. At around 7.40 p.m. we had finished, and we had won convincingly. Johnnie was over the moon!

"We've done it, we've done it, Boyzie, and *you* have been my lucky charm!"

§❧§

We sat in the bar with Eric and Yvonne. The Saunders family had gone home about 40 minutes before, taking Micky with them, and Peanuts and Butch. Jan and Lou were not with us. Jan was looking after the erring Abbie, and Lou was putting her four children to bed in their caravan. They were staying on and would not move off until Sunday evening, they said.

Johnnie, in expansive mood, was buying drinks all around!

Eric, who had come second in the race, and a good second too, giving Johnnie a real run for her money, had found the performance of his car much improved and was also feeling expansive and in high spirits as we all toasted 'Cardinal Puff, Puff, Puff,' for the seventh time!

"I reckon we'll all be getting cabs home tonight," laughed Johnnie Friscoe, placing another large whisky and dry ginger in front of me.

Yvonne, who was only drinking lime and lemonade, said she would be driving me and Eric home. Just as well! Eric was definitely several drinks to the good, and enjoying himself hugely. He was very bullish and extremely matey towards me and indeed towards Johnnie, who had defeated him.

"You drove a magnificent race!" he told her.

"Yeh, I was gud, wasn't I?" she rejoined, smirking behind her hand.

Eric either did not notice or chose not to notice that slight snub.

"I was really impressed; I don't mind coming second to someone who drives like that! You are a great driver," he said, and there was real admiration in his voice.

Johnnie took it all in, and seemed to bask in his approval.

§☙⚫◗§

It was well after ten o'clock before we left the bar and the track at Brawnstone, and commenced the drive home to Cherry Wootton. I was sad to part with Johnnie Friscoe. We had had such a great time together that weekend, and I felt as though a part of me would always be with that young, attractive, fast-living, smooth-talking female, who for the previous couple of days had been one of the mainstays in my life!

I felt sad as we parted.

"You look better now than you did when we climbed out of the car earlier on, Boyzie!" she joshed.

"Aw, what a ride, I'll never forget it! Eric's right, you *are* superb!"

We threw our arms around one another's shoulders and embraced heartily.

"And so are you, mister!" she told me with feeling. "Aw'm gonna
see you again real soon, don't you fret."

"I hope so," I said, and I meant it with all my heart, at least, at
that time I did.

Chapter 26

IT WAS about 35-minute drive from Brawnstone to Cherry Wootton since the roads were clear and Yvonne was a fast and competent driver. When we got in, Libby greeted us with great enthusiasm. Eve made me a big mug of hot chocolate and we sat in the lounge. Libby slumbered at my feet, and snored fitfully. It was gone midnight when we all eventually went up to bed.

As I lay on my bed, I heard a pitter-patter of paws outside my bedroom door and I went and opened it. Libby excitedly rushed in like a mini whirlwind.

"Come on," I said, laughing, and took her up onto the bed to sleep alongside me that night.

She was delighted, and excitedly licked my face and hands before eventually settling down on my right and lying full-length on top of my chest. We were parting as friends, having started as enemies, and I was very pleased that I had made that conquest. I stroked Libby and completely relaxed, and as I stroked and fondled the dog lying across my chest, I fell asleep, reflecting on how well my holiday had gone so far and on what an eventful weekend we had just had in Cambridgeshire—far more eventful than I would ever have envisaged!

The following day, Sunday, after a large brunch-style meal, I would be off up north to stay with Doreen, Fred and their vast clan of kids in Harts Hill, North Yorkshire. I knew that, inevitably, that would involve me in more adventures!

Sleep claimed me, and in my dreams I was once again racing around the track in the company of Johnnie Friscoe! .

Chapter 27

IT WAS mid-evening on Sunday, 31st December, 1989. I played the Patsy Kline track for Johnnie, but she did not phone again, although I had anticipated that she would do so.

The place was packed, stacked out with people. There was nobody in there with me at that moment however, and I was in splendid isolation, very much as I wished! I felt tired, so very, very tired. My head felt fuzzy, my eyes heavy, but I had to keep awake. I had to keep going!

I had received so many cards of congratulations, so many encouraging phone calls. I even had a call from my parents and one from Yvonne and Eric. They couldn't hear the programme where they were, but they all knew what I was doing.

"You're barmy!" my dad had said, when he knew what I proposed to do.

Despite that he had sent me a message wishing me the very best of luck and hoping I would complete the 80-hour broadcasting marathon. My mum had sent me a message on a cassette; she was wishing me a Happy New Year and all the best for the nineties. Good old Mum! I daresay the family would be getting together in their various venues to celebrate the end of an era and the beginning of a new decade. There would be no shortage of people with whom to celebrate at the studios of Sunny Gold Radio.

I started another sequence of easy listening music with a track by The Carpenters, and sat back, letting it all flow over me. I knew Bob was still out there, looking after me with regard to the engineering etc. When he finished his shift Craig would be back on again. The two of them were taking it in turns to see me through during the entire 80 hours. On 20 hours at a time, or thereabouts, they didn't stick to the regime rigidly, but swapped around between themselves as they desired. Me; I had kept going all the time during those past 60 hours or so and, although I felt tired, I also felt duly elated by my efforts. I felt intense pride! I knew I would feel terrific once I had completed the 80 hours, but I would also feel very, very tired indeed. I was going on holiday for a while after that, so I was looking forward to that very much indeed.

The Carpenters' track was superseded by a John Lennon track, and I relaxed completely and felt entirely safe! I was all right, I was well guarded; nothing and no one could hurt me! Could they?

Chapter 28

I AWOKE IN Cherry Wootton on Sunday morning with the sun shining full in my eyes. Eve must have been in and drawn the curtains back. Libby had gone! I looked at my watch, lying on the bedside table to my left. It was almost 10 a.m. I had slept heavily and well.

A knock on the .door roused me.

"Come in," I called cheerfully.

Eve came into the room with a mug of tea for me.

"Time to get up, sleepy-head!" she exclaimed.

"Oh crumbs, Eve, I overslept didn't I?"

She laughed.

"We all did this mornin', I'm afraid."

Libby came bounding in.

"No!" yelled Eve, and the dog stopped exactly where she was, tail wagging, her whole body moving with the great excitement she felt at seeing me again.

"Come on then, handsome, up you come, breakfast's on the way!"

Libby and Eve left the room, and I sat on the side of the bed, swinging my legs and drinking my hot sweet tea from the big breakfast mug she had fetched for me. Later, I got up, went into the bathroom, showered, shaved, returned and stripped the bed. I then dressed and, leaving my bags on the bed, I went downstairs. I sat in the lounge for a brief while then Eve came and called me into the kitchen. After a huge breakfast, I returned upstairs to clean my teeth again and pack my bags for the forthcoming journey north to Harts Hill.

It was about 11 .45 a. m. and my bags were all packed, save one or two last minute articles that I just had to slip in. The phone was ringing, and I picked it up on my way through the hallway to the kitchen.

"Hello," I said brightly.

A dusky voice, with a pronounced accent I remembered well, said:

"How are you, mister?"

"Hi there, Johnnie," I said, pleased that she had phoned, but wondering if I had ever given her that telephone number.

"Are you ready for your long journey north?" she asked.

"Almost," I responded.

We chatted for a while then I had to take my leave. With great reluctance, I said goodbye to my new friend, Johnnie Friscoe.

"It's not *goodbye*, it's only Qllie Voyle," she told me, and we both laughed.

That broke the tension between us momentarily, but then Johnnie became serious again, and spoke with great certainty.

"Don't forget, aw'm gonna see you again real soon! Remember that, yeh, Boyzie?"

"Too right I'll remember, and you make sure that you do too!" I told her as we parted, laughing.

"Who was that, Ian?" Eric asked as I walked into the kitchen.

"Oh, it was Johnnie, Johnnie Friscoe," I told him.

I thought I detected a slight sense of unease within the room. The atmosphere seemed to change for a short time, or was it just me? Anyway, I went back up to my room, opened the windows wide, finished packing, ran a comb through my hair and went to the top of the stairs to call for Eric. He hurried up and helped me with my bags.

At 12.40 p.m. we left the house and I said my farewells to Yvonne and Micky, who was back home and ready for his Sunday dinner.

"See you soon, Uncle Boyzie!" said M icky, who was turning out to be a real live wire.

"You sure will," I told him, ruffling his hair.

He laughed and ran into the house to play with Libby. I hugged Eve and thanked her for a very pleasant weekend. We were off, and I had begun my journey northwards to Harts Hill, North Yorkshire.

Chapter 29

THE NEW city of Southborough, on the Northants/Lincs borders, was about 75 miles north of Cherry Wootton. It was a pleasant drive up there on that warm Sunday afternoon in August. We arrived at bay nine on the bus station at approximately 14.05 p.m. My bus was at 14.25 p.m.

Eric helped me with my bags and we walked over to a bench, where we sat down to await the arrival of the bus that would take me northwards to Harts Hill.

"Give Doreen and Fred all my best, and tell her I hope she's okay when the new sprog arrives," said Eric.

I smiled. It would be Doreen's thirteenth child, and it was due at any moment. Perhaps it would arrive while I was up there, who knew?

"Thanks for a great weekend, bruv," I said to Eric, who sat close beside me on the bench.

"Aw shucks," he said, "we didn't actually see that much of you, did we?"

I felt a bit guilty then! I had spent a lot of time with Johnnie, but then, why not? She had done me a power of good; yes, she certainly had! Eric, reading my thoughts, laughed and said:

"I'm not condemning, but take a bit of advice, eh bruv? Be careful with Johnnie Friscoe, she's got a reputation! She's hot stuff, you know, I'm only warnin' you."

"Thanks," I said, "warning accepted!"

"Good!" he said, and opened up his wallet.

He pushed £100 in tenners into my hand.

"There you are," he said.

I looked at him in astonishment.

"I can't take all that, Eric," I said, but he pushed my hand into my pocket and laughed.

"You might not get any more for ages, so I would take it and be pleased about it! No, honestly Ian, we want you to have it, so please take it, eh bruv?"

We used to call each other bruv back in the 'good old days' when we both lived at home and got along reasonably well, for a time at any rate. I laughed.

"Thanks, Eric, thanks for everything, bruv, I do appreciate it!"

The bus had arrived. Eric helped me aboard with my bags, then took my fare to the driver and paid him for me. After that, he said cheerio to me and then climbed down and stood waiting until we left the bus station. Several people got on the bus, travelling to different places en route, but no one else was going as far north as I was. The driver told me he would be changing over at Ellington, but he would speak to his colleague and tell her, it was a woman called Pat who would take over at Ellingto, that I was going up to Briggthorpe. I thanked him.

As the bus started on its way, Eric banged on the window and I returned his knock, then, a little wistfully, reflecting on the fun I had had during that past weekend, especially in the company of Johnnie Friscoe, I sat back with my bags and relaxed. It was 14.25 p.m. Twenty-five minutes past two on a warm Sunday afternoon in late August, and I was on my way northwards.

§⊷∾§

Shortly after 3.15 p.m. we stopped at the bus depot in the large market town of Granby in Lincolnshire, the second largest county in England. Granby was in North Lincolnshire, and our next stop, Wheatley, in about 35 minutes, would bring us close to the borders of the two largest areas of England; the counties of Lincolnshire and Yorkshire. I had always been good at the geography of the British Isles when I was at school, the only aspect of geography that I really found interesting. I suppose that was because I had travelled up and down the country so many times in the past, and I was doing it again.

We remained in the bus depot at Granby for approximately five minutes, then left, taking the road towards Wheatley. A young woman had boarded the bus at Granby with her four children. She was sitting behind me with two of them. I turned and introduced myself, in the hope that we might open up a dialogue between us and thus make the journey pass more quickly and pleasantly.

"Hi, I'm Ian, Ian Dickson. I'm travelling to Briggthorpe."

There was a pause before the young woman replied.

"Sandy, Sandy Christmas!"

"Hi again," I said.

"I expect you want to laugh now!" she said.

"No, why?" I responded.

"Everyone usually laughs at my name when I tell 'em it's Christmas!"

"Oh," I said, "well, I won't!"

She turned to speak to one of her erring offspring.

"These are my lot," she continued, introducing me to her four children. "Randle is nine, then there's Dominic, he's seven years old, then there's Tyler, she's four years old and the youngest is Dillon and he's two years old."

"Oh, right!" I said.

What unusual names, I thought. She continued, as the bus started on its way from Granby,

"I'm 27 years old and I'm a single mum. I'm going with the kids to stay with a cousin in Harts Hill, and I may decide to look for a place up there. I've no real need to stay in Granby; it's not my home anyway."

"Where is your home then?" I asked casually.

I had detected a trace of a London accent. I liked her and wanted to keep up a dialogue with her.

"I'm originally from Kent," she told me, "but I moved up here with Tyler and Dillon's father. He's gone off an' left us an' nah I jus' wanna move away from there!"

"I'm going to stay with relatives in Harts Hill," I said. "There's a very big council estate on the fringes of the town and it's called Penniwell," I continued.

"Yeh," rejoined Sandy, "that's where my cousin lives. She's my mother's sister's daughter, her name is Norma Townley."

As the bus travelled on towards Wheatley, our next destination, Sandy Christmas and I kept up a conversation about our respective families. Sandy told me that her mother's name was Belle, and she lived in Kent, near the sea. She was a single mum as well. She had left Harts Hill in disgrace, since she was not married and was expecting Sandy. She had had a job as an auxiliary nurse at a local hospital, and had apparently been doing well then she went to a party and became pregnant by one of the doctors. He was of West Indian origin, so Sandy, the result of that pregnancy, was a black woman.

"I'm black, an' I'm proud!" she told me, and then started to laugh.

Belle, who was then only just 50 years old, had moved down to Kent in 1951 when she discovered she was pregnant with Sandy. She took a job for a while until Sandy was born. Sandy told me Belle worked in the kitchens at a hotel near the sea, but the work was heavy and the pay was poor.

After Sandy was born, Belle worked in a laundry, then as a cleaner, then as a cook-housekeeper for a while, but her male employer was a 'randy owd bugger' and she left before she became pregnant again! She took a job as a 'skivvy', working in a pub, cleaning, making sandwiches etc., and working on the bar in the evenings. The money wasn't bad, although the hours were not good for Sandy. During that time, Sandy, Belle's beautiful Anglo-West Indian daughter, was looked after by neighbours on the Brightleys council estate in the seaside town of Marshend, where they lived.

When Sandy was three and a half years old, an attractive, lively, chubby little girl, she went to nursery school. She was fairly well accepted there, although she was the only black child in the nursery, and the same when she started at infants' school. Belle continued to clean, take in washing, bake cakes, undertake work in pubs etc., and she also 'worked at nights', according to Sandy. She said that from the age of five years, she remembers a large number of 'uncles' coming into her life! Some of them did not stay long; all of them were kind to her. Nobody used her badly, but they gave her money or gifts rather than love—and they stole her mother's affections from her!

When she was 13 years old, Belle expected Sandy to continue in the same mould, but Sandy, revolted by the idea, would not do so! She ran away and went to live in Harts Hill. Initially she lived with her Aunt Sarah Townley and her cousin, Norma. However, it was not long before Sandy discovered that her cousin, Norma, only daughter of Sarah and Joe Townley, was also 'on the game'. Sarah Townley, formerly Sarah Christmas, was some eight years older than Sandy's mum, Belle. Sandy lived and worked in Harts Hill for a while, then, about five and a half years previously, she had moved down to Granby with the father of her two youngest children. By then, she already had Randle and Dominic, but her new partner had taken well to the two boys and treated them like his own.

It was soon after the birth of Dillon that Sandy's partner, Mick Priddy, left her. She believed he had gone to London with a girl whom she met while he was working as a vacuum cleaner salesman. She said that all she wanted to do was to move back up north, even though she did not approve of the way of life lived by her cousin, Norma. Norma Townley, who was 38 years old, some ten and a half years older than herself, was Sandy's closest relative apart from Belle, her mum. Belle was still living in the town of Marshend on the Kent coast, and she was still cleaning, working part-time in a laundry, and 'flat-backing' to make extra money! Despite everything, Sandy had a great affection for her mum, and Belle positively doted on her four grandchildren.

We were just outside Wheatley Bus Depot. The time was passing quickly in conversation with that lively, friendly young woman, and I was greatly enjoying becoming acquainted with her.

૯૭≈≫૭

It was 4.05 p.m. on the last Sunday in August, 1978, and we were just pulling out of Wheatley Bus Depot. After a few moments, Sandy began to talk to me again.

"So, I've towd you quite a bit abaht me, nah, what abaht yo', Boyzie?"

I had already told her my nickname, the name by which almost everyone knew me. I was amazed how easy it was to go on and talk to Sandy Christmas about Sue, about her illness, the way she had died, how I had felt and about my present situation.

"I didn't know how I would cope without her," I told Sandy, "but now… well, I'm reunited with my own family, and have been enjoying a smashing holiday here down south with them. My late wife's family are back in Gaynsford, where I live, and there's a network of people up there who are intent on looking after me once I return home."

Sandy listened intently, and despite having occasionally to speak to her erring children, she seemed to be taking it all in. After I had finished speaking, she waited a moment or two before saying quietly:

"You are lucky, Boyzie, it must be smashing to have so many people who care abaht you! Your family sound great and I am glad you are enjoying your holiday, but who are you going to visit up in Harts Hill?"

I started to tell Sandy the story of Doreen and how she had gone up to Yorkshire to live with our Aunt Muriel.

Chapter 30

I T WAS August, 1960, when Doreen left home and she was not
yet 15 years old. She left on a Saturday morning, and Mum and
Dad were both very upset. They had no inkling as to where
she had gone or why, at least so they said at the time. I remember
that Sunday very well. It was late evening when Mrs Taylor came
around to Mum's and said there was someone on the phone for
her, could she please come around and have a word, it was a long
distance call from Yorkshire. Both Mum and Dad went to Mrs
Taylor's, who lived five doors down the street and was the only
one on our side who had a telephone at that time. Funny the way
things change!

The phone call had been from Muriel's husband, Jack Dabbs.
He said that Doreen had turned up at their house, very upset, saying she had hitch-hiked all the way from Essex and that there was
no way she was going back home to Mum and Dad! It was some
time before my parents returned home that evening, and when
they did, the atmosphere between them seemed to me to be very
hostile!

On the following morning, which was Monday, they announced
to Eric and me that they were both going up to Aunt Muriel's
in Yorkshire to bring Dorrie home, and that we would have to
go and stay, temporarily at any rate, with neighbours. I was dispatched to stay with Mrs Ryan and her family. Eric stayed over the
road with Ernie Russell and his family, because Ernie was a good
friend of his.

It was Wednesday evening before Mum and Dad returned to
Essex and it was without Dorrie. They had accepted that she would

not come home with them and that she had said she wanted to stay with Aunt Muriel and Uncle Jack in North Yorkshire. However, she had also said she wanted to find a job, and Mum and Dad were saying she was too young. Dorrie, however, being of a wilful nature, with plenty of spirit, decided to find a job for herself.

In the early part of September, 1960, she started work at the nearby farm. She worked there until the middle of February, 1961, but after almost five months she left, saying the work was too hard and the hours too long. She began to look around for other work and eventually, in the middle of March, she started work as the tea girl-cum-messenger girl-cum-general factotum in a factory where they made bicycles. She worked for Martinau Cycles in Briggthorpe for almost two and a half years, and then, at the beginning of the summer of 1963, she left and began work in a cafe in Harts Hill called Loui's. There she made hot drinks, sandwiches, toasted snacks etc., and waited on tables, cleaned up the floor, wiped the tables, washed up and generally did anything and everything that was required of her. Allegedly, she loved it, every minute of it, although at times it was hard and exhausting work, especially on Saturdays when it got really busy and the place was packed with youngsters.

Dorrie was a cheerful, hard-working girl, and was well thought of by the staff at Loui's. She was very happy living with Aunt Muriel, Uncle Jack and their two young sons, Ronnie and Bobby. The boys adored her, and both Aunt Mu and Uncle Jack were very fond of her. She was a willing help to Aunt Mu, and they were like sisters together!

Chapter 31

"SOUNDS GREAT," said Sandy in a thoughtful way, "but… what abaht your parents?"

Mum and Dad had taken Dorrie's departure from Thamesford very hard indeed. Mum would not correspond with her or Muriel, and saw Muriel as having enticed Dorrie away from them. In no way was that true! Muriel and Jack had both tried hard to talk Dorrie into returning home to Thamesford with Mum and Dad during the two days when our parents were up in Harts Hill with them, but all to no avail. Doreen would not come home. She would not even contemplate doing so, and that was that, 'an' all abaht it', as Granny Annie, my mum's late mother, would have put it! When Mum tearfully confided the news to Granny Annie, she said that it was a pity Dorrie had gone off like that, but she did not express great surprise at what had occurred, and neither did any of Mum's sisters!

Doreen had always been a hot-blooded young female, with fire in her eyes and plenty of sauce and spirit! She was a wilful young lady, who would always do whatever she wanted to do, and what she wanted to do was to be free of Mum and Dad and their constant and, as she saw it, intrusive supervision! Up in Harts Hill, North Yorkshire, with Aunt Mu, who was ten years younger than Dad and more like a sister to Dorrie than an aunt, she could feel much more free and more able to live the kind of life she wanted to live.

Not that Aunt Mu made life easy for Dorrie; on the contrary. Life at work was quite hard at times, and when she got home there were chores for Dorrie to undertake before she could go out, meet her friends etc. Somehow Dorrie did not mind undertaking those chores for Aunt Mu and Uncle Jack, and she loved her two cousins to bits. She would often look after Ronnie and Bobby while their parents went 'up the club' or out visiting friends, and she loved it. She did a deal of housework for Aunt Muriel, more than she had ever done for Mum back home in Thamesford. Although she pretended that she did not miss her, I knew how much Mum really mourned the loss of her daughter, and the hostility she felt towards Muriel because of that never faded away. All very sad!

On arrival at Ellington Bus Depot, we changed drivers. Alan got out of the cab and Pat got in. Pat was smoking, but she put out her cigarette and chatted easily to Alan and another bloke called Goffer. Al told her about me and that I was going all the way up to Briggthorpe. Pat said she would see me out at the bus terminus there, and I told her I was being met. We sat in the bus, Sandy, her four young children and me, eating sandwiches, apples and crisps, drinking from cans and chatting.

The children were really behaving very well considering how young they all were. Dillon, the two year old, was tired, and for a while after we had eaten some refreshments and had a drink, I held him on my knee. As the bus started up on its way to Raughton from Ellington, the rhythm must have rocked him to sleep. He put his head on my chest and was fast off. Sandy and I continued talking.

It was now early evening, and the bus was very sparsely populated; only us and about four other passengers travelling northwards. We chatted easily and pleasantly, and it passed the time, talking, laughing and eating with that new acquaintance of mine—Sandy, Sandy Christmas!

Chapter 31

IT WAS in November of 1963 that Doreen, my sister, first met the man to whom she is now married. The Dingle family, although not large, were nevertheless notorious in the area surrounding Coalbeck, Penniwell and Harts Hill. June Ellen Dingle, daughter of Ellen, who was a forewoman in the pickle factory, was 16 years old when she became pregnant by an American airman called Dave Clover. Dave, who was 26 years old, married with a wife and family back home in California, enjoyed June Dingle's company. June, who worked in the pickle factory along with her widowed ma, was a saucy, high spirited young woman with a temper as hot as Hiroshima! She also had a red-hot passion within, and Dave Clover knew how to turn her on.

Thus, one night in the moonlight, down in the woods near Bryerwood Farm, they made mad passionate love, and the result, just under nine months later, was a fine, healthy baby boy with a strong pair of lungs! June and her ma decided to call him David Frederick Dingle, but he had always been known as Fred. Fred, a strong, sturdy, confident youngster, thrived and grew like a tall oak tree. At the age of nine years he was in trouble for pinching groceries from a local store. As he grew older, his list of misdemeanours grew longer, almost daily! Fred Dingle was notorious and he was a handful for his doting mother and his ailing grandma to cope with.

At 14 years old he ran away to sea! At 16 years old he returned briefly, but went away from home again to become a boy soldier in the army. At 20 years old he returned home again, a fine figure of a young man, more than six feet five inches tall, with a ruddy, healthy complexion, gleaming white teeth, a smile that could break any female heart, a ready wit, an engaging, although cheeky, personality, sandy hair and twinkling baby-blue eyes. He was very handsome, and he knew it! He walked along with his head up and his shoulders back—cockily, jauntily—with immense confidence. The lads flocked around him; he was something of a local hero. The girls just fell at his feet, but Fred only had eyes for one; the young, cheeky, spirited and most attractive girl who worked behind the counter serving drinks and snacks in Loui's Coffee Bar, and that girl was 'our Doreen'!

⁋⋙⋘⁋

One Saturday evening towards the end of February, 1964, after the cafe was closed for the night, Doreen took young, wild, handsome Fred Dingle up the stairs to the four-roomed flat above the shop. She occupied that flat, and had done so more or less ever since she started work at Loui's.

Jack Dabbs, husband of Muriel, had run off with Lilly Turnbull, the barmaid at the Rowe Deer, and Muriel did not know where they had gone. Rumour had it that they were living in Alberta, Canada. Muriel was endeavouring to obtain a quickie divorce on grounds of desertion! Doreen had deemed it prudent to move out of the house, but she was still a frequent visitor to her Aunt Mu, who had done a lot to help her since she arrived in Harts Hill and had done nothing but make her welcome. Dorrie thought of Mu as an older and much loved sister.

Now there was someone else in Dorrie's life, and she loved him too! Oh, how she loved him. She loved him with a wild passion of which she would never have believed herself capable! She loved him hard, she loved him long, and he returned her passion one hundredfold!

So it was that on that Saturday evening in late February, 1964, with the cafe closed, and all the doors locked against possible invasion, Dorrie and young wild Fred found themselves upstairs in the four-roomed flat Dorrie rented, above Loui's Coffee Bar in the mean streets in the centre of the shabby, incestuous, industrial town of Briggthorpe.

What happened between them that night changed the course of both their lives. Dorrie Dickson and David Frederick Dingle made wild, passionate love on Dorrie's bed! As the wind blew outside and the rain battered against the windows of the deserted cafe-bar, they lay together upstairs in the bedroom of the four-roomed flat above the shop in which Dorrie toiled all day. As they lay there, wrapped in one another's arms, they made love again and again and again with a ferocious intensity and an all-consuming passion! They both came at the same moment! A heartfelt cry arose from Dorrie; a muffled groan came from Fred!

The result of their passion, nine months later in the November of 1964, was their daughter, Peggy Sue. Peggy Sue was the first of their 13 children! In the spring of 1965, Dorrie and Fred were married, and by then baby number two was already conceived and well and truly on the way. Frank arrived on the scene in late October 1965, before Peggy Sue was even a year old. By then the couple were earnestly looking for accommodation, and Fred Dingle, family man, was looking for good honest toil!

Seth Daley, the owner and manager of Bryerwood Farm, which was situated off Lumley Lane in Harts Hill, was looking for good, strong and honest labour; someone young and fit, hard-working, not afraid of taking on plenty of work, someone with a head on his shoulders! Someone who would be willing to learn his trade, set his hand to almost anything, and David Frederick Dingle was the man—the answer to all Seth Daley's prayers. The job had a house going with it—Keeper's Cottage, one of two cottages, each containing eight rooms, set back on a slip road off Lumley Lane, just before the road leading down to Bryerwood Farm, but part of the farmland anyway.

Joss Daley, brother of Seth, knew of the family. He told his brother about Fred Dingle and his little family. By then baby number three was in process of being 'hatched', and Seth and Joss interviewed Fred one day in the public bar of the Roe Deer. After that interview, the family were cordially invited to take Sunday tea with the Daleys. Bessie, Seth's wife, made them all very welcome, and Aunt Muriel and her two sons were invited as well. They all sat down to a sumptuous repast in the kitchen of the big house at Bryerwood Farm, and Bessie Daley waited upon them all most solicitously.

By the beginning of Autumn, 1966, Dorrie, Fred and the children were established as the new tenants of Keeper's Cottage, and Fred was toiling long hours on the farm, working for the Daley family and earning his 'daily bread'! He loved it, every moment of it, and the Daley family certainly valued his presence and indeed, the presence of Doreen and the family, which was growing in numbers from year to year! Eventually, it was necessary for the two eight-roomed cottages to be knocked into one, and it was renamed Ploughman's Cottage.

Dorrie presented her husband, Fred, with a child per year until 1970. In that year the twins, Jackie and Freddie, were born. After that, there was a brief lull then Iris arrived in 1972, followed by four more strapping healthy sons. In late August, 1978, Dorrie was expecting her thirteenth child! Fred was now well established as the pig man at Bryerwood Farm.

Bessie and Seth Daley had retired to live in Killesby, between Marson and Macclesborough. They apparently had an eight-berth mobile home there. They had five dogs there with them, and were allegedly as happy as larks. Their son, Matt Daley, was now the new boss at Bryerwood Farm. Matt was a year younger than Fred. He had married Becky Poulson, who was 29 years old, and they had four children. Sarah was nine years old, Belinda was six years old, Adam was three years old and had no hearing or speech, Sophie, the baby, was eight months old, and a bouncing, healthy baby girl. Becky and the children were frequent visitors to Ploughman's Cottage. The two families got on very well indeed, and Fred and Matt Daley were like brothers-in-arms.

Chapter 32

A s WE drove towards Waykely, the second to last stop before the town of Briggthorpe, I was still nursing two-year-old Dillon, who was still sleeping with his head snuggled on my chest. I was looking forward with great anticipation to seeing all my family up in Harts Hill.

ৡৣৢ

Waykely was behind us and we were now on the road to Raughton, the last lap before we headed into Briggthorpe. It would take about 20 to 25 minutes from there to our next destination, and from there, we would travel non-stop up to Briggthorpe. At the bus depot in Briggthorpe, I had no doubt that Fred Dingle, my brother-in-law, would be there to meet me. In the meantime, Sandy and I were still fellow passengers on the bus, and we were still talking, sharing experiences and family information. I was still cuddling the sleeping Dillon on my knee. Sandy was telling me about her cousin, Norma Townley.

It was 1939 and the summer of that year when Belle's 19-year-old sister, Sarah, married 22-year-old Joseph Townley. Joe Townley was a miner's son, and a very handsome young man. He was born of good mining stock, one of seven brothers. Sarah and Belle's mother were delighted at the match. She could not have wished for 'owt better' for her eldest daughter. Belle, then a rather stroppy youngster of 11 years, was the only bridesmaid. The wedding was a big affair, however, and the whole village turned out to see the marriage of those two young people.

It was true that the Christmas family had something of a reputation, but the girls were reasonably well accepted by the other villagers, and Sarah Christmas, eldest daughter, was considered to be quite a beauty in the community. Lads dubbed her a 'bonnie 'un'. Joe Townley was considered a lucky man to have ensnared her.

At the outbreak of war, the couple were just home from a week's honeymoon at Macclesborough, and were endeavouring to set up home together. In 1940, Joe went off to war and left young Sarah pregnant with their only daughter, Norma. Joe came home once and saw her, but in the early part of 1942, he died in action out in France. Sarah and her daughter, Norma, moved back into the family home for a while before setting up in Lennon Street, Harts Hill, where Norma and her family still lived.

Belle, Sandy's mum, who was eight years younger than Sarah, had a good relationship with her niece. She spent a lot of time with Norma, looking after her while her mother worked etc., and she became very attached to her. After Belle left the district and moved down to Kent, Norma missed her sorely. Norma's mother, Sarah, was not a particularly adequate woman; she could not function well without a lot of support, and this usually meant the support of men! Thus, like Sandy, her cousin, Norma Townley, had a lot of 'uncles' in her life, especially during her early years.

Norma's childhood was not a particularly happy one. She did go down to Kent to stay with her Aunt Belle and her cousin, Sandy, and also, Sandy went to Harts Hill to live when she was a teenager. She moved in with Sarah and lived with her in Lennon Street at number twenty-eight. Norma had moved four doors down on the same side and now lived at 20 Lennon Street. She had left her mother's home when she was only just 16 years of age, and had moved in with John Toone, the builder. John was 19 years old, and an apprentice to his Uncle Ernest.

The Toone family had been builders in the town for many years. The trade was passed down from father to son etc., etc. John's father was dead, but his uncles looked after him and were training him to follow in their footsteps. John and Norma had five children, although they never married. The first was George, born when Norma was 17 years of age, then came Barbara the following year, followed by Kenny, then Eddie and, last of all, Vinnie.

After the birth of Vinnie, John Toone, now qualified and working hard as a builder from his uncle's builder's yard in Gallows Street, abruptly left the crowded family house in Lennon Street. He had met and fallen hopelessly in love with a girl called Carol Balmer, whom he subsequently married. They had a daughter called Lesley Ann, and still lived in Harts Hill, although at the other end of town from Lennon Street! John Toone had never seen or acknowledged any of his five children by Norma Townley for many years!

Exit John Toone, the tall and handsome builder. Enter Richard Julian, a gas fitter. He was 23 years old, five feet ten inches tall, rugged and handsome. He was of West Indian origin, and lived in the town with his parents, Claudia and Elias. He had a brother, Oliver, and a couple of younger sisters, one of whom was called Beatrice. She apparently worked at Loui's Coffee Bar, so may well have been known to our Dorrie. Anyway, Rick Julian, the handsome, rugged gas fitter, lived with Norma Townley in Lennon Street for about four and a half years. Their relationship produced only the one child, a daughter called Heather, who was born in 1964.

In 1967, Richard Julian left Norma. He met, and subsequently married, a young woman called Sally, in the early spring of 1968. Sally was already pregnant by Rick, and they lived in Wellbourne Street, Penniwell, and had six children of their own. Rick had acknowledged his daughter, Heather, and she often went around to see Sally and her half-brothers and sisters. She enjoyed visiting them, and Norma apparently had no objections.

So, exit Richard Julian, enter Mike Taylor. Mike, a six-footer, was also black and was a plumber. He worked for John Toone. Mike was 26 years old when he moved in with Norma, who was now in her twenty-eighth year. Their relationship produced three children, Benson, now nine years old, Louise, now eight years old and Julie, a fine, sturdy youngster of seven years. Julie was a most attractive girl, with beautiful long hair, whereas Louise was apparently much plainer, taller and more willowy than her younger sister. All three children, however, were very lively, according to Sandy. She had seen them once, about five and a half years previously. Soon after Julie Ann's birth, there was a tremendous family row, and Mike Taylor left the house one dark damp morning, never to return, although again, Sandy said she understood that he did not live far from Norma.

Her eldest daughter, Babs, had also now left the family home, and Sandy believed she had at least one child of her own. She had not seen any of the family for some time, she said. However, like me, she was looking forward to seeing them all again very soon now.

"Will you find a house and move up here, then?" I asked her.

Sandy did not respond immediately. Dillon was stirring on my knee, and whimpering for his mum. I cuddled him close and kissed his little round face. He remained still on my knee then lifted his head and said sleepily:

"Oishie!"

We all laughed.

"He's not heard your name right," said Randle, who had come to sit on the seat beside me.

Dominic and Tyler were now sitting together with their mum, and Sandy, whilst still engaged in talking to me, was trying to tidy up Tyler's long hair with a large comb she had found in one of her bags. Tyler was not responding very well to Sandy's efforts to make her look less tousled, and she was just beginning to fidget and fret when Sandy suddenly announced:

"You'll do Fanny Ann."

Tyler sighed and sat back, leaning against her brother's shoulder. Randle, who was quite a little chatterbox, was now engaged in talking to me nineteen to the dozen, and that continued until we pulled into Raughton Bus Depot at around 5.40 p.m.

"We'll be here until 6 p.m. then we go all the way up to Briggthorpe, an' then up to Merton," said Pat, who was getting out of the cab to have another fag.

"Do you fancy a quick cuppa?" I asked Sandy. We decided not to bother, since it would have meant all the children accompanying us into the tea shop. However, Sandy sent Randle off to fetch some cans of orange and some chocolate bars for them, and also two mugs of hot chocolate for us. Randle, a most pleasant youngster, went eagerly to do his mother's bidding!

Several more people came aboard the bus at Raughton. Dillon was duly handed back to his mum, despite his protests to the contrary, and soon settled down on her knee and went back to sleep. Randle returned with the goodies that he had been asked to purchase. Pat climbed back into the cab, took everyone's fares, and asked me which were my bags. I was able to describe them to her adequately.

"Fine! Aw'll 'elp yo' off when we get there now, an' aw'll mek' sure your bags are unpacked from the boot, then ye'll be okay, eh?" she asked.

"Sure, thanks!" I said.

"Aw'm gettin' off at the same stop as 'im," said Sandy, "an' 'e's bein' met anyroad."

"Ay, aw knaw that," said Pat.

She was back in her cab and we were pulling out of Raughton Bus Depot on the last leg of our journey northwards to Briggthorpe. It would take us about 40 minutes to get from Raughton to Briggthorpe. We should be there by 6.40 p.m., or rather 18.40 hours, since everyone in the sphere of transport, from those who planned the timetables to the drivers, worked on the European-style 24-hour timetable those days.

Sandy and I had enjoyed our mugs of hot chocolate, fetched for us on the bus by her nine-year-old son, Randle. He still sat beside me, drinking from a can, and he had given me a large chocolate bar to eat. I said I would put it in my bag and perhaps give it to my four youngest nephews, Gordon, Steven, David and Andrew. They were all aged between four years and one year. It was a very big bar of chocolate, and too large for me to eat on my own. In any case, I knew that Fred and I would probably be going for a few pints before we arrived back at Ploughman's Cottage, Lumley Lane, Harts Hill, and that, once we arrived there, Dorrie would have a huge meal ready for our consumption. Therefore, the idea of eating a large block of Cadbury's chocolate was not particularly appealing to me at that moment.

The young boy seemed to understand, and I told him I would give him back the 20p it had cost him, but he said:

"Naw, it wor a present from me an' Mam!"

I laughed.

"Thanks then, pal, I'll buy you summat if I see you arrahnd while I'm up here, eh?"

"Yo' can cum to tea one day wivv us an' ahr Norma an' all her lot if you want to!"

That was from Sandy.

"Aw yeh! Please cum to tea wivv us, mister!" said all three of the older children, speaking in unison.

I laughed.

"Yeh, yeh! I'd like to do that. Thanks, kids, and you, Sandy!"

"Right, that's easy enough to arrange. A Sunday afternoon 'ud be nice, eh?" said Sandy.

"Yeh, we could mebbee go out somewhere—for a walk or whatever," I suggested, adding, as an afterthought, "if it's nice."

"Yeh, why not?" enthused Sandy. "Aw'll get ahr Norma to pack us up a big picnic, an' we can go to Donkey Meadow."

"Aw yeh," said Randle, jumping up and down on the seat beside me. "That'd be great, Mam!"

So that was at least one Sunday afternoon sorted, and all the time the bus drew nearer and nearer to our destination. The excitement within me was mounting. It was some considerable time since I had been up to Harts Hill. I began to think about it and realised that the last time I had been up there to stay I was with Susan, and young Iris, Dorrie and Fred's eighth child, had not long been born. I had not seen any of my youngest nephews, or any of the other children, since they were all quite small. I would certainly notice some changes.

I finished the pack of sandwiches that Eve had made up for me, and the Christmas family finished their refreshments. We then sat, anticipating our imminent arrival in the town of Briggthorpe.

§❧§

It was a little after 6.50 p.m. when we arrived at the bus depot at Briggthorpe, North Yorkshire. Briggthorpe was a large bustling town, with a population of almost one hundred thousand. There were many factories within its boundaries, and it bordered pit country, farming country and colliery villages, all of which still had working pits, even into the late seventies. The town itself and the general area around it were fairly rundown and poor, but the people who lived there were the salt of the earth!

On arrival in the busy bus depot, we duly dismounted from the vehicle. I was a little stiff after sitting for so long. Randle jumped down the steps and ran to his cousins, who were waiting to meet the family. Sandy, after hugs, kisses etc., introduced me to Norma's sons, George, Kenny and Vinny. She then helped me to find my bags, and unloaded hers and her children's belongings from the bus, before saying cheerio to me and going off with her cousins and her offspring, who were all very excited, and had received a promise from me to go and visit them at Norma's on Sunday week, so that we could undertake our proposed outing.

As they left me, Fred, my brother-in-law, approached me. We quickly gathered up my bags, and we walked together from the bus depot and crossed the road to where he had left his Land Rover. Fred's loves and hobbies were many and varied, and among his loves were his vehicles; two Massey Harris tractors, four motorbikes, including a Harley Davidson, and his three 109 Land Rovers, good, strong, sturdy dependable vehicles, very suitable for farm use, but that one, whom he called Bella, was for the family's use.

The Dingle family loved to go camping, and when they did, then

Bella and the Morris van that they possessed, plus the trailer they hooked onto Bella's rear, were the vehicles they used for transporting themselves, their dogs, plus all the equipment they would require for such an expedition. Fred had been engaged with the older lads of the family in cleaning Bella up for my arrival, and now, as we approached her, I was assured she looked quite magnificent, standing there in the car park opposite the coach station, arrivals and departures depot. Fred piled my bags into the back of the vehicle, and we climbed up into the front seats.

"Belt up," said Fred with a grin!

I duly did so, and we were on our way.

The evening was pleasant, although rather chilly for the time of year. Fred drove to Briggthorpe Working Men's Club, on the corner of Tudor Street and Haigh Street, and we climbed out of the vehicle, which he secured before we walked into the lounge bar together. Fred signed us both in. We sat down at a table and he went striding up to the bar and ordered two pints of best bitter. He also fetched a plate loaded with sandwiches for our consumption.

"Isn't our Dorrie getting a meal for us when we get in?" I asked him.

"Away!" he rejoined, his mouth full of food, "but we've got some serious drinkin' te do a'fore then, eh? So, we need summat to keep it dahn, eh Boyzie?"

I nodded.

The room was hazy with smoke and swirling with the sound of many voices. It was warm, and the food and beer were good. I relaxed in the easy chair in front of the laden table, and felt very happy, warm and comfortable. I was greatly looking forward to the next couple of weeks, spent in the busy, bustling community of Harts Hill. I took a huge bite from a doorstep ham sandwich and finished my second pint of foaming best bitter. I licked my lips; I was really beginning to feel good now. Fred, my 20-stone brother-in-law, was up at the bar getting two more pints for us. I relaxed completely as the club secretary called the room to order before the evening's entertainment began. I felt good; it was grand to be back up north!

I sat back in the chair, supped my third pint, ate ravenously from the huge plate piled high with thickly cut meat sandwiches, and realised I felt entirely at home. It was a good feeling, right enough. As I finished my third pint and munched away at the last of the sandwiches, it occurred to me that I had hardly thought of Gaynsford while I had been away. Perhaps I had been too busy enjoying myself? Well, I had certainly done that over the previous couple of weeks or so… and now? I was greatly looking forward to the next couple of weeks before I had to return to the town I called home.

That was a couple of weeks away, and for now, we were leaving the Briggthorpe Working Men's Club and were intending to stop and have a pint or two at the Coalbeck Miners' Club, and probably at least one at the Penniwell Top Club, and maybe another at the Harts Hill Social Club! We would drive home to Ploughman's Cottage and our Dorrie several pints to the good.

Chapter 33

I HAD A very eventful fortnight in Harts Hill, and the events that occurred had quite an effect upon my life, so that, later on… oh well! Now I am jumping the gun, so to speak! Let's go along at a slower pace, and I will make matters more clear.

As I. have already intimated, the next few days were extremely eventful for many different reasons. On that first night of my holiday, the Sunday, after alighting from the bus in the depot at Briggthorpe, we travelled first to the Briggthorpe Working Men's Club, and then onto the Coalbeck Miners' Club. After a pint in there, we moved on to the Tanners Club and had a pint in there, and after that, we went onto Penniwell Top. That was packed out; they had good entertainment on there, apparently, also, National Bingo. We just had the one half in there before moving on to the Harts Hill Social Club. By then it had turned 9.30 p.m. We drank down another half in that establishment then went on to the Roe Deer, which was just down the road from Lumley Lane.

The landlord and landlady of that establishment were Carrie and Tom Fisher. They were a couple in their late thirties and were doing very well with the running of that very popular venue. We had a pint in there, and Fred collected the two seven-pint flagons of cider that Tom had kept for him. We loaded those into the rear of the Land Rover, and then moved on to Mcguigan's, the bakery. They were already baking for the following morning's deliveries. Barney Mcguigan greeted us. He was about five feet five inches tall in his socks, 50 plus, with a beard and a shiny bald head. He was small and very plump. A jolly, red-faced bloke, who loved his job, adored his grub and could drink like a fish!

"How then, bonny lad!" he said to me, shaking my hand heartily until I thought he would pull it out of its socket. "Aw've got all your bread an' pies packed oop for ye," he told Fred.

Together, they commenced loading the food into the back of the Land Rover. Two baskets of bread—it smelled wonderful, the loaves being still hot from the ovens—two, great big boxes of pies, four home-made cakes and a couple of big trifles, well wrapped in deep glass dishes.

"Okay?" said Barney as they finished loading the food into the rear of the vehicle.

"Aw'll bring the eggs an' the goats' milk, and all the vegetables rahnd temorrer," said Fred.

"Ay, that's fine, monn," said little Barney Mcguigan, and he stood on tiptoe to pat Fred on the shoulder. "Aw'll see yo' temorrer then."

"Thanks," said Fred.

We were then off to Ploughman's Cottage!

§≈≈§

I received a very warm welcome from Dorrie. As I had anticipated, she had a meal and a half ready for our consumption. She had cooked faggots with pease pudding and loads of bubble an' squeak. A good, old-fashioned Cockney-type meal; and there was plenty of it! It went down well, followed by a home-made Stotty cake and plenty of cider.

As we sat, eating, drinking and talking, we heard footfalls on the stairs. Suddenly, there was an invasion of the main living room! The five eldest children, Peggy Sue, Frank, June, Archy (Arthur) and Ellen, had come down to see me.

"Boyzie, Boyzie!"

Such tremendous enthusiasm! I was delighted to see them, but they were soon shooed back to bed, as it was school the following day! They started back to school at the end of August in that part of the country.

It was well after two in the morning when I finally got to bed on that first night. On the following morning, when I awoke, the sun was shining. I got up and went over to the little high window in my room. I pulled it open; it was a gorgeous morning corresponding well with my mood!

I heard a noise outside the bedroom door! I was in the box room at the end of the long landing on the second floor of Ploughman's Cottage. The door was flung open and Jackie and Freddie, the seven-year-old twins, came racing in.

"Boyzie!" they breathed, both speaking together.

"Hi there, trouble!" I said, and they both jumped on top of me.

We wrestled on the unmade bed for a moment or two before Fred's voice called out sharply.

"Cum on, yo' two, it's school in a bit."

"Ah naw, Dad!" both boys exclaimed. "Wae wanna stay hoame wi' Boyzie!"

"Cum on, ye'll see 'im tonight. School nah, lads," said Fred, coming up the stairs.

The lads reluctantly left the room. They scampered down, ready to put on coats and shoes, and go off for their first day back at school. It was the end of August and the long summer break, at least for the kids up in that part of the country. I knew the kids in Gaynsford would not be going back for at least another week or ten days. Pity I could not have gone up there before, still, never mind eh? I would see them all later and there were the weekends to look forward to.

I waited until all the kids had gone off to school then went to the bath room and washed from head to foot. Afterwards I returned to my bedroom, the box room, which had been newly decorated and furnished just before my visit. It was small, compact, but very comfortable nonetheless.

I dressed casually and put on my new slippers that Mum had bought me. I went downstairs to the large, inviting front room.

I was greeted by the four youngest boys, Gordon, Steven, David and Andrew, plus several dogs, cats and the three loudly chirruping budgerigars, Daisy, Dickie and Dolly. What a noise! In the midst of it all, our Dorrie was smiling, welcoming, helping me over to the rocking chair where I sat while she handed me a large mug of hot sweet tea.

The four little boys, whom I had never met, were all a little wary of me at first, but once David approached me with a toy car, they were all around me, and fighting to get onto my knee and show me their toys. Dorrie was delighted. I could tell she was very tired with the baby she was carrying, kicking and moving inside her. She told me that later the four lads would be going to the nursery, and that their two grannies, June and Muriel, would be down in a while to have a pot of tea, then they would take the four of them to the nursery for the afternoon session. The nursery was in Gallows Lane, part of the newly extended Gallows Street Primary School.

I had another mug of tea and Dorrie placed a dish of cereal, cornflakes, before me with a plate of hot buttered toast. The lads went out to play in the garden with various animals. The family possessed the following livestock, apart from the 13 children. To begin with they had seven dogs. There was Cassie, the four-year-old springer spaniel bitch, Heidi, the Yorkshire terrier, who was about ten years old, Fliss, the seven-year-old collie, Barley, the two-year-old lurcher, Ruby, the red setter, about a year old, Scrap, the Jack Russell terrier, two years old and very pregnant, and lastly there was Purdy, a six-month-old whippet. Fred was training Purdy to the gun.

The four cats were Pebbles, Roxie, Fifi, and Lulu. They were almost always pregnant and wandered around the house, the garden and the land adjoining the farm. There were also the three budgies, Daisy, Dickie and Dolly, which were very noisy, and two of them talked. Daisy and Dolly both chatted away, but Dickie, the cock bird, had never talked.

There were eight rabbits, 25 guinea pigs, 16 bantam chickens, nine ordinary hens and a cock bird, known as 'The General', because of the way in which he strutted around the yard, caring for his flock! In the pond at the end of the orchard, there were seven ducks. There were also three geese that made a heck of a noise. In their dovecote in the orchard, there were approximately 20 white fantail pigeons. There were three nanny goats, Holly, Clover and Bracken, all young and apparently all good milkers.

Star was an eight-year-old sheltie Shetland pony. He was not yet broken in for riding, but the kids loved him all the same. Star lived in a paddock, and had a stable there. Last of all, although by no means least of all, there was Mabel! Mabel (Mab) was Fred's pride and joy. She was a huge, black Tamworth pig. Not yet 18 months old, Mab was expecting her first litter, and Fred, who looked after over 700 pigs at Bryerwood Farm, believed it would be a big one, possibly as many as fourteen!

Whenever he was not with his pigs on the farm, or with his large family, or training his gun dogs, or racing his pigeons, or down the club for a pint with his mates, then Fred could always be found down by Mab's sty, making a fuss of her, stroking her back, talking to her and making her as comfortable as possible! Fred was a big softie, but he was a brilliant pig man and good at many other tasks on the farm as well. Dorrie and the kids worshipped him, and quite rightly so! He was a great bloke, right enough.

Chapter 34

IT WAS Wednesday morning of the first week of my sojourn in Harts Hill—4 a.m.

I had heard Fred go downstairs earlier on and believed he was still in the house. Everything was peaceful and then I heard Dorrie moaning. I heard her call out for Peggy Sue, the eldest daughter. No response, so I got up and went down to where I could hear my sister calling. Dorrie was lying on their bed in the room at the other end of the landing from mine.

"Aw, Boyzie," she said, sounding a little slurred. "Fred's down with Mab. She started having her litter earlier on this morning, and now—*ooh!*" She stopped speaking, then after a moment, she went on. "An' now—oh, Boyzie, *I'm* starting an' all!"

I was standing in my pyjama bottoms and bare feet in the doorway of my sister's bedroom. I immediately spun around. I went and hammered on the door of Peggy Sue and June's room.

"Quick!" I said through the open door, "your Mam's starting in labour and your Da's out, down with Mab, who's having her litter at the moment!"

"Okay, Uncle Boyzie," said Peggy Sue, who was a very capable young lady, "aw knaw wot to do!"

Within no time, Peggy Sue had organised us all and we all knew exactly what we had to do! I was put in charge of looking after all the younger children, assisted by Frank and June. Peggy Sue started boiling water and attending to her Mam's immediate needs. Arthur, the ten year old, was dispatched to run over to fetch Mrs Peacock, the midwife, who would ring Dr Fletcher. He would come over immediately, Peggy Sue was sure. Ellen was sent over to the orchard where Fred would be sitting with Mabel. She had to run over there and let him know what was occurring.

We all knuckled down and got on with our jobs, under the very capable management of young Peggy Sue, who seemed to be enjoying herself, but underneath all the bravado, she admitted later that she had been quite terrified!

§≈≤§

By the end of that mad, hectic Wednesday morning, when it was time for elevenses, Mabel had given birth to a family of 14 piglets, everyone of them perfect, little Scrap had had seven puppies, and at around 8 a.m. our Doreen had given birth to a ten pound 13-ounce baby girl, with a more than perfect pair of lungs!

For a day or two the household was in near chaos, but on the Friday, both grannies, June and Muriel, my aunt, arrived and 'bottomed' the place between them, doing lots of baking, changing all the beds, cleaning all through, doing plenty of washing and generally making the whole place habitable again!

Dorrie had not been to hospital, although she had had quite a bad time being sick, but by then she was up and sitting in the rocking chair in the main living room, with little Muriel, now three days old, lying beside her in her home-made cradle. She was a lovely baby!

"That's it!" explained Dorrie to me as we sat in the sun-filled main living room on that serene Saturday morning. "I'm not having any more now. That's the last, and I've told Fred so an' all!"

I smiled. If she has told Fred that, then she must definitely mean it, I thought.

§≈≤§

Fred came in at about one o'clock that afternoon and we had pies, beans and chips, great platefuls of food, for dinner, and also the two grannies had made Stotty cakes and bread pudding, so we had some of both of those too—wonderful fare! Just the kind of food I loved. The two grannies, June, who was Fred's mum, and Muriel, Dorrie's aunt, got along very well together. They had descended upon the house and made tremendous strides. By the end of that Saturday, when they both left to return home, Dorrie was back on her feet and feeling much more able to cope. They would be back daily for the foreseeable future, because Fred was so busy with all his responsibilities on the farm, as well as with Mabel. She was looking after her 14 offspring like a 'good 'un', and they were all doing really well.

I was as happy as a lark in the midst of that vast and totally chaotic family!

Chapter 35

SUNDAY DAWNED bright and sunny, the first Sunday of September, the Sunday when I had promised Sandy Christmas and her family that I would go and visit their cousin, Norma Townley, in Lennon Street. I had put the idea to Dorrie and Fred, who seemed quite happy about my doing that, provided I wanted to go.

I thought it would be fun and so, on the Sunday morning, I telephoned Sandy on the number she had given me as we had parted at the bus depot the previous week. A man's voice answered.

"Hello, the Townleys' residence."

"Oh hello, my name is Boyzie," I said. "I... I wanted to speak with Sandy Christmas."

"A'huh," replied the young man, "aw'll get her for ye, wait on a tick."

After a moment, Sandy's voice came on the line.

"Boyzie!"

"Hi," I said. "So, you remembered, eh? Is it still on for our picnic?" I asked her.

"Ooh ay!" said Sandy. "We'll send a car around for you at twelve. Sound okay with you?"

I said it sounded grand, and that I would look forward to seeing them all again soon. In the meantime, Fred had invited me to the orchard to meet Mab's new family.

"Would yo' like one?" he asked me.

I laughed.

"How can I?" I said.

"We'd look after it for yo' an' kipp it 'ere, an' all," said Fred, with great enthusiasm. "The bairns 'ud luv to look after another 'un for yo', Boyzie."

I thought about it and then said:

"Okay, why not? Will you choose one for me?"

We chose her together; a sturdy little 'un she was. I held her for a few moments and she was very lively and squealed a lot. That seemed to be giving Mab cause for concern, so we put her back in the sty with the others.

"Wot yo' gonna call her, Boyzie?" asked Fred.

I thought about it and then decided I would like to call her Fay. I became the owner of a piglet called Fay. Fred said that when she grew older she must have a sty of her own, and he, Frank and Arthur would build one adjacent to Mab's when the right time came.

We returned to the house and ate a hearty breakfast. I spent the remainder of the morning playing with the youngsters and some of the dogs. Little Scrap was doing her best to care for her puppies, one of which had died soon after birth, and there were now three dogs and three bitches left alive. Scrap was exhausted, so the girls and Frank were doing their best to help her to care for her six surviving pups. I was able to help give them some milk through a dropper that morning, and I think I was fairly successful.

Two of the cats were pregnant again! Honestly, that household!

§•§

At approximately midday, a big black Vauxhall of the old family saloon type arrived outside Ploughman's Cottage, and I was taken to the gateway by Peggy Sue, Frank and Arthur. They said cheerio to me and I told them I would be back later that evening.

The car was driven by Eddie, one of Norma's sons. He introduced himself and his girlfriend, Jan, and then we drove off. Within about 15 minutes, we were at the house in Lennon Street, which was in the midst of the vast Penniwell Estate. The estate had a reputation for being rough, but the people there were the greatest and, if they liked you, they would do anything in the world for you. If they didn't—then brother! Watch out and keep looking over your shoulder!

I was warmly welcomed at the house by everyone present. Eddie introduced me to his three brothers and their girlfriends. There were George and Meg, Kenny and Sue and Vinnie and Sam (Samantha), who was a tall leggy blonde, and a mouthy young lass, but nevertheless, she was hearty and very pleasant—somewhat over-friendly, if you know what I mean! Also in the house were Norma and her current 'fella', whose name was Charlie Ford. Chas was in his mid to late thirties and worked as a milkman. Sandy was there, with her four offspring, Randle, Dominic, Tyler and little Dillon, all of whom were delighted to see me. Also, Norma's daughter, Heather, who was almost 15 and a fine, well-made young woman, plus Norma's three youngest children, Benson, nine years, Lou ise, eight years and Julie Ann, who was seven years old. Quite a house full!

Later, Babs, Norma's daughter, was coming with her partner, Tommy Twigg (Twiggy, the rat-catcher), plus their six young children, all under six years old. We would certainly be quite a party for our trip to the Donkey Moor that beautiful sunny Sunday afternoon.

The women of the family had been very busy. The picnic hampers were packed, just a few last-minute items to be placed in them. Three big bags were also packed with items that might be needed for a day on Donkey Moor. Although the afternoon was beautiful, fine and warm, macs had been packed for the youngsters because, well, you never knew! Everyone seemed in a state of high excitement!

At approximately 12.30 p.m., after I had been in the house at Lennon Street for about ten minutes, another car arrived. That car contained the rest of the family who had not yet arrived; Norma's eldest daughter, Babs, plus her partner, Twiggy, and their six young children. I was in the parlour talking to Norma and Sandy as they arrived. I could almost feel Norma's attitude change as they paraded into the already crowded house! Sandy must have felt it too, but neither of us said anything at the time.

After a short while we all began to walk out to the waiting transport. Most of us who were older were carrying bags or coats or something with us. There seemed to be so many people, so many children. I wondered how we would all get to the picnic site on Donkey Meadow.

The two youngest of Norma's sons, Eddie and Vinnie, with their girlfriends, Jan and Sam, went off on motorcycles. George and Kenny, the two eldest lads, plus Chas Ford and Tommy Twigg, managed to pack the rest of us and all the other belongings into their own four vehicles, including the big black family saloon, in which I had travelled earlier, and once we were all settled, we set off in a small convoy, with the two younger sons acting as outriders.

It was all very jolly, at least it should have been, but somehow there was an atmosphere! I could not tell why. It was not straight-forward; it was like a strained atmosphere between two factions. I puzzled about it as I sat in the car with Sandy and her four children, plus Kenny and his girlfriend. Sue, Kenny's girlfriend, was a most attractive redhead, and she was full of chat and fun. When she eventually subsided into silence, sitting close beside her 'fella' as he drove towards Donkey Meadow, Sandy, who was sitting in the back of the vehicle with me and her two younger offspring, spoke.

"Aw knaw you are wonderin' abaht Norma an' Babs. Well, when we get there, an' we can get a chance to be on ah r awn with the bairns, aw'll tell yo' things, an' then you'll understand all abaht it!"

"Okay!" I said, intrigued.

We arrived at the picnic site on Donkey Meadow in the midst of the North Yorkshire Moors. It was mid-afternoon by then. The drive had been pleasant, but quite long, and Sandy's children were all rather restless. We played some games before we sat down and enjoyed our marvellous picnic. There was certainly plenty of good food, and there was wine, beer in cans and plenty of soft drinks for the bairns.

I bit into a doorstep ham sandwich and asked Sandy, who was seated beside me under some shady trees, what she had meant when she talked about telling me everything when we were travelling in the car. Norma came over to us, so Sandy again deferred in telling me what I wanted to know.

"Well now," said Norma, a short, rather plump woman in her late thirties, who wore her hair loose so that it flowed down her back. The fringe seemed to hang in her eyes and hide her elfin face. Norma looked younger than her years, even though she was rather on the 'hippy' side! "Are you enjoying yoursel', Boyzie?"

"Oh, it's all smashing!" I exclaimed, feeling wonderful.

Norma laughed.

"We're all havin' a great time," she said, and turned to walk back to where her sons, their girlfriends, plus Heather and the younger children, and Babs and her tribe were all seated.

Randall and Dominic were with them, but Dillon and Tyler were with Sandy and me. We were picnicking in the shade, laughing and talking while Dillon dozed idly in the sunshine and his elder sister picked daisies for a daisy chain, allegedly for her mother's hair. Tyler was a lovely child, full of romantic ideals, and she was so innocent.

Sandy was engaged in telling me the saga of why it was that there was a terrible atmosphere between Norma and her eldest daughter. Apparently, after Mike Taylor had left her, Norma had set her cap at little Tommy Twigg, the rat-catcher. Tommy, who was 26 at the time, was more than flattered that a woman like Norma would want him, and he moved in with her right away. They lived together for the best part of two years, and then young Tommy began to notice Barbara! One day when Norma arrived home, she found Tommy Twigg in her bed with her eldest daughter, and she threw them both out on the spot! Later she learned that they had moved in together and that Barbara was pregnant by Tommy. She was furious! She vowed and declared that she would have nothing to do with the family from that day onwards! Barbara had three sets of twins by Tommy Twigg! Jamie and Alex were two and a half years old and very lively. Ruth and Rachel were 16 months old and they were both walking and talking, after a fashion. The youngest set of twins was Thomas and Emma, just a few weeks old. The family was completed by the presence of two dogs, a two-year-old Dobermann pinscher called Bilko, who was very large and very boisterous, also a six-month-old Rottweiler bitch called Anna. Two most unsuitable dogs for a family in which there were three sets of twins under three years old, at least one would have thought so!

Barbara, not yet 21 years of age, seemed totally oblivious to anyone's thoughts or remarks regarding the size of her family etc., and kept making 'sheep's eyes' at her beloved Tommy. Norma, however, although she adored all her grandchildren, tried her best to ignore her daughter and her daughter's 'consort', but it did make life rather difficult.

All in all, the day went well up on the moors. That was until towards six o'clock that evening.

§❧§

At around that time, we were starting to pack up in order to go home. The kids were tired and the dogs had had enough. Apart from Bilko and Anna, the two dogs belonging to Babs and Tommy, Norma had also taken along her old dog, an ageing Scottie called Bridie, who suffered from arthritis and was not the most friendly or pleasant animal in God's world! Norma thought the world of Bridie, and liked her to be near her. As we were packing up and rounding up the strays, dogs and children alike, we suddenly heard a loud anguished cry from Babs.

"Aw, my bairns! Where are my bairns?"

Immediately, everyone stopped doing whatever they were engaged upon and looked over to where Babs and Tommy Twigg stood with four of their children, and Norma, Heather and Chas Ford. Chas was a deaf mute. Although he was a milkman and ran his round extremely efficiently, he was, nevertheless, a deaf mute, having neither hearing nor speech. He was a tall, strong, macho man, however, and a marvel around the house. He could apparently turn his hand to anything in the practical sphere and, according to Norma, passed on to me by Sandy, he was 'good in bed an' all'!

He stood beside Norma and Babs, a strong arm encircling the shoulders of each woman, while Tommy stood behind Babs, one of the younger set of twins in each arm, with Ruth and Rachel whining, one clinging to each of his legs. Norma was endeavouring to talk to Babs. At that moment Sandy suddenly realised that Randle and Dominic had gone off with Jamie and Alex, and that they weren't around either. We had four little boys missing. For the next couple of hours life was positively frantic!

Although we tried to keep things low key, so as not to upset the other children, everyone among us adults was very worried indeed. The moors were vast. Four little boys having adventures together could literally be anywhere, and before the heavy mists of the night fell we had to find them!

§❧§

It was very late in the evening when we eventually discovered the four of them, huddled up together beneath some trees. They were some distance from Donkey Meadow, where we had played games and had our picnic earlier on that day. Randle and Dominic were thrilled and delighted to see us as we all went towards them. Everyone had been involved in the search, and had left Tommy and Sam to look after the rest of the bairns. Bilko and Anna had come along with us, and they had romped on ahead and had unearthed the four little scallywags, and forced them from their hidey-hole. They were all mightily relieved to see us!

Jamie and Alex ran crying into their mother's and grandmother's arms. Randle and Dom came over to us, and Randle was excitedly telling us what had occurred and how they had come to be where they were found.

"We were in the woods, walking in deeper and deeper, then Jamie and Alex got tired. Me and Dom was having adventures, and we didn't want to come out, but the twins kept crying. We started to find our way out of the woods and as we came to the top of the path where we had started, Dom thought he heard the ice cream man! When we got out of the trees, we could see it wasn't an ice cream van, it was a smashing little sports car! A lady got out of it and she started to talk to us. She asked if this was Donkey Meadow. I told her yes, it was near to Donkey Meadow. Then she said..."

He stopped speaking and waited for a moment or two as though unsure if he ought to proceed. My mind was racing! A smart little sports car, a horn that sounded like an ice cream van, a lady driver. No! No! It couldn't be! She was miles away from there.

"Go on, Randle, what happened next, son?" I asked encouragingly.

Randle came and stood beside me, putting his hand into mine.

"She… she asked us if we knew someone called Boyzie," he said.

There was an uneasy silence, and I was the one who felt the most uneasy! So, Johnnie was up there, but why? What did she want, and why on earth had she tried to kidnap four little boys? I did not understand, but I kept remembering how concerned Eve and Eric had been about our continuing relationship and the closeness of our time spent together over that wonderful weekend. Yes, I was remembering, but nothing I remembered was making any sense. Randle was continuing his monologue of the afternoon's events.

"So, me and Dom said, yes, we knew Boyzie. We said he was a friend of our Mam's!"

Yes, of course, they would say that wouldn't they? Two innocent young kids, they wouldn't think there was any harm in that! I was beginning to understand. Everyone else remained silent, so I again encouraged young Randle to proceed with his account of what had occurred that afternoon.

"Yes, go on, son, you're telling it ever so well! What happened then, Randle?"

The little boy, still with his hand in mine, now laid his head on my left shoulder. He started to cry.

"Oh, Boyzie, I hope we never done nuffink wrong! I like you, Boyzie. I hope you and Mam's not too cross with us, cos the lady wanted to know, so we towd her!"

I put my arms around his small, shaking body, which was now racked with sobs! He snuggled into my arms and Dominic came and stood beside me on my right. Everyone else gathered around.

"Hush, shh now, Randle, it's all right, mate. Nobody's angry with you, you did right to tell the lady what she wanted to know, but maybe you should have thought a bit, son. You see, it's not a good idea to get too friendly with strangers!"

"But… but she said she knew you and she knew our Mam," said Dominic, since Randle was crying hard now and could not speak to me!

"Oh, she said that, did she?" I replied, and, still holding Randle close to me, I placed a comforting arm around the shoulders of Sandy's second eldest child, Dominic.

Sandy moved in and took Randle from me, patting his back and telling him gently and soothingly not to cry.

"It's all reet nah, mate, you're safe nah an' back with us! Boyzie is right; you should have come back an' checked with us if it was all right to go off with that lady in her sports car."

Randle spluttered into life again.

"But we did, Mam, we started to come back towards you. The lady said she wanted to see Boyzie and you and everyone. She had come to Donkey Meadow to join us, she said! So we all started walking back to you and then…"

He stopped again and burst into fits of crying, so while Sandy held him close and consoled him, Dom went on with the story.

"So, as we got nearer to you, she stopped, and she was looking straight ahead, at you an' Mam, Boyzie! After a few seconds she said would we all like to go into the village with her and find a shop where we could buy lemonade and ice creams. It was warm and we were all thirsty, so we said, yes please, then we all got into her car and off we went to Bow Bridge."

Bow Bridge was the village about four or five miles down the road, and there, apparently, was a thriving shop that sold everything, and at the back, there was a cafe. It seemed they went there, and Johnnie, for I had no doubt now whom it was who had taken the four lads for a ride in her sporty little car, had bought them big milkshakes, burgers and French fries, and had then left, taking with her bottles of lemonade, huge bars of chocolate and five very big ice creams, each with a chocolate flake stuck in the top. The lads had thought it all wonderful, and why wouldn't they? All that attention from a stranger, but she wasn't a stranger was she? She had said that she knew both Sandy and me, and she had gone to Donkey Meadow to join us on our day out, so of course the lads thought it was all right to be with her. We managed to console them all then we finished packing up our things and drove back to Lennon Street in convoy.

I was not invited into the house when we got back, but Jan and Eddie said they would drive me back home to Ploughman's Cottage. I said my goodbyes to everyone else, and felt the atmosphere around me was rather cool. Norma would not say anything to me and Sandy said a very hurried, 'goodbye Boyzie' then, as an afterthought, 'thanks for helping out with Randle and Dom, you know!'

I sat in the back of the big Vauxhall as we travelled towards Ploughman's Cottage in a state of some apprehension. I also felt rather angry, angry with Sandy, Norma and everyone for believing that I had anything to do with what had happened. I hardly knew Johnnie Friscoe! I had no idea what she had planned or why she had decided to go up there to find me. Perhaps she was under the misapprehension that she and I really meant something to one another, but we had had a pleasant evening together! Everything had been right, so the evening had been a tremendous success, but that was all! We were not engaged or anything like that, so I could put my arm around Sandy and kiss and cuddle with her, and there were no strings. That was what Johnnie had seen! That was what had enraged her and why she had taken the four little boys away from us that afternoon—to get back at *me*!

As I was dropped outside Ploughman's Cottage and said my farewells, somewhat hastily, to Ed and Jan, I found myself wondering what else she might try. The feeling persisted within me that Johnnie Friscoe was nearby and that she could possibly be a threat to me and to those I loved. Therefore, I had only one course of action—to cut the holiday in Harts Hill short and return to Gaynsford somewhat earlier than planned.

Chapter 36

ON WEDNESDAY morning, after a substantial breakfast of home killed bacon, fresh double-yolk eggs, tomatoes, mushrooms, baked beans, black pudding and fried bread, followed by toast and marmalade, and several mugs of hot sweet tea, Fred drove me to Harts Hill Railway Station in time to catch the 10.45 a.m. train to Briggthorpe.

I had decided to go home by train rather than coach, which meant purchasing a single ticket from Harts Hill to Gaynsford, however, that was not a problem. The 10.45 a.m. from Harts Hill was a slow train and did not arrive in Briggthorpe until approximately 11.35 a.m., where I would have to wait a short while before catching the 12.02 p.m. train to South borough, which got me into that city's station at 3 p.m.

I had over three-quarters of an hour to wait at Southborough, so I got the porter to take me into the cafe bar where I was able to have a mug of hot chocolate. As I sat with my bags surrounding me, I drank from the large mug and ravenously tucked into the big bag of sandwiches that Doreen had insisted the girls made up for me to take along that day. Doreen had been very unhappy about me cutting the holiday short, and she and Fred had sat down and talked to me about it for some considerable time, trying to persuade me to stay. I was determined to go, primarily because I wanted to ensure the safety of my relations and friends. I did not wish anything else to happen!

"Who is she?" asked Doreen when we were discussing my main reason for leaving. "How did you come to know her, Boyzie?"

I told them how I had met Johnnie while staying with Eve and

Eric, and how we had become friends. I told them that we had made love together and that she had driven with me in the last race of the day on that Sunday, despite the misgivings of Eric and the concerns of Eve. I said that she must have reckoned we were going steady or something, because she was pursuing me from one part of the country to the other, or so it seemed!

"Are yo' sure it wor her who tried to kidnap the bairns on Sunday?" asked Fred.

"I'm pretty certain," I said, "going by the description of the car and everything that Randle was able to tell me!"

"Then we ought to tell the police!" said Aunt Muriel decisively.

"No!" I said with equal decision. "Everything is okay now, the lads are all back home, and nothing would be gained by telling the police!"

"But if she tries it again?" said Doreen.

"She won't," I said, "not if I'm back in Gaynsford."

"But wot abaht yo', Boyzie! Will yo' be aal reet, mate?" Fred's voice held real concern.

"I'm sure I'll be fine," I said with feeling.

As I sat there on the train, which was now pulling into Southborough Midland Station in the late afternoon of a warm Wednesday at the beginning of September, I was not sure! I was anxious. I was afraid, and I was quite certain that I had not heard the last of Johnnie Friscoe. Of course, I was right! She would manifest herself again and again in the course of the next few years of my life, culminating in a fairly frenzied attack upon my person, but at that time I did not know about that. That was to happen a long way in the future.

I was in the cafe bar on Southborough Station, surrounded by all my bags, awaiting the train that would take me back to Gaynsford.

CONCLUSION

I T HAD just turned 8 a.m. on Monday, 1st January, 1990—the
start of a new year and a new decade, the last of that millen-
nium. I had done it! I had successfully completed my 80-hour
music marathon on Sunny Gold Radio, the best songs all year
long, to ring the old year out and the new year in. I had so much
to look forward to in the future, and it had all started with great
hope!

At midnight the place had been packed to the rafters with people, and the celebrations had gone on long into the early hours of
the morning. At around 4 a.m. there had been a temporary lull,
and some degree of sanity had been restored, but at the culmination of my 80-hour broadcast, the celebrations had started up
again in earnest. The first record I had played after the chimes of
Big Ben and the bells to ring out the old and ring in the new was
'Happy New Year' by Abba. That was playing as my music marathon came to an end. I had had so many cards from listeners all
over the county. I had had so many phone calls congratulating me
on my performance. I was feeling cock-a-hoop then, and not a bit
tired, but I knew as the record finished that tiredness would kick
in very shortly and that when I finally got to bed I would sleep the
sleep of the just. What I did not know was that there was someone
lurking very close to me who wished me to sleep the sleep of the
damned!

At the end of the Abba record, I turned on my mike for the last
time for a while.

"This is Rick Dee saying a heartfelt thank you to everyone who has been listening and everyone who has been working with me over the past 80 hours. I never thought we would crack it, but we've done it, you and me. We've come through it together, and I want you all to know that I could never have done it without all your good wishes and your phone calls and all. Bless you and thank you all from the bottom of my heart! This is your mate, Rick Dee, signing off for now, but I'll be back again very soon. Don't you touch that dial now, you hear?"

I then played in the Sunny Gold Radio jingle, and the news jingle. Trevor Brock was then reading the news summary and I was leaving the studio—the room in which I had spent most of the previous 80 hours alone—with a large escort all around me. We walked out of the studio, through the main ops room then out to the visitors' room. There I was stalled while even more people wished to speak to me, patting me on the back, rubbing my shoulders, pumping my hands, everyone congratulating me on my great achievement! Bill Grundy was absolutely thrilled by what had transpired, and he was now my ardent devotee!

"Well done, mate, well done indeed," he said, squatting at my feet and pumping both my hands until I thought they would come off my wrists.

I laughed. Now I was starting to feel tired and my eyelids were drooping. I had a raging thirst!

I eventually stepped out into the sunlight of a frosty, but fine and pleasant, morning in January. I was still being congratulated. I stood for a few moments, just drinking in the good clean fresh air—it was so good! I was still surrounded by people, so I did not l take too much notice of the voice behind me.

"Happy New Year, mister!"

I then felt a blow between my shoulders and a stabbing pain in my chest! I fell forwards. Pandemonium ensued all around me! I was aware of voices shouting my name, a young woman scream-ing, someone being tackled and eventually being brought down to the ground by one of the police personnel. It was Johnnie!

Vaguely, through a haze all around me, I could hear her

screaming obscenities at those who held her down! Someone was bending over me. My whole body was shaking. The voices and everything happening around me were becoming more and more hazy. I heard the sound of a police siren and then someone shouting for an ambulance for me. After a few moments I heard another siren and deemed that the ambulance must be on its way.

So! She had done for me at last, and on the first day of a new year and a new decade. Johnnie! Johnnie Friscoe, the psychopath. Well, she'd had plenty of practise and now she had succeeded! She would pay, oh yes, she would pay dearly for her crimes, and if she thought I was done for, well, she was very much mistaken. Oh no, I may have been down, but I was not yet out of the game. As far as I was concerned, even if what she had done to me left me permanently in a wheelchair, I would have my day in court with Johnnie Friscoe! I was determined about that. I would see her go down for all the crimes she had endeavoured to perpetrate over the previous years.

A police van came and took her away. Detective Sergeant Jane Bonnier and Detective Constables Joe Capper and Andy Mullins were all kneeling around me, waiting with me until the ambulance arrived to take me into hospital. Bill Grundy was also close by and there were several other people around me, but I knew very little about that; I was hanging on by a thread. I was still thinking about all I had to live for!

I thought about Sandy and her family. I thought about my mother-in-law, Lizzie, and about Trudy and Mick, and Dave and his new young wife and family. I thought of all the lads who had formed a network to protect me! I thought of all the drivers who worked for Phoenix Cars and who had been such good mates to me. I thought of Wayne Clarke, Chris Braun and Kev, his brother. I thought of all my wonderful friends, the staff who worked with me at the Family Support Centre in Bread Street. I thought of my great mate, poor Rob McCallasky, who had been killed in Glosport on that fateful Saturday night at the end of 1978, and as I thought of Rob, suddenly his cousin, Father Martyn, the priest, was kneeling beside me, holding my right hand in both of his and talking to me quietly. Dear Father Martyn!

I thought of Marjorie and Alice May McNault. I thought of my family in various parts of the country; of Mum and Dad, of Doreen, Fred and all their tribe, of Sid and his new wife, Brenda, of my aunts, uncles, cousins, and of my lovely late Granny Annie. I thought about my late and still lamented, and indeed much loved wife, Suzy.

No! I was not going to die—not yet. Not to satisfy someone like mad Johnnie Friscoe. I would live to have my day in court with her—and I did!

Well, that's another story, maybe even another book!

Book Three

Stumbling On!

INTRODUCTION

Tuesday, 23rd January, 1990—7 a.m.

I WAS VERY comfortable! I was lying snug and warm in a fresh white bed, spread over with a clean white quilt, in a small private room off the main hospital ward. Sister Brennan had just been in with one of the nurses—I think it was Nurse Baxter!

"Wash him, and be gentle with him, nurse!" she said quietly.

"Yes, Sister!" said Nurse Baxter, dear Joy Baxter, who among all the others had been so kind to me since my arrival there at the County Hospital in Gaynsford, North Midlands.

Gently, carefully, Joy Baxter, talking to me all the time, lifted me up in the bed and prepared to wash me all over! I had to have blanket baths at that time!

"You might sit out of bed today for a while, Boyzie!"

Joy watched for a response from me! I nodded my head vigorously, and she laughed.

"Yes! I reckon as how you'd like that, wouldn't you, my love?"

Yes! Oh yes, Joy! I would! She washed me all over, gently and thoroughly, before laying me down again in a nice comfortable bed!

"The doctors will come around after breakfast and they will say if you can get up or not," said Sister Janet Brennan, who had just walked into my small private room.

It was being paid for by my brother, Eric. He had been visiting me on a regular basis since the episode on 1st January, the episode of my life in which I had been beaten over the head and so cruelly and heartlessly stabbed by that crazy woman, my ex-lover, Johnnie Friscoe!

I could feel my face becoming hot as I thought of her! Immediately, the Sister's cool hands were upon me! Stroking my forehead, feeling my face and the heat that was rising in it!

"Shh! Hush now, Boyzie! It's aal reet, luv! It's aal reet, mon! There's nobody here to hurt you now! Shh! Hush now! It'll soon be breakfast time, and we'll get you a nice big bowl of cereal and some toast and marmalade, eh, and a big mug of tea! How's that sound, luv, eh?"

Dear Sister Brennan! I knew she was being kind, and the tears began to well up in my eyes! She gently and patiently wiped them away, and then propped me up in the bed and gave me my head-phones! I put them over my ears and listened to Sunny Gold Radio, the sounds of summer all year long! Of course, I did not work for them any more! They could not keep me on, and I understood that, but Bill Grundy, the station manager, had been very kind to me! He and his family had sent flowers for me and he had visited me and brought fruit, chocolate etc., also my wages up to the last day I had worked for them.

I still remembered with pleasure the 80 hour music marathon I had managed to achieve to see in the New Year! I still remembered all that had happened afterwards, and how I had ended up in that small private room at the County Hospital. Oh yes, I remembered! As I sat up in the bed, my head resting against four or five pillows banked up behind me, I closed my eyes and let my mind wander—back to 1978, back to the Christmas of that year, but first of all I thought back to the time after my return home from my long Summer holiday, that wonderful holiday during which I had visited all my family in various parts of England!

Chapter 1

As I thought back over the years to 1978, my memory was like a diary. I could remember past years and past events during those years with amazing clarity, but when I tried to remember more recent events clearly, it was like a screen came down and intervened between my thoughts and my idea of dates, times etc., and the order of the events! Thus, more recent events were not nearly so clear to me!

I was told that I must not worry! That was apparently how things occurred when someone had been through what I had experienced over the previous few days and weeks. Still, it didn't worry me! I wondered if I would ever be able to think of more recent events clearly again. I clung to the hope that my fuddled brain and confused mind would clear and that once more I would be able to read all my thoughts clearly and have perfect understanding of everything that had transpired!

Chapter 2

Wednesday, 6th September, 1978.

IT WAS a pleasant warm day to travel. I was up early. Fred and the girls ministered to my requirements. Peggy Sue, the eldest of our Doreen's 13 children, prepared a very large pack of sandwiches, scones, cake, etc., for my consumption on the journey home to Gaynsford, and Fred cooked me an extremely large breakfast!

Later I said tearful goodbyes to Doreen, Peggy Sue, Ellen, Arthur and other members of the family. They made me promise faithfully that I would soon go and visit them again!

"He's got to come back anyway!" boomed Fred heartily. "He's got a new pet nah!"

It was true. I had been given one of Mab's young piglets. Mabel (Mab), Fred's own 'pet' pig who lived in the barn at the end of the large orchard adjacent to the yard and kitchen garden at Ploughman's Cottage, had borne a litter of 14 piglets on the very same day when our Dorrie had given birth to baby Muriel. Fred and the boys of that large and boisterous family of Dingles, based at Ploughman's Cottage, Lumley Lane in Harts Hill, had talked me into having one of them. Jackie and Freddie, the twins, had helped me to choose the sturdiest of them and we had christened her Fay. She was delightful, and I had told my twin nephews that they would have the care of her and bring her up for me! They were very thrilled!

Later, Fred drove me to the railway station at Harts Hill and I caught the train down to Brigthorpe. From there I boarded a train direct to Southborough Midland, where I had to wait a while for a connection to Gaynsford Parkway.

I was now going into the home straight, and would soon be stepping from the train after my long journey, then I would get a taxi, one from Phoenix Cars, and would soon arrive at 23 Rutland Close—home!

§❧§

I alighted from the train with all my bags and was immediately greeted by young Danny Shaw. He worked on the station and was a friend of mine.

"Hey-up then, Boyzie! Home from your holidays, yeh?"

"That's right, Dan!" I told him, and we walked together to the taxi rank outside the main entrance of the station.

Danny Shaw and Barry Barnet loaded my bags into Baz's cab, and we drove off towards Rutland Close, Parkside. It felt good to be back home again, although I was still angry about having to cut my holiday short because of what had occurred on that Sunday when I was out with Sandy Christmas and all her family, picnicking in Donkey Meadow! I dared not take the risk of anything else happening to my relatives and friends in the north-east, and it may well have done if I had not left accordingly. Oh yes, it may well have done and perhaps events at that time would not have turned out so well! Who knew?

I consoled myself with the fact that I had used my head rather than my heart on that occasion. My heart was still up there in North Yorkshire! I loved it up there. I had thought that maybe I had found a new love up there, but Sandy had been very cold towards me when we parted on that Sunday. Despite my hopes to the contrary, she had not telephoned me or tried to get in touch with me before I left Harts Hill. Ah well, so much for holiday romances! In my secret heart, I knew it had been more than that between Sandy and me!

We were turning into Rutland Close, and pulling up outside my house. Ooh, it felt good to be home!

ౘ౸౨

The first thing I did when I got in, after removing my coat, kicking off my shoes, and after Baz had helped me to carry all my bags upstairs and stow them together on my bed, was to go into the kitchen, light the stove and put the kettle on for a nice cuppa! I was ready for one! I had only had cans to drink from on the long journey, but I had eaten very well! Doreen's daughters had supplied me with plenty of grub, but I would probably cook myself a big fry up later on! In the meantime...

I heard the urgent ring of the doorbell. Oh help! I knew, before I even went to the front door, who would be standing outside waiting for me! It would be Don, Dave and Dek, the Williams boys, and perhaps even some of their Gypsy mates! I had only just arrived home, so I did not want their company at that moment! Nevertheless, I left the kettle merrily boiling on the gas stove and went to the front door.

Yes! I was partially right anyway! There on my driveway stood the three Williams boys, Don, Dave and Dek, all in their twenties, all big, strapping lads, each one being well over six feet in height! There in front of them stood their Uncle Basil. Basil was smaller than his three nephews! He lived with Vera and her husband, Cyril, his brother.

"Hello, Boyzie!" said Basil. "Have you had a good break?"

"Hi! Yeh, I've thoroughly enjoyed it! I've only just got in lads, so-"

Basil cut me short.

"We've got some bad news for you, Boyzie!" he said.

He shuffled his feet, and the three Williams brothers moved in so they were standing all around me, leaning their full weight against me! Don stood on my right, with his head planted on my shoulder! Dave stood on my left, his face buried in my left shoulder. Dek leaned against me and buried his face in my chest! I felt acutely embarrassed! Basil, their uncle, shuffled his feet and spoke awkwardly.

"They are very upset! Their dad's in hospital! The County! He-he had two heart attacks while you were away, Boyzie! Vera's down there with him nah! They-they say..."

He hesitated there, as the three big men gathered around me were all crying hard and I was endeavouring to console them! Basil went on in a querulous voice:

"They say they reckon he won't last the night, Boyzie!"

Chapter 3

BREAKFAST WAS over on the ward, and I had had mine! The night staff had gone off and Sister Janet Brennan had been replaced by Sister Christina Rayfield, a big jolly Jamaican woman, who was always laughing! The staff at the County Hospital were really lovely with no exceptions! Sister Rayfield was making me ready for the doctors' visit!

"Dey may say as how you can get up an' sit in a chair today, my dear!" she told me. "How would you like that eh, Boyzie?"

"I'd love it, Sister!" I freely admitted.

"Well," she said, as she tidied my bed with the help of Nurse Helen Tidy, a very appropriate name for a young nurse, "we'll jus' have to see what happens!"

There was a smile in her voice, which told me that Sister Rayfield had a notion as to what would happen, and that to all intents and purposes, I would find myself sitting out in a chair either by my bed or out on the balcony, although perhaps it was a little fresh for that!

Later, the two doctors made their tour of the ward and visited me in my little private abode! Dr Chen was male and he was Chinese. Dr Mishra was female, and she was from India. They were both young, and both very friendly and pleasant towards me.

"So," said Dr Chen, "you want to get up today, Boyzie?"

"Yes please!" I said with feeling!

"Good!" he said, and squeezed my hand.

While he took my blood pressure, Dr Mishra spoke.

"You must promise to behave yourself, Boyzie! No flirting! No chasing the nurses all around the ward, mind!"

I laughed! We all laughed! They had realised that my sense of humour was very acute!

"Aw! I can't say about that Dr Mishra, but I reckon perhaps I'm too poorly to chase anyone around, as yet anyway!"

"Aw well!" said Dr Chen. "Perhaps you shouldn't get up yet then, Boyzie!"

Again, we all laughed, and I made them both solemnly promise that I could get up and sit out beside my bed with my headphones on. Yes! I could do that, so later on, I was helped from the bed by Sister Rayfield, who settled me in the chair and gave me my headphones!

The radio was my own and the headphones also! Eric had brought them for me. Good old Eric! He had been so good to me since all that started, and it was strange, because hitherto, our relationship had never been all that great. Still, he had certainly come up trumps when required to do so!

"Now den, my dear, are you comfortable enough at the moment?"

"Yes! Yes! I'm fine now, Sister, thank you!"

She laughed.

"I'll get one of the nurses to bring you a drink in a little while!" she said, and then she had gone!

I was left alone! Left alone, to continue with my own thoughts, which were playing back like a long-playing cassette with pictures in my head!

Chapter 4

CYRIL WILLIAMS died on Friday, 8th September, in the early hours of the morning. Vera was beside his bed when he died, but his sons were not there. They were all at my house, sleeping there! I felt it was the least I could do to help my friend and dear neighbour, Vera, who had been a tower of strength to me when my lovely Susan died, and who had always been there for me ever since.

While I was away, for example, she had had my keys. She had cleaned all through the house for me and had stocked up the fridge and the freezer before I returned home. Good old Vera. I would pay her for all that stuff when things calmed down a bit, but not then! No, not then!

The three lads were very quiet, often tearful, and I had all on to look after them and motivate them. Basil, if you please, had found himself a lady friend! I was glad for him. Baz deserved some good luck and some fun out of life, and I was pleased that he had met Joyce and that they were going steady. He was spending most of his time either with Vera at the hospital or around at Joyce's at that time, so I had said I would look in on the house and feed the animals, etc., etc., and that the lads must come around and stay with me—and so they had done!

On the day of the funeral, I attended, primarily out of affection for my late neighbour, but also to look after Don, Dave and Dek. I knew they would need me! Vera was inconsolable, and she had her brothers, sisters and other relatives around her. Two more of Cyril's brothers went, along with one of his sisters, who seemed rather severe, and also Baz, who took Joyce along with him! Not the most tactful of moves in my opinion, but nobody said anything about it! The three lads, tall, well-built, shaking in their shoes, smart suits and ironed shirts, stood all around me, leaning heavily upon me for support!

When they were reading the last part of the service concerned with the cremation of Cyril's body, all three lads buried their faces in various parts of my body and rocked on their r feet as they sobbed fit to beat the band! I tried in vain to put my arms around the shaking shoulders and trembling bodies of all three of those stout young men, none of whom was the brightest star in the firmament, to endeavour to comfort and console, but my efforts were largely worthless. The three young men clung to me pitifully for the rest of the day, and would not leave my side!

I had to travel home with them and then, because I was concerned for Vera, I allowed them to stay with me one more night! We ended up sleeping together, the four of us, in my king-size bed! The three of them cuddled tight up against me and cried themselves to sleep then they snored for all the world as though they hadn't a single care among them, and I was kept awake all the rest of the night! Still, what could I do? Vera and Cyril had always been good neighbours to me, so it was my turn to repay their kindness to some extent and endeavour to look after those three lost, lonely and unhappy young men to the best of my ability!

Poor Vera! She never fully recovered from her husband's decease. All she wanted to do was to move from the close and settle down somewhere where she felt she and the lads could make a new start. They had gone by the end of October!

At night, for the few weeks before they moved, I would go home regularly from work surrounded by my network of youngsters, to find the three Williams boys and a large number of their Gypsy friends sitting together quietly on my front garden wall!

They would be smoking, talking, listening to music, with their shoes off, feet stuck out in the roadway! I always felt so sorry for the three Williams lads, but Vera needed them. She needed them to be strong for her, and I tried with all my courage, kindness and confidence, to instil this strength into them. I don't really think I succeeded, however!

Chapter 5

On 21st September, the first day of autumn official, the fair arrived on The Green around the corner from Rutland Close. There had been a vast number of vans, buses etc., parked there for some time, but at last, a working fair had arrived and set up for the autumn. The first night it opened for business was actually on the Thursday, the first official day of autumn.

I went along! I took the three Williams boys with me! Loads of the lads from Gunners Lane Academy had said they would be there too! I knew lots of people in the community who were going, and all in all it was a wonderful evening.

The weather was autumnal, but the night was fine. It could not have been better if it had been made especially to order! The smells of the hot dogs, beef burgers etc., wafted over my garden and I could hear the music playing and the stallholders and masters and mistresses of the rides shouting about their wares and the various adventures one could have at that quite large fair! I went on that wonderful night, and several nights afterwards! I usually went at around 7 p.m. and stayed until 10 p.m., when the last ride took place and the fair closed down.

The three Williams boys all got jobs at the fairground, and they thoroughly enjoyed their duties, although those were fairly menial! They positively blossomed as they mixed in with the crowds, undertaking their 'work', either gathering up litter, guiding people to rides, minding other people's stalls or working on some of the game shows etc., etc. Anything, in fact, they were called upon to undertake, those three willing 'giants' did, and for very little in the way of pay or praise. Still, they enjoyed doing the work!

They stayed with me more or less until the family left the close! They moved away on Friday, 27th October, and on the Sunday, after a fantastic night on the previous Saturday, 28th October, the fair trundled off The Green and suddenly summer was gone for good! With the lights, equipment, stalls etc. from the fair, went all the vans, buses etc., and all the Gypsy lads and families! I don't know where they went, but I never saw any of them again.

The Williams family moved to Boston -Drive on the Mount Carmel Estate, and I visited them there. Vera was delighted with her new house, and with her new friend, Frank, whom she had met. The three young men, Don, Dave and Dek, clung to me when they saw me! I gathered they were not mad keen on Frank! Baz married Joyce and they spent their honeymoon in the Isle of Man. I was very happy for Baz; at last he had found someone!

After the departure of the Williams family and of the autumn fair from our area, life continued as normal in the locality of Rutland Close, Parkside! I eventually had new neighbours, but more of them anon.

Chapter 6

I HAD MADE a new friend at the hospital! It happened this way! One afternoon, Sister Rayfield came to me and said:

"You can go an' sit in de day room if you would like, Boyzie! Would you like to do that, my luv?"

Everyone there was so kind to me, and they all called me by my nickname, Boyzie!

"Oh! Could I, Sister? That would be smashing!" I said, with feeling!

Later on, Nurse Gerrard took me through to the day room. There were several blokes in there and one or two women as well. I was talking to a guy called Bryan Lennahan, who came from the Mount Carmel Estate and knew the Williams family who used to be my neighbours in Parkside.

Vera had married her new fellow, a guy called Frank. The three lads, Don, Dave and Derek, never cared for him, but Vera and he worked on them so that eventually the family gelled together into some kind of unit, but he was never really accepted. Apparently, within less than three years, he and Vera had parted, and she now lived on her own with just her three boys for company. They were getting older too! Well we all were, weren't we? I was now in my forties. I would be 43 years old the following June!

Anyway, I sat talking with Bryan Lennahan, and he went off, so two other blokes came to chat with me; a young fellow in his twenties called Scott Jacklin, who was in because he had had a motorcycle accident, and a fellow called Andy. I discovered his name was Andrew David Gange. He was 27 years old, and was ex-army. He had joined the police five years previously on discharge from the army, and then just before Christmas he had had some acid thrown into his eyes! They had managed to save the sight in one eye, but he had lost it entirely in his right one. Still, he was grateful that he still had the full sight in his left eye, and he was going back into the police, although he would probably have a desk job, he reckoned.

Andy and I hit it off straightaway! We had many of the same likes and dislikes as far as sport, music, cars, food etc., were concerned. We were friends right from the start! I was sorry to have to leave him after supper, although I did feel very tired. He came back to my small private room with me, and said, as he sat on the bed, talking to me:

"How abaht this, Boyzie? Why dun't I move in wi' yo'? I'm gonna be here for some time, an' so are you presumably! So, why dun't we ask if we can move in together? What say, mate?"

"Yeh!" I said with enthusiasm "Great, Andy! I reckon that would be smashing!"

He was going to ask them if we could do so, and I would have a word with Eric, who would probably be pleased because I was sure my private room was costing him a packet and a half of money! It would be good to be in a small ward with someone else, especially someone with whom I got on so well. Yes! I would enjoy being friends with Andy Gange, the policeman!

Chapter 7

THAT NIGHT, as I lay in my bed, I went back over the years again! Back to 1978, and the Christmas of that year! It would be my first Christmas without my lovely Susan.

I remembered how wonderful the Christmas of 1977 had been. We had chosen the tree together, and gone carol singing in the cold wind, all around the local neighbourhood! We had delivered cards to everyone we knew in our close and the locality. We had decorated the tree, and Sue had made a wonderful Christmas cake, mince pies, sausage rolls, trifle, a meat loaf, a cheese and tatey loaf, as we called it, and loads and loads of sandwiches for a party we had held on Boxing Day night.

We had pulled our crackers, opened our presents together, and it had all been wonderful! We had been over to Sue's mum for Christmas dinner and then we went over to Trudy and Mick for Christmas tea. Again, it had all been good fun, but the best of all was the huge Boxing Day dinner that my darling Sue had cooked for me! We had roast pork, crackling, stuffing, Yorkshire pudding, honey roast ham, sausages wrapped in bacon, roast potatoes, boiled potatoes, croquette potatoes and just about every vegetable you could think of! Before that, we had pate on French bread, then soup, then the marvellous dinner, followed by mince pies and Christmas cake, all well washed down with a white wine and dry cider—marvellous!

Poor Susan had been so very ill later on in the year, and our New Year was not so good, but she perked up again before finally succumbing to the illness—the fatal illness that took her life in May.

I could feel tears welling up in my eyes as I thought along those lines! I still missed her sorely, and perhaps I would never truly get over that, but Sue was dead. I was still alive, and I ought to try and get on with my life, even though she was no longer a part of it. Wasn't that what she would have wanted? I knew without asking the question that that was absolutely what she would have told me to do if she could have returned to me!

Yes! Go on, Boyzie! Get on with it, man! I'm still around you! I still love you, and that will always be, and I know, my darling, my dearest Boyzie, that you will always love me! You are down there, and I am up here, so you must get on with it!

Okay, lady! That's what I'll do, but it won't be easy!

Chapter 8

I RECEIVED SO many invitations to visit people or stay with them that first Christmas I was on my own! Everyone I knew seemed to want me to spend the day or part of the day with them!

Danny Shaw, who was a porter on Gaynsford Parkway Station, invited me to go to his home for Christmas dinner and tea, saying his wife would be delighted to entertain me to both meals! I knew Dan very well, but had never met his young wife. The couple had several small children, and it would have been lovely to see them open their presents around the tree on Christmas night!

Chris Braun, the newly promoted office manager at Bread Street, in place of Pat Lenham, had invited me to have Christmas tea with him, his parents and his five younger brothers! I thanked him profusely. Chris's promotion had happened because Pat Lenham, our previous office manager, who was then the personal secretary to Kate Cox, had been appointed as the new centre manager. Chris Braun was now the office manager, Jacky Paternoster was the chief clerk and we still had three audio typists, but Sandra Couchman was now the senior typist! Mandy Moss and the new girl, Alison Hockley, were the other two audio- typists, and we had a new accounts clerk named Ben Marcello.

Ben was 28 years old, married with a three-year-old daughter, Kinsey. He was Irish-Italian! He possessed a keen sense of humour, but had a fiery temper. He could also be quite bombastic at times, and did not always endear himself to other members of the staff. However, from the start, he and I got along quite well, and we became good friends in time. Ben was a clever bloke, and certainly knew his stuff!

He had asked me to go around for drinks on New Year's Eve and maybe to spend some time with the family on Boxing Day, but had said that on Christmas Day, his family and his wife's family would descend upon them en masse! Perhaps I would find all that company rather too much? I had laughed, and said no, I wouldn't, but had thanked him for the invitations anyway and had said I would certainly think about it! Whatever happened, I really did not want to be on my own.

Marjorie McNault and her daughter, Alice May, invited me over to dinner on Christmas Day and said I could spend the remainder of the day with them if I chose. That was very kind! Rob McCallasky and his family invited me over to their house for all or part of the day, whichever I chose. Paul Copley and his mother invited me over to their place, and several of the 'Apostles' said their parents would be glad to see me on Christmas Day. I was very touched.

Wayne Clarke, one of the social workers who worked at Bread Street, also asked me to join him and his family for the day! Wayne was of West Indian origin, and he was a very good friend of mine. Several neighbours in the close had asked me around for drinks etc., on the day. Vera Williams and her three sons invited me to their place. I thought seriously about that one, but Vera now had a new fella in her life, Frank Davey, and I knew there was friction between him and her three sons, so I decided to pass up that invitation!

Will Mooney and his ma, Agnes, invited me over to their house for all or part of the day! Aggie Mooney was as Irish as they came! She was a 'rag' woman and she and her son, Will, lived in Allerton. Will, her young son, was known as 'Steptoe' because his ma was the 'rag' woman! Will Mooney was 15 years old. He was too tall for his age! His feet were too large for a lad of his years! His hair was always long and lank, or too short! His eyes were always watery, as though he had been crying! He was very thin! Tall, leggy, gangly, awkward, always wearing hand-me-downs, which never seemed to fit him adequately, Will Mooney presented as a poor figure! He was teased and bullied, despite his height and the size of his hands and feet, which were too large in proportion with the rest of his long lean body! Will was one of the vast numbers of lads who followed me home each and every weekday night and hung around at the end of the close! I had a soft spot for that young man! I always felt I wanted to protect him, protect him from all others around him, to protect him from himself! It was more a fatherly feeling than any other, but it was, nevertheless, very prevalent. I thanked Will and his ma, Aggie, for their kind invitation!

Bob Douse and lots of the drivers from Phoenix Cabs had invited me over to their houses for all or part of that special day—a day when it was felt that nobody should be on his or her own. Jean and Terry Barradell asked me over to their house for dinner on the big day! Pat Lenham and her family had said they would be delighted to see me, so had Sue Garlick and her tribe, also Jacky and Keith Paternoster, who had only recently been married.

Naturally, Lizzie, Sue's mum, thought I would be going over there for Christmas tea, and Trudy, Mick and Dave thought I would be spending Christmas Day, or at least have Christmas dinner with them!

Oh yes! I had plenty of invitations, but I did not really want to accept any of them!

My parents wrote to me! Nelly and Alf Sunley had invited everyone in the family down to Seaport for a good, old-fashioned family Christmas! Was I interested? Again, I responded by writing back to say I did not as yet know what I wished to do, and to leave me out of any family plans for the festive season.

I was very grateful to all those people for their kindness, and for inviting me to spend the day or part of it in their company, but I did not want to be gregarious that Christmas! I merely wished it was all over!

Chapter 9

ANDY GANGE and I had become good friends. On Friday, they moved us into a four-bedded ward. There were Andy, me, young Scott Jacklin, who was injured in a motorcycle accident, and a young fellow called Paul McGowan.

Paul had come in the previous Wednesday apparently, having been injured when he collapsed under a rugby scrum. They were playing on that Wednesday evening, and Paul had gone into a rough tackle with a big bruiser from the opposing side! Suddenly he had found himself on his back with about eight or nine of them sitting or sprawling on top of him, and someone kicking him in the head! He had lost consciousness! He was recovering, but he had a heart condition, they said, and that was why they were watching him and keeping him in.

His young wife, Karen, had been in to see him! She was a smasher, so I was told! She was very pregnant, and they already had three young children under the age of four years; two daughters and a little boy, Jamie, who was the pride and joy of Paul's existence!

"It wor like winnin' a million pounds when he cum along!" Paul told us proudly when we were talking on the Friday night! "I'll get Kas to bring them all in some time, an' you can see my lot!"

We all agreed that would be good! Yes, things were picking up nicely! I was feeling better for the company and for being able to get up during the day! The four of us young blokes, well, I still counted myself as young, even though I would soon be 43 years old, we were all getting on great together! We had formed ourselves into an unholy alliance!

Chapter 10

28 Lanton Street
Harts Hill
North Yorkshire
Monday, 6th November, 1978

Dear Boyzie

*H*OW ARE *you? I'm sorry it has taken me so long to write to you following your holiday up here and our time together!*

Boyzie! I know what happened to Randle, Dom and Babs's twins, Jamie and Alex, wasn't your fault, but, well, when it happened, we were all so upset, Boyzie, and I wasn't thinking straight! I am ever so sorry, love, and I hope you can forgive me!

I have missed you ever so since you went home to Gaynsford, Boyzie! I would love it, and I know the kids would love it too, if you could come up here for Christmas and the New Year. We could have such a smashing time, and as you see from the top of this letter, I've got my own place now! It's a four-bedroomed council house, converted from a colliery house, at number 28 Lanton Street, not too far from our Norma. She forgives you too, by the way!

We would all love to see you again, Boyzie! The children send their love!

Boyzie! There's something I've got to tell you, but I can't write it in a letter. Please say you will come up for Christmas and the New Year!

I am so looking forward to seeing you and to having you to stay.

Yours, with love,
Sandy Christmas and all the family!

Chapter 11

So, NOW I had yet another offer on the table! To spend Christmas and New Year, if I desired, up in Harts Hill with Sandy and her family!

The more I considered it, the more it appealed! Granted, Sandy had not been very friendly as I had left her on that Sunday evening, but then, if I had just had my two eldest boys kidnapped, or almost had them kidnapped by a complete stranger, and that stranger was a friend of Boyzie, whom I had met and fallen for on a bus on route to Harts Hill, then maybe I would have reacted in the same way as Sandy had!

She had not been exactly cold to me, but neither had she been friendly, understanding or forgiving, and I had been angry because even though Johnnie had been involved, or believed to have been involved in the near kidnapping of those four youngsters, it was not my fault! People who did not know me obviously believed it was!

Yes, I had been angry and hurt, but now, as I saw it, an olive branch was being offered! Sandy had thought about it, had indeed thought about me a lot since I had left the district, and now, well, who knew? She was asking me to go up there to spend Christmas and the New Year with her and her family, and that had to mean something! At least, I reckoned it had to mean more than we were just good friends! In the course of her letter she had written, *Boyzie! I've got something to tell you, and I can't write it in a letter!* I wondered for a while what that might be!

She had told me they were in a new house! She might have something to divulge about the family in general, but surely she could have told me that in the course of her letter! Ah well! Perhaps if I rang her, she would tell me then. She had enclosed her new phone number in the context of the letter she had just sent me.

I received that letter from Sandy on Tuesday, 7th November, and I replied on the following day—the Wednesday!

23 Rutland Close
Parkside
˙Gaynsford
North Midlands
8th November, 1978

Dear Sandy and family,
It was good to hear from you again! Yes, I would love to come up and spend Christmas and the New Year with you all!
I will ring you in a week or so and let you know times of trains etc. Could you arrange for me to be met at Harts Hill Station or maybe even at Brigthorpe, if I came up on the bus?
I do hope everyone up there is well! Please give them all my best! Cheers for now!
Love and best wishes to you all
Boyzie!

Chapter 12

Sunday, 4th February, 1990—8 p.m.

I T HAD had a super day at the County Hospital! It had been warmer than usual and the sun shone for most of the day!

Yvonne (Eve), Eric, Michael and Mike's mate, Grant, plus my parents, Mary and George, all came up to see me that day! Several of Andy's mates arrived! Scoff Jacklin's family came in force. There were a lot of them! He was one of seventeen! Also, Karen McGowan, Paul's young wife, and her parents, plus Paul's mother and brother came to see him, and with them, Kas and Paul's three lovely children!

We all went out into the grounds, and the staff, Sister Rayfield and the nurses on our ward, provided us with drinks while we all ate a huge picnic, which was provided by all the visitors! We all shared in whatever people had brought with them, and it was all smashing! Everyone chatted away, and the children ran riot! It was a really great afternoon and early evening, where everyone got on really well together!

Our Eve and Eric's son, Mike, and his mate, Grant, were the life and soul, taking the McGowan children and others of similar age on shoulder rides all around the hospital grounds! Little Jamie McGowan and his two sisters thought it was a hoot! Eric bore it all very patiently and well, and laughed about it later on with the rest of us. I was surprised at the change in our Eric. He had mellowed almost overnight! He had been so much more easy-going since the episode on 1st January, when I had nearly died at the hands of that crazy woman! My family had just left, having helped me stack up my locker with all sorts of goodies! Eric was not too bothered about me giving up the private room. He thought I had put on weight and that I was looking and coping much better since I had had some company. I was sure that was true. I felt so much better in myself. My friendship with Andy was going from strength to strength. The family all liked him, and were glad I had made good friends there. I know they all hoped I would be leaving the hospital soon, as indeed did I, but I didn't know where I would go afterwards! Somehow, and I don't know why, I did not feel that I wished to return home and be on my own, and yet I didn't know what else I could do, unless I went to a convalescent home for a while! I had been told that I could do that if I chose, and Eric had offered to find somewhere for me down nearer the family, and to pay for the accommodation. No, I couldn't allow him to do that!

Chapter 13

S ATURDAY, 11TH November, 1978, turned out to be a very long day, but a most memorable one, and an extremely busy day for me!

I arose early, as was my wont at that time. I had no alarm clock, but always kept my Braille watch on the dressing table beside my bed. I sat on the side of the bed for a moment or two before rising and padding through to the bathroom. I performed all my necessary ablutions then returned to the bedroom, made the bed and dressed, quickly and casually.

I no longer had a dog at home. I had never had a guide dog, and never wanted one! My mobility was extremely good just using a white cane, and whenever I was out alone, that was the method I chose to help me to get around. I had met people who owned guide dogs, and who swore it was the best and most trusted method of getting about if one was visually handicapped, but I preferred to use good 'old faithful', my white cane! It had never let me down yet! More often than not, however, I was out with someone, so it did not matter.

As regards my dog, Meggie, I had decided on my return from my long holiday to allow her to remain with Trudy and Mick. When I took my Meggie over there, they already had four dogs! While I was away, the eldest, Lucy, had died. She was 14 years old, and had been suffering somewhat with arthritis, like my poor old Badger! Libby, the 11 year old, was still very active, as was Jody, the seven year old, and Amy, who was about three years old! All four of those dogs were mongrels! Meggie had gelled very well with Libby, Jody and Amy, and although they occasionally had their falling-outs and all possessed an equal loathing for the four cats, Smokey, Fluff, Tiger and Whiskers, by and large they had formed themselves into a happy little quartet! So, since she was happy, and since the three Williams boys were no longer around any more to care for her, take her for walks for me etc., I had decided to leave her with Trudy and Mick, who adored her, and were most grateful for a replacement for Lucy!

Dave was primarily in charge of walking all the dogs, although Libby did not want to go so far those days! There was a park nearby—a large and spacious park—and Dave and Mick often took all four 'girls' over there, especially at weekends! They loved to take them for a good run there on a Sunday!

Meggie was happy and I was mightily relieved, but I missed having an animal around the house!

৪৯৫৩

Downstairs again, I made myself a mug of hot chocolate! I sat in the conservatory and drank it! The weather was still reasonable and, although not hot, it was nevertheless fine and sunny! The sun was low in the sky, a watery sun, growing weak now as the year advanced!

As I finished my drink, the telephone rang!

"Hello," I said.

"Hi, mister!"

I immediately knew that voice, and I went tingly all over! I should have been angry and upset to hear her, but instead, I was thrilled and excited! I did not know why! There was a short silence between us then I spoke.

"Hi, Johnnie!"

"Mr Cool!" she responded mockingly.

I could hear that laugh in her voice!

"Is that all you've got to say to me?"

I was beginning to bridle then!

"Well, what did you expect, a royal welcome?"

"No," she said, "but I did think you might have been more civil;

more pleased to hear from me!"

"Johnnie," I asked her, "where are you?"

She laughed that strange, almost maniacal laugh!

"I'm at home, Boyzie! Here in Buckinghamshire where I live!"

"How do I know that?" I asked, rather truculently.

"Well, you'll have to trust me won't you, mister?" she countered.

"Because I trusted you before, and look what happened. You turned up in North Yorkshire and caused no end of a fuss on that Sunday, 3rd September!"

Again, there was a short uneasy silence.

"I came up to North Yorkshire, where I knew you would be, in order to find you and see you again! I've missed you, Boyzie!"

"We've made no commitment to one another, Johnnie!" I said.

"No, but you made love to me and you told me you were in love with me, didn't you, mister?"

Her voice was becoming excited and high-pitched as she talked!

"Yes, and we had a wonderful time over that very special weekend, but I am still allowed to have other female friends! I have not committed myself exclusively to you, Johnnie!"

Her voice was chilled as she replied:

"I came up especially to find you and surprise you, and it was me who got the surprise! When I found those four little boys walking on the outskirts of the woods, and they told me it was Don key Meadow I asked them if they knew someone called Boyzie. The eldest lad said, 'Aw yes! He's with us here, ma'am! He's a friend of my mother's'!" She stopped speaking, but then continued before I could say anything. "So he told me he would take me to see you! I followed them back to where you were all picnicking, and then, well, you know what I saw. Who was she, Boyzie?"

Now, I could feel my face becoming flushed, and I was getting angry! How dare she cross-examine me like that! Who the hell did she think she was?

"Sandy is a friend, in the same way as-as you are, Johnnie. You know I can't have a permanent commitment to anyone as yet. You know I am still grieving!"

She laughed a mirthless laugh.

"*Grieving*? You sure weren't grieving that weekend when *we* were together, Boyzie!"

Now I really was angry! She had done it! She had lit the 'blue touch paper'.

"That's not fair, Johnnie! You know very well I can't commit because as yet, I'm-"

She cut me short.

"Because I'm not yet over Susan," she said in a cold cruel voice. I was shaken, shaken to my foundations by the hard cruel sound in her voice.

"Johnnie! That was cruel and heartless," I said with great emotion.

There was a moment's silence before she responded.

"I'm sorry, Boyzie! Yes, I know you are still hurting. I remember all the lovely things you told me when we were together! I remember how much you loved your Susan and... and I am truly sorry, Boyzie. I'm a cow! I do care for you, Boyzie, and it really upset me to see you with that young woman on that Sunday, so I asked those four little boys if they would like ice creams, and they all said, 'Aw! Yes please, lady'! So we went off together and had ice creams, sweets, cold drinks and a lovely afternoon altogether! It was great fun! You know I returned them all in great shape, didn't I, Boyzie? No harm done eh, mister?"

I was calming down a bit by then.

"No, physically there was no harm done to them, but technically that was an incredibly stupid and heartless act, Johnnie! Just because you thought you were getting back at me."

"I'm truly sorry, mister! That's all I can say to you," she said, and I felt she was genuine.

"Well, all's well that ends well, I suppose," I said, acquiescing.

I did not really want to fall out with Johnnie Friscoe! Perhaps I realised how destructive an enemy she could have been! I don't know! Anyway, I was not anxious to quarrel with her.

"So," she said, wheedling, "am I forgiven then?"

I waited a moment before replying.

"Yes! You're forgiven, Johnnie!"

"Aw gud!" she said, taking the mickey. "So, can we start afresh from here?"

"I guess so!" I told her.

We chatted more amiably for a while, before she suddenly said:

"So, what are you doing at Christmas then, mister?"

That took me somewhat by surprise.

"Er… as yet I don't know! I've… I've had lots of invitations!"

"So," she said slowly, "here's another one! How about coming down to me for the Christmas break?"

I was poleaxed! That had completely caught me off guard! For a long moment, there was again silence between us and then I blurted out:

"Well… I… er…!"

In truth, I did not know what to say! She was laughing!

"Well, what? Don't you want to come down to me for Christmas?"

"No! No, it's not that! Well… if I am completely honest, I don't really want to

travel, but…"

My mind was working overtime then! If I went to stay with her, I would be on her territory, and if anything untoward should occur I would be at a distinct disadvantage! Hell! Why was I thinking like that? Now, if she came to stay with me? Yeh! That would be okay, because then she would be on my territory, and if anything appeared to be about to happen, I had plenty of people who could come to my aid, and anyway, I could easily get rid of her! I shouldn't have been thinking like that. Surely it would be great to have her up there for Christmas? I could always go to Sandy's for the New Year then I'd have the best of both worlds! Yes, that was the way to play it!

"You could always come up here to me for Christmas!" I said. "We would have a super time, I assure you. I could introduce you to all my mates, or we could just spend time together on our own—you know, Johnnie! I reckon we could have a superb time!"

She seemed to be considering that for a few moments before replying brightly.

"Yeh! Yeh, I reckon you're right, mister! Yeh! If that's a definite invitation, that's what I'll do! I'll come to you for Christmas!"

After I had replaced the receiver on its rest, I stood for a moment at the foot of my stairs, a half-finished cup of hot chocolate in my right hand! Oh, my God! What had I done?

I busied myself preparing for a shopping expedition with Trudy and Dave, as Mick could not help me that morning. I began to warm to the idea! Johnnie was good fun, there was no denying that, and on her day she could be the best! I was sure that over Christmas she would positively bloom! Oh yes! Everybody who met her would be most impressed. They would all love her instantly, as I had done. Yes, I had been right to invite her. I had not wanted to go down to hers, but if she came to mine, I would be the person in charge, and we would be on my home ground! Yes, it would be fine—Johnnie and me at mine for Christmas! We could buy the tree together, decorate it, put lights on it and a star on the top! We could pretty up the house so it was right for the Christmas season!

I was sure Johnnie would be able to give the place a good clean through for me! Since Vera had left, the place had lacked that touch of a woman around it! I did the best I could and, on occasions, Trudy would come by and give the place a once over, but she was not as clean and house proud as my lovely one had been, or even as much so as dear Vera, who had liked to 'bottom' the place for me every so often! Trudy's house was not the cleanest or the tidiest abode in Gaynsford, although I was sure there were a lot worse than hers! Still, Johnnie would, I was sure, come up trumps for me! Yes, we would perhaps have a good Christmas, all

things being equal! At least I hoped so anyway!
It did prove to be so, but more of that anon.

Chapter 14

A T AROUND 10 a.m., Trudy and young Dave arrived to take me shopping in Allerton. Shopping was not a pain, but a pleasure to me, even for ordinary everyday commodities, therefore, I thoroughly enjoyed shopping that day! Saturdays in that quarter of Gaynsford were always extremely busy. The place was bustling, full of life, crowded with people all busy with their own chores, but, as was the way of the people in that suburb of Gaynsford, they were never too busy to chat or be of help if you require assistance! I knew that for certain! It was like the people up in Harts Hill, North Yorkshire. If they liked you, you were in, and they would do anything in the world for you! If they didn't like you, well, get out of town fast! That was the best thing to do. I knew right from the start when I first went up there to live in the North Midlands town of Gaynsford that I would be happy there, and so, by and large, it had proved to be!

We started off at James Blume's, the bakery, and I bought four large white uncut loaves, plus one large and one small brown, also uncut. I bought half a dozen cream cakes in a box and also a large strawberry jam sponge cake. I loved visiting James Blume's, but I always purchased far too much! We then went on to Gregsons, the supermarket, and I bought all sorts in there! After that, we went to North Midlands Counties Dairies, which was originally Cresta Dairies, and I bought milk, butter, eggs, home-grown potatoes, cheese and two pots of double cream, as well as a load of pots of fruit yoghurt, which I was very much into at that time! I liked to eat yoghurt for breakfast those days.

From there we went onto Westall, the greengrocer's, and I

bought plenty of fruit and vegetables. I was into fruit those days such as melon, grapefruit and pineapple. At Trotters, the butcher's, I bought ham, two or three different kinds of sausage, liver, kidney, gammon rashers, sliced pork with stuffing and two chickens for the freezer. I also bought some black pudding. Whilst in there, I ordered a large piece of boiling ham and a 14 lb turkey for Christmas, as well as two, 1 lb. Christmas puddings with brandy sauce! I know Dave, who went into the butcher's with me, was a little surprised, but he did not say anything to me about it, or at least, not immediately anyway! The subject of Christmas came up later on as we drove home together.

We went and had a coffee in Ruby's Cafe. After coffee and a bun apiece, we went to Fine Foods, where once again I bought plenty of tinned fish, tinned fruit and more items for the freezers. I had two freezers! I know it was daft for a bloke on his own, but I entertained so often that it proved to be economical really, so I kept both of them!

We went home with the car weighed down with shopping for all of us, and Trudy and Dave helped me to unload my bags at my house, and were all for coming in to help me put all the stuff away! However, I said I could manage, so they helped me in with all the bags and left me to it!

During the ride home, the subject of Christmas came up. I told Trudy and Dave that I was having Johnnie Friscoe over to stay with me for Christmas, and that I was going away for the New Year!

"Great!" said Dave.

He thought the world of me, young David!

"Yes!" said Trudy. "That will be smashing for you, Boyzie! We shall look forward to meeting Johnnie! She sounds very nice from what you've told us already!"

"Yes!" I enthused. "I am sure you'll like her."

I was sure because I knew damned well she would be on her very, very best behaviour while she was staying with me over the Christmas period! Oh yes! I was very aware of that!

It was 2 p.m., I had put all the shopping away and was sitting eating cheese and tomato sandwiches and drinking a mug of hot tea! The pot was full, and I would have another one in a bit! I was making inroads into a large plate of sandwiches and pork pie! I had the radiogram on! An LP by Joan Baez, of whom I was very fond! It was peaceful. I was happy and contented then I heard a knock on the front door! Oh hell! Who was that? I did love visitors, but sometimes I loved my solitude more, and I was just enjoying that time on my own! Nevertheless, I had to answer the summons at my front door, so I walked into the hall having placed my plate of sandwiches and my half-finished mug of hot tea on the table.

"Hey-up, Boyzie!" said a familiar voice at my front door. "I bet you never expected te see me today, eh mate?"

It was my ex-neighbour from The Circle, Terry Barradell!

"Hi! What on earth are you doing here?"

I motioned Terry to follow me into the lounge.

"Excuse me! I'm finishing my lunch! I'll get you a drink in a tick!"

Terry laughed his deep throaty laugh.

"Aw, it's okay, man, I'm not stopping! I jus' came to tell you you've new neighbours movin' in next door at number twenty-one!"

"Oh!" I exclaimed, immediately interested.

Number 21 had been empty for some considerable time. Apparently the Skinner family, who had occupied it just before I moved into my house, smashed the place up good before they left! It also required to be fumigated! The Skinners were a filthy mob, and apparently no one in The Circle was sorry to see them go. I never knew them, thank goodness.

"So, who's moving in then?" I asked Terry.

"My eldest lad and his family! Ahr Tony and Heather and their four kids!"

"Oh!" I said.

I was thrilled! I had known the Barradell family ever since I first moved into The Circle, and good friends they had proved to be! They had been a wonderful support to me when my Susan had lost the baby, and through many other difficult times. Yes, it would be good to have Tony and his family living close by.   I

"Me an' Jean are jus' ovver 'ere 'elpin' 'em settle in, you knaw!"

Good old Terry! I knew he would want to help Tony and his family settle into their new abode, as indeed he and all his mates had helped Sue and me when we had first moved onto The Circle. How well I remembered that night, when, crammed into the bar of the Gunners, we had talked—me and loads and loads of Terry's mates, who all turned out to be *my* mates in the end—about all the things we were going to do to number 48 The Circle to make it habitable for me and my lovely Sue! Oh yes! I had had some wonderful help from some damned good mates in the past and I knew that would continue.

Terry and I had a chat then he shook my hand and left me, saying he would give my best to Tony, Heather and the four kids, and would suggest that they call upon me at their earliest convenience!

"Yeh that will be great! I'll look forward to seeing them, and to welcoming them as new neighbours!" I said.

Chapter 15

I T WAS 3.45 p.m. on Saturday, 11th November, and I was sitting in my lounge, waiting for Rob McCallasky. We were going to 'hit the town' that night, but not Gaynsford! We were driving to Glosport, Merseyside, on Rob's motorbike.

The outing had been planned since the previous Friday evening, when Rob and I had gone out 'on the town' in Gaynsford! We had commenced by having a huge meal down at the Laughing Cow, after which we had gone for several jars, and then several more, at the Gunners. Rob and I had ended up being driven home in a taxi, and deposited outside my front door by Bob Douse!

We had helped one another inside, and, after sitting around for a while, had managed to assist one another upstairs to my room! We had stripped down to our underpants and socks, and slid into bed beside one another! We awoke in the morning, mouths dry, heads pounding, having been totally rat-arsed the night before! Before drifting off to sleep, we had sworn undying friendship and brotherhood to one another, and had agreed we would go out the following Saturday night, and that we would take the bike and go up to Merseyside!

Rob knew a club in the City of Glosport where we could go, but would not give me any details about it, saying it would be a surprise when we got there—and so it proved to be, but more of that anon.

§⊷⊰

At around 3.50 p.m. that Saturday afternoon, a knock came on my door, and I went to answer it, believing it to be Rob arriving slightly early. In fact, there was a young woman standing there, with two small children, one a babe in arms! The other a young boy of indeterminate age and size, clung to his mother's right hand while she stood and talked to me!

"Hello!" she said. "I've not long moved in across from you! I live at number 22 Rutland Close! My name is Maryjane Cauldwell, but everyone calls me Jinny. I'm a young mum with six growing children, including a little boy with Down's syndrome! I've come over to see you because one of your neighbours, Tracey, from down the end of the close says you might be interested in someone to clean, wash and cook for you two or three times a week!"

I smiled what I hoped was a welcoming smile!

"Well, Jinny, I *was* thinking about advertising for a cleaner-cum-cook to help me out!"

"Aw, good!" she said. "Would you consider me for the job please?"

I thought for a moment:

"Look," I said, hoping that I didn't sound as though I wanted to get rid of her, "I'm just about to go out, but I would like to have a chat with you! Suppose I come over sometime tomorrow, say in the mid to late afternoon, could we have a talk then?"

Jinny hesitated a moment.

"Okay! In the meantime, you won't give the job to anyone else, will you?"

I laughed. Despite myself, I quite liked that young woman, who seemed very genuine!

"As I said, I'm just about to go out now, so I won't be talking to anyone else about it! No, I give you my word you will be the first one I consider if I do take someone on, I promise you that!"

She removed her hand from that of her clinging three-year-old son, who immediately began to holler!

"Now now, Deano! Thanks very much," she said as she offered me her hand. "I could do with the money you know, and it would help me to have a little job of some kind! Thanks, Boyzie!"

I had already introduced myself to her by that name!

"That's okay, Jinny, I'll look forward to meeting you again to-morrow at yours!"

"Yeh!" she said. "We're not going anywhere! I hope you can put up with five rather boisterous boys! They will be all over you, and will want to ask you loads of questions!"

I laughed. "I'll be ready for them!" I told her.

"See you soon then, Boyzie!" she said, and with that, she had gone!

I closed the front door and went upstairs to put a comb through my hair. Ten minutes later, at approximately 4.10 p.m., the door-bell rang and when I went downstairs, there was Rob waiting for me!

"Hi!" he said. "Are you ready?"

I secured the house front and back, and we walked out together to where Rob's gleaming motorcycle stood by the kerb. Rob's mo-torbike was like a god to him! He loved it with all his heart, and he looked after it so well, but he *used* it too! By that I mean that when we were on the road, he thrashed it and really made it work for us! I loved it when we were riding on that wonderful machine together. It was almost like flying! The wind whipped around one, and one just felt so happy and carefree. It was wonderful! I was re-ally up for it, and tremendously looking forward to the long ride into Glosport!

Rob helped me to put on the gear; one lined jacket, to keep me extra warm, and one helmet! He then assisted me to climb on board. Once settled comfortably on the pillion at the rear, with the back-rest to lean on, so I felt safer, Rob said:

"Can you find the switches for the music?"

I felt around the helmet. On the left was one switch, which I moved downwards. The music came on very loud. I pressed the button in the middle and the volume went down. It was all great! It was a continuing cassette that would play for as long as an hour, and then turn itself over to play the reverse side! Rock music while we travelled up to Merseyside—fabulous!

"Right!" said Rob, as he put on his gear and climbed aboard in front of me!

I wrapped my arms around his ample waist, and then he was kicking the machine into life, revving up the engine and suddenly, with a word to me to 'hold tight now, Boyzie!' we were off! From the start, it was totally thrilling!

I was mad about motorbikes! It started when I was very young and my Uncle Jack Dabbs had one. My dad, George, bought a motorbike and sidecar with money my Grannie Annie gave them when I started school. That was to help Mum and Dad to visit me while I was away at boarding school! Later, Eric had one, but not for long! Mum disapproved of them, although I loved it whenever Eric took me on the back of his, which did not occur often, but on occasions, he would do so!

There we were, flying along towards the north-west on Rob's F and S Phoenix, Mark 3, the 'superbike' of the Phoenix range—a truly magnificent and wondrous machine! It was a real pleasure to feel that beast of burden bursting with all that pent-up power being released. Truly fantastic and wonderful!

⊰❧⊱

At around 5.40 p.m., we drove into the town of Lyttleton! Lyttleton was situated about 45 miles north-west of Gaynsford, a busy, bustling little town with factories, several pubs, amusement arcades, cafes, restaurants, a hospital on the outskirts etc., etc.

I liked Lyttleton! It had a famous opera house and a very beautiful theatre, The Landau. Yes, Lyttleton was a very pleasant town, and we were heading for Rose's Restaurant in Cable Street. Rose's was a very ordinary restaurant where the helpings, like those served in the Laughing Cow, were huge!

We arrived at Rose's at around 5.50 p.m. and, after removing our gear and chaining up the bike, we went in together. We had drinks first! I had a pint of bitter shandy and Rob had half a pint of rough cider!

Rose West was a grand woman! She was about 50 years old, and very friendly! A large jolly woman, she was the chief cook and bottle-washer at Rose's, supported by four of her large family of daughters. Rose had eight daughters! The four who worked along with her in the restaurant were Midge, Babs, Fifi and Lulu. They were all grand girls!

Rose had a husband, Harry, who helped out by delivering, as they also took food out to people's homes, and driving the van to the cash and carry etc., when required. There were also a couple of stout tall sons, who did a g rand job as security guards for their mum! Apart from that, Rose employed waiters etc., to work in the restaurant, which served plain, home-made food for all who wanted it!

That night we certainly made in-roads into a sumptuous repast at Rose's Restaurant, in the town of Lyttleton! I had the chef's special; soup of the day, which was thick farmhouse vegetable, with two enormous thick slices of French bread! Rob had spaghetti Bolognaise, one of the house specialities! I then had a very large plate piled high with meat and potato pie, mashed potatoes, carrots, peas, cabbage, parsnip and gravy. Rob had a 14-ounce rump steak with all the trimmings, plus a huge quantity of French fried potatoes, cut thick! Delicious!

Afterwards we had coffee and another beer apiece, and then set off for our night in Glosport, feeling very comfortable and well catered for as far as the 'inner man' was concerned!

§❧§

It was soon after 8.15 p.m. when we drove into the City of Glosport, having travelled some 90 miles from Gaynsford! A long way to go for a Saturday night out, but Rob had assured me it would be well worthwhile, and so it proved to be!

Rob swung off the main drag and into Cowlishaw Street, down near the docks area of that bustling city! We turned left onto Pye Street then right onto McCugh Street and later, into a small street known as Percy Street, where a long low building known as the Beehive Club was situated. We pulled into the long driveway leading up to the building, and Rob found a place to stow his bike. I switched off the music and we both dismounted. We took off our helmets and jackets, and Rob took off his over-trousers, which he always wore to ride in. We stored those underneath the cover that Rob put over his beloved machine when we had secured it in its parking space.

By the time we had done that we were surrounded by four young hostesses from the Beehive Club! Sami, Carla, Tasha and Judy escorted us into the building! They were very friendly and chatty, and immediately conducted us down to the cellar bar, where they invited us to buy drinks! I bought a Black Russian cocktail with plenty of ice, made up in a long glass! Rob had a pint of best bitter. I didn't feel like drinking beer, but was happy enough with the vodka-based cocktail.

We sat down at a table and the four girls were very pleasant and attentive hostesses! The music began to play. It was sixties and seventies disco and pop music! Very good, and although it was loud and reverberated through the cellar bar, it was not too loud so that we could not hear one another speak!

Carla, a small freckled, but nevertheless pretty and petite, young lady from Merseyside, had taken quite a shine to me! She suddenly said:

"Cum an' dawnce wi' me, my lad!"

Sami, who was from Australia, managed to persuade Rob to get up onto his feet, and we all four took to the dance floor! Tasha and Judy went and acquired more drinks for us at the bar. Carla loved to dance, and she was most thrilled and excited at the way I enjoyed it too!

"You know what, Boyzie," she told me excitedly, "you are one of the best dawncers I've been with for ages, lad! You may be blind, but you sure can move your feet to the rhythm, can't you? I just *luv* a good dawncer!"

We were on the dance floor for what seemed ages, and although I felt tired, undertaking one dance after another, I was pleased and proud that I was holding my own with that rather attractive young woman. She was thrilled and delighted with me, and we danced on until I thought my legs would collapse beneath me! "Ooh! I'm going to have to sit this one out, Carla!" I told her after the eighth or ninth dance we had shared together.

"Cum on then, my lad!"

She laughed, and led me back to the table, where Rob was engaged in resting his feet and finishing his third, or maybe his fourth, pint! We sat close together on a couch before a table laden with drinks, Carla and I! Close together! Her perfume was hypnotic! Exotic! I wanted her!

After a short while, maybe ten minutes or so, when I was well down my third cocktail, Rob rose to his feet and spoke to Sami.

"Come on then, luv! Are we going upstairs?"

"Sure! As soon as you are both ready, we'll escort you upstairs, lads!"

Carla protested.

"Me an' Boyzie wanna dawnce some more, don't we, luv?"

"Yeh, we do!" I said, with great heartiness.

Rob seemed a little put out, but nevertheless, he and Sami went off upstairs, taking their drinks along with them! Carla and I finished ours and went back onto the dance floor again. It was crowded, but we were by far the best dancers on it that night! We were thoroughly enjoying ourselves, at least I was, and I thought she was too.

After about half an hour or so she led me back to the couch. She sat close beside me while I had another drink, stroking my hair, blowing gently into my left ear and snuggling up very close to me! I liked her! I wanted her ever so much, but somehow something was stopping me from showing my feelings. Something was standing as a barrier between us.

Carla continued to try and cajole me into having sex with her, but eventually, with a friendly peck on the cheek, she went to the bar, brought me another drink back and then left me sitting alone at my table in the cellar bar! Now what should I do? I hadn't a clue where I was and there was nobody to help me, but I would not panic! Surely, someone would come down there and then I could ask them where I was, and perhaps they would kindly show me the way upstairs! With that comforting thought in my head, I settled down on the couch and finished yet another long cold drink!

§֍֎§

I did not hear her approach. Somehow I was aware of her presence, but I had not heard her arrive. She came so silently, almost like someone or something from another world! She sat down beside me on the couch! Her perfume was wonderful, like a whole midnight garden of beautiful, exotic flowering plants! When she spoke to me her voice was soft, velvety, sensual, like dark chocolate flowing all over me! Warm, sensuous, wonderfully relaxing! The whole effect of her presence beside me was entirely hypnotic!

"Well," she breathed in her wonderful, slow, West Indian drawl, "so my gurls are not good enough for you eh, Mr Man?"

"Oh no!" I said quickly, endeavouring to hide my embarrassment. "Your hostesses are lovely! It's just that I... I-"

She cut me short.

"It's ju'st dat you decided to wait for de Queen of de Beehive? Well, here she is, sittin' right beside you!"

I was flattered! She had pressed all the right buttons!

"What's your given name my Queen of the Beehive?" I asked, moving closer to her and putting my left hand into her right.

She squeezed it hard!

"My name is Honey, Honey Lavern, an' aw'm waitin' to escort you upstairs, Boyzie!" she said, snuggling up tight against me and burying her head in my left shoulder!

Oh boy! I felt as though all my birthdays had come at once, and in a very short time I was walking with Honey Lavern up several flights of carpeted stairs to the room that she called 'her own heaven above'. There she gave me my initiation! For as long as I live, I'll never forget Honey Lavern or the wonderful love we made together that Saturday night in November, 1978.

We arrived in her room, which was very large, or seemed so to me! She gently, but firmly, conducted me to a sofa, into which I sank down.

"Now, Boyzie!" she breathed, moving very close to me and placing an arm around my shoulders. "I'm going to help you to strip, den I'm going to wash your feet boy, an' annoint dem with my special cooling creams! I'm den going to help you to bed, an' we'll make wonderful music together, yeh boy?"

I was hers! Hers completely, for her to do with exactly as she liked!

She helped me off with my clothes! Eventually, without protest, I stood completely naked before her! Now, she too was naked, and suddenly we were in each other's arms—me and the Queen of the Beehive Club in one another's arms! Her body was gorgeous! Soft, velvety, sensual, warm, like honey and sweet flowers! Like hot chocolate being poured all over me! Ooh, how I ached for her!

She cooled me with her balms and creams, and washed my feet thoroughly, drying them on a big warm towel then carefully, quietly, coolly, she conducted me into the bedroom and helped me into bed! The sheets were satin. The pillows smelled of her exotic perfume.

She was in bed beside me! She was stroking me in all the right places, and I was growing! Suddenly, I was on top of her as she lay beneath me! I was in her, and she was giving me all the help she was able. She was talking to me, encouraging me, and soon we both came together—the effect was entirely wonderful, like an explosion! A wonderful coming together of bodies and souls that would be linked forever!

We did it again and again, and yet again! Oh! How I wanted her, and how she responded! She was rough! As rough as a butcher's dog! She liked hot, sweaty action, and that was what she got from me! I performed as I had not done for ages, even better than I had for Johnnie or Sandy Christmas. I thought not of either of them, or even of young Carla, but only of that wonderful, sexy, ferocious, hungry creature who lay in bed beside me, the Queen of the Beehive—Honey Lavern.

꧁☙❧꧂

Eventually we lay together quietly, pleasantly tired after our exertions! As we lay together, we wrapped our bodies around one another, and stayed like that for who knew how long. It was truly wonderful!

Later, as I showered, as she gave me a cooling drink, as she helped me to dress, as she ran a comb through my hair, as she laid her head on my shoulder, as she showered kisses upon my face, as she led me downstairs again to the main reception, where Rob was waiting for me, Honey told me in her deep, soothing, sensual voice:

"You a lucky man, Boyzie! You picked the flower of the flock tonight! She loves you! She wants you to come back an' see her again very, very soon, you know, an' you will, my darlin'! You know you will, Boyzie!"

As we stood together in reception at 2 a.m. in the warmth of the Beehive Club, I knew she was right. I *did* want to see her again, and I would most certainly do so! I could not wait for the moment!

It was hard parting with her, but eventually we were walking together, Rob and me, towards his beautiful machine where it stood in the moonlight! The night, or rather the early morning, was cold, and our breath was freezing on the chill air! Honey and some of the other hostesses stood waving us goodbye, and as we roared out of the car park I heard Honey Lavern's voice calling out to me over the still, chill air.

"You will see me again, Boyzie, very soon!"

My whole body tingled with pleasure as I thought of her and the wonderful, passionate love we had made together in her 'heaven above' that fantastic night!

The night of my initiation—and what an initiation!

It was almost 5 a.m. as we turned into my close and pulled up outside the house! I knew Rob was very tired. We both climbed off the motorbike and I said:

"Would you like to stay over, Rob? You could sleep in my room or the spare, whichever. It would be best, eh mate?"

We had hardly spoken since we had left the Beehive Club. We sat together on my front garden wall, and Rob put an arm around my shoulders!

"Yeh," he said, "that would be good, Boyzie! Aw'll sleep in your room on the floor for the rest of the night if you give me a pillow or two!"

In the event, we both slept in my bed! We were both extremely tired, and after Rob had fetched the motorbike into the front driveway and covered it over, we went inside, kicked off our shoes, stripped to our underwear and socks, and went upstairs. We both showered and cleaned our teeth then climbed into bed—and we slept until well after midday!

We both awoke with splitting headaches! Rob got up and found his socks!

"Sounds an' looks like you might be havin' new neighbours in today, mate!" he told me, and he went to open the window so he could tell me more!

I moaned and pulled the bedclothes tighter up around me. There was a helluva noise going on in the close!

"Oh yes!" said Rob. "There's a jockin' gret coal lorry pulled up outside, an' a load of scruffy kids in the close!"

Oh no! Who on earth was coming in next door?

The Starlings arrived and made their home at number 25 Rutland Close—Bessie and Jim Starling, who was 50 years old and a coal merchant! Bessie, his plump, loud and rather plain wife, was 44 years of age when the family arrived. The couple had eight children still living at home, and one daughter, Carol, aged 19 years, who was married. The Starlings had settled at number 25, and the close would never be quite the same again!

In the space of one weekend, I had had new neighbours move in on each side of me! Well, life would certainly be more interesting from now on with new neighbours living each side of me! Oh boy, if only I had realised how true that was going to prove to be!

As I lay in bed beside Rob that morning, I could not have cared less about anything, especially my new neighbours, the Starlings, but more of them anon. Much more, in fact!

§⤙⤚§

Rob and I eventually arose and I made the bed. I decided to change the sheets and do some washing later on. I also had shoes to clean and other domestic chores to undertake,

and later on I had promised to go over and visit Jinny Cauldwell and talk to her about the cleaning job. I certainly did need a cleaner, and the sooner I found someone, the better!

Yes! All things being equal, I would take her on a couple of times a week, and worry about the consequences and how she would cope with the care of her kids etc., later!

Rob stayed with me and together, after taking pills and lying down again for a while, we tidied around as best two blokes could, then we made a brew and a huge fry-up to make us both feel better! Somehow or other, that always seemed to work for me!

Rob left me later and, before doing so, we both pledged to go back to the Beehive Club as soon as possible, preferably before Christmas, but that never came to fruition, for reasons I will disclose later on!

Chapter 16

ROB LEFT me at around 4 p.m. that afternoon, and 20 minutes later I was out of the house and on my way over to talk to Jinny Cauldwell, my neighbour over the road at number twenty-two.

As I went out of the house, I was hailed, first by Tony Barradell, who was outside number 21, cleaning his cab! Tony worked for Phoenix Cars.

"Hi there, mate!" he called out to me.

"Hello Tony! Welcome to the close," I told him brightly.

"Fanks," he responded. "Cum rahnd an' see us when we're settled in loike, eh?"

"Love to!" I told him, and was just about to go on my way when, from the other side, I was hailed by a young fellow carrying stuff through into the house where the Starlings had settled!

"Watcher!" he said. "Aw'm Mal, Mal Starling. I'm glad to know yer!"

"Hi!" I said. "Welcome! I heard you and your family moving in this morning!"

He laughed! Malcolm Starling was 16 years of age, a small, tough, wiry young man, with plenty of good old honest-to-goodness cheek!

"Aw," he said, "we're still at it, yer knaw!"

"Keep going!" I said, and then, with a cheery wave in his direction, I went across to number 22 and knocked on Jinny Cauldwell's door!

The door was answered by a young man!

"Hello!" he said. "How can we 'elp you then?"

299

"I'm Boyzie from across the road! I came to see Jinny!"

"Aw!" said the young man, who had now been joined at the front door by several noisy children and a very lively dog. "You better cum in then, mate! She's upstairs wi' the babbie, but she'll be down in a tick! Cum through an' sit dahn! Mek' yersel' at 'ome, an' aw'll bring yer a drink! Wot's yer poison, owd mate?"

I liked that young fellow; he seemed very ready to please and was extremely friendly towards me! It turned out that he was a little older than me, and his name was Jason, although Jinny referred to him as Jake! Jake Cauldwell was Jinny's partner, although the couple had never married. All six of the children were his! He had 'done time' he told me as we sat drinking pint shandies together in that cluttered lounge, surrounded by his five very active sons and the barmiest dog I had ever known, but now, he was home, and 'going straight' he vowed!

"Aw'm not goin' back in there again! Not if aw can 'elp it anyway!"

Jake had a strong West Midlands accent and told me he came from Walls Hill in Staffordshire. I said I knew it vaguely. I had been to college in Shropshire, and we used to pass through that district on our way there. Jake and I were sitting chatting and drinking happily, with our feet up, surrounded by the kids and the crazy dog, when Jinny came into the room. Jake got up and offered to pour his 'wife' a drink!

"I'll 'av a whisky please, luvvert," Jinny said.

"Commin' right up!" said Jake and, whistling, pursued by his five sons and the crazy dog, Daisy, he went through to the kitchen to make up her drink!

Jinny sat down on the sofa beside me! In her arms was the six-month-old baby, a plump, rather fretful little girl called Ruby Ann.

"She's not very happy this afternoon!" said Jinny. "I think she's teething or summat!"

Jinny, who had endeavoured to speak so well and clearly the day before, had obviously decided it didn't matter that day and that she could, and should, be herself!

I was glad because I felt much easier in her company when she was relaxed.

"Can I hold her for a bit?" I asked.

The three-year-old son, Dean, known as Deano, who had Down's syndrome, commenced climbing all over me, and thus, Jinny was compelled to put Ruby Ann back into her cot and hope she would sleep despite all that was going on around her!

"She's a good babbie," she told me. "She con sleep for ages as a rule!"

I was pleased! The couple had enough on with their five erring sons without the further pressure of a fretful and difficult baby daughter to add to the quota!

The dog, Daisy, was a nine-month-old Labrador retriever, and had been bought for the boys to keep them happy prior to the arrival of the baby. The boys simply adored Daisy, who appeared to have carte blanche to behave just as she wished in the house, although I was assured she was thoroughly house trained, but totally undisciplined apart from that! Still, she was undeniably adorable!

Ruby Ann seemed to drift off to sleep after a short while, and Deano settled down on my knee to play with a toy car or two! He later thoroughly enjoyed some of the chocolate I had purchased and taken with me to pacify the boys! It seemed to work! They were suddenly all my friends and great fans, especially Deano, who was three and a half stone, although he was only three years old! He was big for his age, tall and solid, and that would prob-ably stand him in good stead when he started at the nursery, as he would not be taunted or bullied by other kids, being the size he was!

I took a shine to that lovely, but totally disorganised, family! I did wonder about Jinny's efforts, cleanliness and tidiness over at mine, but she assured me she could and would cope with the job three times a week! Further, Jake told me that come the spring and the summer he would be over to help me with the gardening!

"I don't want nuffink for that! It'll be a pleasure, Boyzie!" he told me in his broad West Midlands accent!

I was completely at ease in the company of those good, friendly, but down to earth people. The five little boys, Adam, who was nine, Ashley, who was eight, Errol, who was six, Owen, who was four and young Deano, were all over me, all chattering at once, asking me questions and climbing all over me until Jake, laughing, rescued me and took them out into the garden for a game of footy.

Daisy madly rushed out to join them, which left me inside with Jinny and the baby girl, Ruby Ann, who was still fast asleep in her cot! At last Jinny and I were able to have a proper talk. We could get down to the real nitty-gritty! We agreed that Jinny Cauldwell would start that coming Tuesday and would do two hours for me on a Tuesday morning and a Friday afternoon, during which times she would ensure that the house was cleaned, and also undertake any other small chores for me, of which I would inform her on the day. I would drop my spare set of keys off at her house each morning when she was supposed to come. It was not that I didn't trust Jinny, but I was a bit concerned that her children might get hold of them if I left a spare set there all the time, and she agreed that the arrangement we had made was the best one, indeed, it proved to be very satisfactory!

Chapter 17

TIME WENT on, and Christmas was fast approaching! I was
greatly looking forward to the arrival, on the Thursday before the 'big day', of my lovely and much missed Johnnie
Friscoe!

Oh! What a tangled web we weave when first we practise to de-
ceive! That was how it was with me! I had utterly convinced myself that I was head over heels in love with Johnnie. I was pretty
nigh certain that the same applied in relation to her and, although
I knew of what she was capable, I could not help myself! 'Come
into my parlour!' said the spider to the fly! Yes, and how willingly
I went into her parlour!

Chapter 18

23 Rutland Close
Parkside
Gaynsford
North Midlands
14th November, 1978
Dear Sandy and family,

*I*T WAS *grand to receive your letter, and the totally unexpected invitation.*

Yes! I would love to come up and stay with you in your new house on Lanton Street, but unfortunately I can't come for Christmas! I could, however, be with you for the New Year!

If this is acceptable to you, Sandy, I could arrive late afternoon on the Thursday, 28th December, and remain with you until the following Wednesday, 3rd January. I am off all that week, so maybe we might even get a couple of extra days in! What say?

Please write back or phone me as soon as possible!

I am greatly looking forward to Christmas with my family and, of course, it will be wonderful to spend New Year with you, if you are able and willing to have me!

You've got me wondering now when you tell me there's something special I have to know! If you wait, you can tell me as the New Year strikes! Okay? I'll look forward to you reply!

Love to you all!
Yours sincerely,
Boyzie!

I posted the letter the same day! I felt bad, telling her the lie about going to stay with the family, but what could I do? I could hardly tell her the truth, could I?

Chapter 19

I

T WAS a damp, chilly morning in early February 1990, a Friday morning! The night before there had been high drama in our small ward in the County Hospital!

We had been talking until late, the four of us, me, Andy Gange, young Scott Jacklin, who was due to go home in a few days, and Paul McGowan! Paul's wife, Karen, had visited him, also Scott's parents, but nobody had been to see me that night, or indeed Andy. He had been expecting one or two of his mates, so he was a bit down earlier on, but he brightened up as the conversation among the four of us intensified and reached a crescendo, so that Sister Brennan, who was on duty that evening, had to come in and tell us to quieten down a bit!

We carried on chatting until well after midnight, then Nurse Joy Baxter came in and offered us last drinks! I had a hot chocolate. Scott and Andy both had hot chocolate too and Paul had a mug of tea.

"Two sugars please, ma' am!" he joked with Joy Baxter.

She brought in the drinks on a tray then came in a few minutes later to settle us down! When she did so, Paul McGowan, who had not drunk his tea, told her he felt a bit poorly. She and Sister Janet conferred briefly and then decided to send for Dr Mishra, who duly arrived, checked Paul over and decided there was nothing to worry about.

Thus, we all settled down and I was soon asleep!

I was having a nightmare! In my nightmare I was running from Johnnie, who was pursuing me with a carving knife!

"I'll get you, mister!" she screamed in my head, and my legs turned to jelly!

I could not run! As I heard her breathing behind me, I found I had an excruciating cramp in my left leg, and awoke with a start!

I was sweating!

I was shouting!

Nurse Joy Baxter quickly came over to my bed to help me! She consoled me, and managed to make the cramp in both my legs go away after a while. She gave me two quinine tablets and a drink. She also helped me to change my pyjama jacket because I was sweating, then I settled down again!

I soon drifted off to sleep again then I was suddenly awake— wide awake and aware of activity in our little ward. Dr Mishra was there, so was Sister Janet. Two nurses were in the room! I heard Dr Mish ra say:

"Give him more oxygen!"

Sister Janet seemed to be trying to obey, but whatever they were attempting to do and to whom, it was not working out! Suddenly I heard the awful words from Dr Mishra:

"He's gone!"

Oh, my God!

Who?

Not Andy?

Please, not my mate, Andy! I also didn't wish it to be either of the others! I had become quite fond of both Scott and Paul, and I was horrified that one of the four of us had died! Which of the other three was it?

I lay in bed, struck dumb by the horror of the idea that once more death had come so close to me!

ह≈≈ॐ

Later that morning, as they were changing Paul's bed, the three of us sat together on my bed, me in the middle, Andy on my left with his arm around my shoulders, Scott on my right. We sat close together, heads bowed, and the three of us discussed the late Paul McGowan.

He had been so young! So vital! He had left three small children, including his son, whom he idolised—and there was another on the way! Poor Karen! How would she ever cope! We all felt desperately sorry for her, but we also missed Paul! His jovial chatter, his banter with the nurses and Sister Chrissie! She was very upset when she came on duty, but of course, being very professional, she tried not to show it.

We had a new bloke in the ward before the end of the day! He was a cockney guy named Albert Conlan, and he was of Irish stock! He had originally come from London's East End and had been up in Gaynsford for approximately 18 months! He was about 50 years old, married with five 'saucepans' as he called his kids, and as strong an East End accent as though he had just left London! Bert Conlan turned out to be quite a character!

Two days later, on the Sunday, Scott Jacklin left us, and Dave Spinks joined us in our ward. He was about 38 years old, and a bus driver. The four of us got on pretty well together, but I could not forget young Paul McGowan. I could not get him out of my mind for ages after his decease!

Chapter 20

November, 1978.

DURING THE week following our trip to Glosport and the wonderful evening spent at the Beehive Club, two things of significance happened. First, I sent off the letter to Sandy in Harts Hill, saying I would love to visit the family for New Year.

I subsequently received a phone call from Sandy, saying yes, please come, but she and the kids were sorry I could not make it for Christmas! Nevertheless, they would look forward to seeing me on Thursday, 28th December, and if I went up on the train and would let her know the time of my arrival in Brigthorpe, she would make sure one of her cousins was at the railway station to meet me—so that was sorted!

The other event of significance that week occurred on the Saturday, 18th November, and had a profound effect upon my life and the lives of many others in the North Midlands town of Gaynsford.

On the Saturday, in the mid-morning, I was driven up to Glosport, Merseyside, in a 26-seater minibus, with Rob McCallasky beside me on my left and his cousin, Father Martyn, the priest, on my right. The three of us lads were sprawled out on the bench seat at the rear of the vehicle, which was full of soccer supporters on our way up north to give vent to our full-hearted support for 'our gracious team', our gallant heroes from Gaynsford United.

Earlier in the year, during May in fact, we had won the FA League Challenge Cup playing against Glosport County, and we knew it would be a real 'needle' match, and that they and their supporters would be out for revenge, but we never in our wildest dreams realised the cost of winning that game!

Rob and I were determined to enjoy the match, and all that would follow, win or lose! Later that evening we would not be returning with the others on the minibus, but would go together for a meal at Rooney's Restaurant then on to the Beehive Club, where I knew I would once more be with my Honey, Queen of the Beehive, whom I was itching to see and make love to once more.

Oh yes, I was sure I loved Johnnie Friscoe and I was pretty sure I cared something, although I had to admit it was not real love I felt for her, for Sandy, at least I did not believe it was, but whatever it was I felt for Honey, the 'Queen Bee' was very real, and I had thought a great deal about her during that past week.

What a strange concept! There I was, almost literally juggling with three women in my life. All of them seemed to want me, and I wanted all three of them, but in different ways, if that makes any sense. I could readily understand my own feelings and emotions, but seriously doubted if anyone else would be able to do so! Yes, I could understand how I felt about all three women, but I could not explain my feelings to anyone else, not even to my best mates, or any member of my family, so I did not try. I merely balanced them all in my mind and kept them pent up in my heart, believing that what I felt for each of those three very different women was real and genuine, and that whatever those tangled, jangled emotions were, they would sort themselves out in time—maybe.

৪৯৯

The game on that Saturday afternoon proved to be very thrilling, and we won six goals to two! We were all standing in the terracing, cheering loudly and waving wildly as the last goal went in, just two minutes from the end of the second half.

"Isn't it jockin' great, mate?" Rob McCallasky roared in my right ear.

"Bloody fabulous!" I yelled, and a big bloke, propped against me, turned and said something to me in a broad Scouse accent! On the terracing were supporters of both clubs, all mixed in together—thousands and thousands of us—and it was considered safe for us to be mixing, at least so the police and those in authority at the Wayfarers Hall Ground in the centre of the docklands area of Glosport decreed, but we could scent the danger all around us! When that big thug turned to speak to me, Rob and Martyn, standing one each side of me, glowered at him and his four mates, who all made a growling noise in their throats! A great deal of chanting started up among the thousands of loyal supporters of the Wayfarers.

"We'll meet you all outside! We'll meet you all outside! We'll meet you all outside!"

We made the usual rude response:

"Bollocks!"

They then began to chant in an evil manner, or so it seemed to me anyway.

"There's more of us than you! There's more of us than you! There's more of us than you!"

Our communal response to that was a great and mighty roar of:

"Yeh yeh!"

There were more than 50,000 of us crammed on the terracing at the Wayfarers Hall Ground that afternoon, and getting out was quite tricky once the game had ended.

We were all positively jubilant as we left the ground, walking together because we believed there was safety in numbers! Once out in the bustling streets around the Wayfarers Hall Ground, we found ourselves utterly besieged by young louts, big, strapping dockers, loads of thugs, hooligans and stacks and stacks of beefcake, each and every single individual amongst them just itching for a fight!

We were in good humour, well, we would be wouldn't we, after a win of six goals to two over the opposition, and on their home territory at that, so we did not particularly want to fight, but they did! In veritable armies, they made their way to the vehicle compound where our minibus and many other vehicles, which had taken our supporters up from Gaynsford, were waiting, and commenced letting tyres down, bursting tyres, smashing windows and attacking drivers waiting with their vehicles to convey our supporters out of danger!

Rob and I made our way along the teeming streets, both having removed our football scarves from around our necks, deeming it safer to do so, and queued to get into Rooney's Restaurant. The establishment looked as though it was very busy that evening, as one would have expected on a night when the 'main team' was at home!

Eventually, Rob and I, with Martyn and some of the other lads behind us, acquired a table for ten near the back of the packed room. Rob and Martyn went up to the bar with Wayne and Danny Guthrie, two young brothers from the Mount Carmel Estate, and left me and five other guys, including Delroy, the younger brother of Rue and Oscar Henry, sitting together at the table. The place was positively heaving that evening! We merrily drank pints of beer or ice-cold cider, and were engaged in earnest, exhilarated and intense conversation as we surveyed the menus to choose what we would eat, when suddenly, from outside there was pandemonium in the street!

Everyone turned towards the huge plate glass window situated at the front of the establishment! Without any preamble, someone flung a smoke bomb through the window, then another and another! Those smoke bombs were followed by several fire bombs, which set light to the interior of the restaurant!

Complete panic ensued! While everyone was choking in the smog, there was an almighty crash and a huge solid object was hurled through the plate glass window! Although the glass was reinforced, the heavy object, which had been thrown with great force and accuracy, shattered it into fragments that flew everywhere!

Complete chaos! Utter confusion! As one, everyone made a rush for the only exit to get away from what was occurring! I was between Delroy and Father Martyn, with the two Guthrie brothers at my back! We valiantly fought our ways outside into the teeming streets of the docklands area of that mad City of Glosport, the city where a few moments before, we had been feeling so good. Now I was feeling absolutely drained and utterly terrified! The stampede of people behind me, and the roars and yells from them were too terrible to contemplate.

People were still pouring from the burning restaurant and spilling into the streets!

All I could hear was the sound of police sirens, blaring out everywhere, and the sounds of many voices and many pairs of feet running, running all over the place! Where was Rob McCallasky? I was dragged out into the street, and found myself standing shaking beside Martyn McCallasky, who draped protectively around my shoulders! Delroy Henry was on my other side, leaning against me, his hand resting on my left shoulder.

"It's okay! It's okay, Boyzie," Father Martyn, cousin of Rob McCallasky was saying quietly, trying to keep me calm. "It's okay now. You are safe, mate!"

"Where's Rob? Where is he, Martyn?" I asked, still shaking in my shoes!

I heard someone shouting.

"More jockin' ambulances, we need a fleet of jockin' ambulances here!"

Something, or someone, then hit me on the top of my head, and I blacked out at young Father Martyn's feet...

Chapter 21

THAT WAS a black night indeed!

I was taken to casualty, and had my head bandaged, also I had to rest because they were afraid of concussion setting in. They thought the blow to my head had cracked my skull, but fortunately, however, that diagnosis proved to be wrong!

The casualty department at the Royal was extremely busy that night—so was the mortuary! In the terrible crush in Rooney's Restaurant, and the subsequent fighting that had gone on in the streets surrounding the Wayfarers Hall Ground on that fateful evening in Glosport, many people were injured and several were killed. Among those who died from Gaynsford was my great mate, Robert McCallasky! Rob McCallasky! I missed him so much following his decease, and the death of Paul McGowan at the County Hospital during February of 1990 had effectively brought it all back to me!

That afternoon after dinner, I sat and cried hot tears, not just for young Paul and his young wife and children, but for Rob, my very best mate, and for my darling late wife Susan! I desperately tried to pull myself together. Such raw emotion was not deemed proper in such a wild display, particularly for a bloke, but I could not stop. Once the taps had been turned on, the floodgates opened, the tears just poured from my hot and swollen eyes, and I let them fall unchecked! I was on my own.

Dave and Bert had visitors and were out of the ward. I did not know where Andy Gange was that afternoon, but I wished he was with me! I felt so utterly, utterly wretched, and gave myself up to the torrents of tears welling up inside me and threatening to overwhelm me!

Suddenly, I felt a hand on my right shoulder. Andrew David Gange was sitting beside me on my bed, his arm draped comfortingly around my shaking shoulders.

"Hey, man! What's all this about nah?"

I could not speak immediately, but was just so glad to have someone alongside me for emotional and physical support! Andy sat beside me and began to talk quietly to me, and gradually I calmed down and pulled myself together again.

"How about a walk out in the grounds, eh Boyzie? It's a fine afternoon, and it's quite warm for the time of year! What say, eh?"

"Yeh! Yeh, I reckon I'd like that, Andy!"

"Good! Get your coat and shoes on and we'll have a turn around the grounds."

It was a warm and pleasant afternoon and we walked down towards the lake and sat on a bench under some shady trees. Nurse Helen Tidy came and found us there a short time later and said she would bring us both out a mug of tea apiece. We sat close together on the bench beneath the shady trees at the bottom of the long garden, and we talked. We talked about all kinds of things, and I told my mate, Andy, that I was not sure where I would go once I left the warmth, comfort and relative security of that annexe of the County Hospital in Gaynsford.

"Well now," Andy told me, "I am looking to share a flat when I leave here! I have a very big flat on the ground floor of an end-of-terraced house in Depot Street, opposite the park, in the town centre. I can't afford the rent on my own, although I hope to be returning to the Force, they have offered me a job in the personnel department at the Bread Street headquarters, so... well, Boyzie, we get on pretty well together, don't we?"

I thought for a few moments before replying. Yes! I did get on pretty well with Andy Gange, and had met lots of his mates, who all seemed decent enough. I had also met his mum, and five of his eight sisters, plus their husbands and partners, and yes, they all seemed very accepting of me. Could I share accommodation with someone else?

I still had the tenancy of a house in Gaynsford. On my return from Harts Hill, I had been fortunate enough to obtain the tenancy of a two-bed roomed property in Milling Street, on the Heath Road Estate in Osleston. My brother, Eric, bless his heart, had paid up six months' rent in advance on the accommodation, and I knew the neighbours were keeping an eye on it for me until I decided to return, but I was unsure whether or not I wished to return! After everything that had occurred, well, perhaps I ought to contemplate making a new start! Moving in with young Andy Gange the policeman, would be a golden opportunity for me to undertake such a massive change in my life. He wanted me to move into his large and spacious accommodation with him, and, yes, I reckoned as how I could get used to living with him there! It needed some thought and I ought to discuss it with my brother and perhaps one or two of my closest mates and acquaintances before I made a definite decision one way or the other.

"It sounds great, Andy, but I need time to consider it."

"Well, you will have plenty of time won't you? Neither of us is ready for discharge for a week or two yet. The offer is there if you want it—you know you would be most welcome to take me up on it, mate. You're a good bloke! Loads of my mates reckon you, an' I fink we'd get on real great togevver! Wot say, Boyzie?"

Relaxed, Andy adopted his strong North Midlands accent once more!

"Okay, Andy! I'll think about it and let you know, and… well… you know! Thanks! Thanks for everything, you know! Thanks for being there for me, pal."

He playfully nudged me in the ribs!

"Aw shucks!" he said. "Here's Nurse Tidy wivv the tea an' all!"

Chapter 22

I LIKED THE night time again! There was a time when that was not so, a time when the darkness frightened me, a time when being alone in the dark held great terrors for me and the night was no longer my friend. I now loved the darkness and the relative peace after lights out. Why? Because at night, when all was quiet, I could think!

Once more, my mind went roving back over the years! Over all that had happened to me since the decease of my beloved Susan, and my involvement, first with Johnnie Friscoe and later with Sandy Christmas and her vast clan!

As a matter of fact, I discovered that I was more involved with Sandy than I had ever realised.

Chapter 23

Christmas, 1978.

I SPENT CHRISTMAS at my place with Johnnie. We had a wonderful time—a happy, never-to-be repeated occasion of ultimate joy and pleasure in which we both basked, and from which we both derived considerable satisfaction! Our love, which had begun when we first met, blossomed and grew from a small acorn into a burgeoning oak tree!

In my heart I was still a little unsure. I still had a soft spot for Sandy, and was determined to keep my promise to her to visit the north-east for New Year and spend it with her and her family. Of course, I said nothing of that to Johnnie otherwise all hell would have broken loose! No! At that time I was not prepared to divulge my plans for the New Year, only to say I was 'going away', and Johnnie, who was also intending to spend New Year with 'friends', accepted it, and subsequently departed from my place on 27th December, quite happy to contact me in order to make further arrangements for future visits.

"We've had a wonderful time together haven't we, Boyzie?" exclaimed Johnnie as I hugged and kissed her prior to her departure. "Let's not leave it too long before we're together again, eh?"

I made a promise, more to satisfy her than for any other reason, that we would get together again very soon. I stood at my front gate and watched her drive away down the close, turning right and driving off towards the motorway and the South of England. Yes! I would miss her company! We had enjoyed a splendid Christmas together, but it was time to look forward to the New Year and my time with Sandy.

Oh, how do we ever allow our lives to become so complex?

Chapter 24

I HAD HIGH hopes for 1979! I hoped that it would be better by far than 1978—so far in life, that past year had proved to be my worst, what with the decease of my adored, and still lamented, late wife, followed by all the problems of readjustment, then the meetings with Johnnie and Sandy, and the problems those had brought upon me! Also there had been the death of my late neighbour, Cyril Williams, and all that that had entailed with regard to the family moving from the close!

I missed Vera sorely. Okay, Jinny Cauldwell was a good. cleaner, and she looked after me as best she could, but she had so many other commitments in her life that I came a pretty poor third or even fourth, despite the fact that I paid her handsomely for what she did to help me in the course of my daily life. Vera and her family had given me so much more than just practical help. Theirs had been a rough kind of friendship, but, nevertheless, a warm all-embracing friendship with no strings attached. Of course, there had also been Honey, Queen of the Beehive, and my wonderful time spent with her, and all that that had evoked.

Almost at the end of the year had come the terrible tragedy that had taken place in Glosport, culminating in the decease of my good and loyal friend, Rob McCallasky. The day prior to his funeral was a very emotional one for me and for lots of his mates and members of his family. In the evening my house was positively heaving with people, all there to be together, so that we could remember dear Rob and how he had lived amongst us, the kind of bloke he had been and how he had touched all our lives in so many different ways!

As we sat, altogether in my house, smoking, drinking, talking quietly among ourselves, listening to the music Rob had enjoyed, or which had meant something to him, I went through the whole gambit of emotions!

It was in the early hours of the morning of the day of his funeral before the house was empty that I went up to bed, completely exhausted, as I had not only felt great emotion myself during that time, but had had to listen to the endless outpourings of emotions from so many others who had been present at my house that evening and during the course of the night! As I climbed into bed, I said a silent, but heartfelt, prayer that the funeral would not be too hard to get through. It would be only the second one I had attended since being present at my late wife's funeral, and soon I was in floods of tears and my whole body was racked with sobs!

I lay in bed and managed to calm myself sufficiently to drop off into a fairly untroubled slumber, but the following day was hard nonetheless, and I certainly would not wish to go through that day again!

Rob's mum stood up to it all magnificently, more so than any of his brothers and sisters, or indeed myself or his cousin, Martyn, the priest, who part conducted the Mass prior to Rob's internment at the Mill Town Cemetery in Gaynsford. Dear Robbie! I missed him so very, very much.

ౕ౿ఌ

A new year beckoned, and I was up north staying with Sandy and her family! I had to prepare myself to look forwards, not back over my shoulder all the time! I had high hopes for the coming year, and believed it would be better than the last one had been!

Oh boy! If I had only known then what I know now, but I didn't! It was the start of a new year—every reason to hope things would be better!

Chapter 25

WITHIN THE space of only a few hours following the commencement of the new year, my hopes for a better one lay in tatters!

It was around 4 a.m. on the first day of 1979. Up in the North-East of England, we had held the party to end all parties! Sandy and all her family had been present in the Harts Hill Top Club until the early hours, as indeed had Dorrie and Fred, leaving Peggie Sue, their eldest, to care for the 'Tribe of Dingle'. Peggie Sue had been somewhat reluctant to undertake that duty, but was bribed with promises of presents, extra treats etc., etc., and thus, she had relented.

Dorrie and Fred had had a wonderful evening with all the rest of us adults and indeed some of the older kids, and later we had all gone back to Lennon Street and Norma Townley's house where the party was continuing!

Sandy and I were alone in one of the downstairs rooms for a brief moment, and she pulled me down onto the sofa beside her.

"Aw, Boyzie!" she breathed. "It's bin a smashing New Year, an' we're all so glad you could cum up and be with us, luv!"

I was several drinks to the good.

"Yeh!" I slurred. "It's been great, Sandy. I luv being here with you an' all the family!"

She snuggled up close beside me on the rather tatty sofa, and put her head on my shoulder.

"You remember I wrote you an' told you I had summat special to say?"

Just for the moment I could not recall the letter then suddenly it came back to me.

"And?" I said.

"Well, I wanted to wait until the new year had dawned to tell you, Boyzie. I don't know how you'll feel about this! The last thing I want to do is trap you in any way..."

I was becoming nervous!

"Well?" I ventured, after a moment's rather heavy silence between us.

"Boyzie," she said, trying to sound casual, but excitement mounting in her voice. "Boyzie, my luv, I'm pregnant, an' I'm sure it's yours!"

Suddenly I was completely sober again! Suddenly I was sitting upright, and pushing her head off my shoulder rather roughly as I struggled to move over on the tatty couch.

"Er... are you sure, Sandy? Are you absolutely certain?"

She started to cry, to shake with sobs.

"Aw! I knew you wouldn't be pleased! I told ahr Norma you wouldn't want it! Oh, Boyzie! I'm so sorry! I'm sorry to have put you in this position! You-you don't have to marry me if you don't want to, luv!"

So, right at the commencement of the last year in the decade, my hopes for a better and more peaceful and tranquil year had already been smashed! There was Sandy Christmas, someone I hardly knew, talking earnestly to me about my becoming a 'dad' in the near future, something I had never achieved with my beloved Susan, and also talking to me about the prospect of marriage! Marriage—so soon after the decease of my late and still lamented Bunny, my pet name for Susan.

No! I did not want to marry Sandy! Come to that, I did not want to marry *anyone*!

No! Not Johnnie Friscoe, not Honey, Queen of the Beehive, and... and definitely not Sandy! Oh yes, I liked her company! We had, until that moment anyway, enjoyed a great New Year, with plenty of festivities involving all the family, and plenty of fun with the kids, who adored me and loved me being present in their lives, but no, I did not want to marry Sandy, or even to permanently live with her and her four offspring!

I wanted to return to Gaynsford, pick up the pieces and get on with my life, but how could I? How could I turn my back on that woman who alleged that she was expecting my kid? I ought to do the right thing by her, and yet... and yet...

*

I awoke at about noon on New Year's Day, 1979, with my head thumping and a sense of gloom and doom hanging over me like the sword of Damocles.

Sandy breezed into the room with a tray containing two hard-boiled eggs, several thick cut slices of hot, buttered toast and a mug of hot chocolate!

"Hello, sleepyhead," she chirruped. "I fought as 'ow you'd never wake up this mornin'! Here's your breakie, darling. The kids are waitin' downstairs for you! Oh, luv, how's your poor head today?"

I hauled myself up in the three-quarter bed we shared, and did my best to do justice to the breakfast she had brought me. It was a poor best, however. I was not in the mood to eat or enjoy a hearty meal! How would I get through the next few days before returning home to Gaynsford?

Conclusion

Late February, 1990.

IT WOULD be impossible for me to precis the events of the past ten years, even if I wanted to do so, so I won't try at this juncture! Instead, I will save those for another book!

I had had some good news that day! When the doctors and Mr Lane, the surgeon, came around to see me, they told me I could go home at the weekend, and I had made a definite decision—one I hoped I wouldn't live to regret!

I was going to move to 10 Depot Street, to share the large, ground-floor flat with young Andrew David Gange, my new mate.